THE SCARY PARTS

Allan MacDonell

PUNK ★ HOSTAGE ★ PRESS

Foreword
Joe Donnelly

Editor-in-Chief
Iris Berry

Editor
Richard Modiano

Cover Art
Georganne Deen

Visual Arts Department
Julai Kwong

Interior Design
Penny Dawson

Punk Hostage Press
Hollywood, USA
www.punkhostagepress.com

*All my heartfelt appreciation to writers
Mike McPadden, Alex Maslansky, and
Evan Wright for clearing the way.*

PRAISE FOR THE SCARY PARTS

The Scary Parts, Allan MacDonell's new riveting and wildly entertaining book of short stories, is a one-of-a-kind, deeply felt, alternately hilarious and heartbreaking collection. It's impossible to read this gem without thinking of John Fante, John Cheever, or Ruth Rendell—writers who pull off the literary equivalent of close-up magic: showing us their characters' flaws and terrors, and in the process making us love them all the more. *The Scary Parts* is an absolute wonder. Allan MacDonell has heart for days, and a fearless, unrelentingly original voice that's all his own. The world is a better fucking place with this book in it.

> **—Jerry Stahl, Author of**
> ***Permanent Midnight, Nein, Nein, Nein!***

Can you talk about needing to evacuate your bowels in a book blurb? If the author, with great aplomb, found it worthy to include in this volume, I see no reason why not. So he was in a car, and I was in a tight, windowless room after a meal that tasted too good to be healthy. The driver was with a gentleman; I was in a crowd of young women I was hoping to impress. I wasn't caught in traffic—I was trapped twenty feet from a door I knew I wouldn't reach, with a sphincter that had betrayed me before. Jesus, Allan, you had to remind me? Life is full of scary parts. And the world is full of authors afraid of Allan's talent—afraid of coming up short, and rightly so. Some fears come true. Some people are better than you. Enjoy it. I did.

> **—Jack Grisham, Author of**
> ***An American Demon: A Memoir, Transmission***

The Scary Parts is a perfect harmony of outrage, humor, and all the ways in which we try to be human. MacDonnell is a skilled observer of absurdity, bliss, grief, and joy. I'll read anything he writes.

—Crissy Van Meter, Author of
Creatures

In Allan MacDonell's masterfully constructed collection of short stories, fear is the current running through inflicting itself on the characters who are caught in moments of time they cannot escape. These moments, different in each story, are similar in that the fear isolates them from life. They are living, don't get me wrong, but the fear encroaching upon them creates a disconnect. Loneliness is the river rising. MacDonell writes, "Fear is not some energy that infects us from the outside. We inherit our own bogeyman. Our scary parts all come from within; only the triggers are outside."

—Nicca Ray, Author of
Ray by Ray

"In *The Scary Parts*, Allan MacDonell takes no prisoners--no one in these stories escapes his wise and knowing gaze, but there's affection undergirding the brilliant irony. His characters are flawed and sexy, bewildered by the choices they've made in a world that's at once ruthless and amnesiac. We all end up heartbroken in the end, but it's no crime to enjoy it all a little more, MacDonell implies here, while it lasts."

—Christine Sneed, Author of
The Virginity of Famous Men, Please Be Advised

FOREWORD
by Joe Donnelly

American Disquiet: Allan MacDonell's
Landscape of Civil Dread

The Scary Parts, with its keen eye for the internal gyrations we subject ourselves to while attempting to navigate the Kafkaesque cabaret of contemporary life, is exhilarating and exacting. It's exhilarating for the sheer precision with which Allan MacDonell paints us into our commonplace, frightful predicaments and exacting because it forces us to see our own roles in the cavalcade of misapprehensions that confound us.

In one of my favorites from this collection, "Fear of Starting Something," MacDonell examines the precarities of being an abashed urban pioneer:

> *"From the beginning, when the Connells first moved in, installing the outdoor decorations has been a delicate process. You don't want to outdo the long-time residents, also known as your neighbors."*

When the everyday is so fraught, even date night at a coveted fine-dining establishment can become a minefield, as it does in "Fear of Success," one of the collection's most relatable follies. Here, we find Meghan and David, waiting too long for their menus while insinuations fill in the dead air like dirty dishes in the sink:

> *"Oh, Meg," David says in muted wonder. "Be careful looking over there. Phil and Bonnie were just seated."*

> *"The Shapiros?" Meghan's neck twists in a subtle, rubberized snap. A very attentive staffer, she sees, is*

> *handing menus to the Shapiros. "They've got a great table," says Meghan.*

This stitch-by-stitch account of being unintentionally and effortlessly outshined unfolds like a *Twilight Zone* sitcom. It will hit close to home for all but the most oblivious of you and remind us of the petty perils of simply leaving the house.

It's been said that all politics are local. It might just as well be said that all politics are personal. Here, they are both. MacDonell, it should be noted, is no stranger to attack politics, especially of Richard Hofstadter's looming-threat variety. From 1983 through 2002, MacDonell worked at Larry Flynt Publications and *Hustler* magazine, a time memorialized in his 2006 memoir, *Prisoner of X: 20 Years in the Hole at Hustler Magazine.* That era encompassed the modern proliferation of the paranoid style of politics with its weaponized and televised (now internet-ized) performative outrage and conspiracy-tangled epistemology. Then, the mode was mostly a trademark of the political right (the good old days). Now, all of us are outraged, suspicious and befuddled all the time.

Prior to *Hustler*, in the first-wave Los Angeles punk scene, MacDonell's mordant observations were a key component to seminal *Slash* magazine. His 2016 memoir, *Punk Elegies*, is an essential read for anyone who wants both the street-level and bird's-eye view (often at the same time) of this generally sentimentalized slice of history. He followed it up in 2018 with a wry first-person observation of his own funeral and ensuing afterlife in *Now That I Am Gone.*

Next comes *The Scary Parts.* The common thread through all this writer's work is politics, or, better, politesse: The contemporary social conventions by which we dance tragicomically around a wild proliferation of contested subjects. The scariest parts of *The Scary*

Parts may be how aptly MacDonell pinpoints the internal gyrations and semiotic mishaps that leave us second guessing ourselves and others. With unnerving narratives and the surgical compassion only a misanthrope's eye knows, MacDonell guides his indelible characters (us) through the accelerating difficulties of finding solid ground in an era when nobody knows where they stand.

In other words, the paranoid style in American politics has become the paranoid style of America. The fears MacDonell's characters and their travails summon—such as how easily one false move can result in imposed abnegation—are almost universal now. That most of the lives and scenarios found in this collection are everyday ones only raises the stakes. *The Scary Parts* slowly charts an EKG at the heart of our collective misconceptions and misconnections. Or, as the protagonist in "Fear of the Unknown" puts it:

> *"I am free to be plagued by monsters of my own creation, to be menaced, to believe and live a portion of timeless terror, of terror unbounded by time since it's a fear spawned by creations outside reality."*

Do not be afraid. MacDonell's light touch and shots of subversive humor keep us smirking and nodding, even as our skin crawls with the recognition that we are the scariest parts.

From "Fear of Success":

> *The husband and wife bid farewell in passing to the Shapiro party, who linger over cordials. The bold faces supported by Meghan and David stay in place until the valet pulls up with the Chevrolet Volt. The car is two kids and one income short of being a Tesla. Dropping into the Volt's optional luxury-like upholstery, David sinks into his*

shallow, mediocre, despair. Nothing like the deep, singular anguish of Jonah Hill.

What a relief that someone, especially a writer this deft, has finally given *The Scary Parts* their name and their due. I feel less afraid, and I bet you will, too.

— **Joe Donnelly**, Author of
L.A. Man: Profiles from a Big City and a Small World,
and *So Cal: Dispatches from the End of the World.*
Senior Lecturer, Whitter College.

ACKNOWLEDGMENTS

All praise to Iris Berry and Punk Hostage Press for choosing to run with this book.

Joe Donnelly's foreword knots *The Scary Parts* anxieties and fears into a defining bow of context and exigence.

Chill and erudite Richard Modiano's chisel-sharp mind and eye copyedited the rough shit out of the original manuscript.

Julia Kwong's icy graphic details delivered a cold visual concept.

Georganne Deen lent two chilling illustrations toward the cause of a perfectly disquieting cover:

For their 25th anniversary, he made her the principal shareholder of a white-collar prison outside of Houston (2016).

Closed for renovations—thank you for your continued patience. The Management (2017)

CONTENTS

"Fear is a man's best friend."

—John Cale

IT'S TIME TO MAKE FEAR YOUR FRIEND

Like everybody, I have this nagging twinge that I should be doing better. I should have provided more for myself and for those who depend on me. Right at this moment, it's not too late to catch up. It will be soon.

I'm a doctor. I practice my medicine in a hospital. I'm the head of the geriatric department. The medical field particularly at administrative levels has long been male dominated. Several talented and energetic women of my acquaintance are motivated to counterbalance that gender disparity. For instance, Marcia White who chairs the review board that has the most impact on my career advancement and stability, and two particular female PhDs operating under my direct supervision on the geriatric wards have all expressed a primary career goal of integrating more women into the upper branches of hospital hierarchy.

Marcia White and I have met, at Marcia's casual suggestion, for an off-the-record coffee in the visitors' cafeteria in the hospital's shiny new oncology wing.

"Old people don't respect you, Jerry, do they?"

"Excuse me," I reply. "I beg your pardon."

No pardon is harbored in Marcia White's gray eyes. Her focus on me is evaluating, frankly dissatisfied and degrading.

"Your patients," says Marcia. "Your specialty. The aged. The senescent. Frail and ancient beings. They seem to not take you seriously, as a personality to be reckoned with."

"After all their years, with all they've seen and experienced, having come face to face with the final absolute, honestly you can't expect these patients to be fazed by personality, policy or social constraint. The patients on my wards have moved beyond constraining mores."

"Nice deflection, Jerry." Marcia's gaze twinkles with false admiration. "Deflection I read somewhere is the mirror of anarchy. Rather than reflecting upon pertaining circumstances to determine causes and conditions, deflection creates blind angles, segmented linear surfaces and distorted perspectives in which anarchy takes on a normalized aspect."

It seems paranoid, but I would need to be unconvinced that Marcia White had not prepared and committed to memory her theory on refraction and chaos. The geriatric ward was seeing some disregard for strict procedural adherence among the patients. An influential core group had refused certain medications and dietary regimens, an exercise in personal preference that an expanding rank of impressionable patients has adopted as its own inspiration and taken further. The old rebels are hoarding pills, trading, mixing and matching, bartering sexual favors for extra dessert, demanding specific recreational prescriptions. Slightly out of hand is a long shot from anarchy.

"If you mean the current uptick in elective medication and picky eating habits among the long-term patients," I say, "the supply chain is very much under control, though it may seem to have slipped approved channels."

"No, Jerry." Marcia's eyes have switched now to pitying me. I cannot pinpoint when that change took place. "This talk I'm having with you, outside the governing board's purview, this chat has slipped the track of established channels. What you have on your ward is a situation bordering on patient insurrection. Among the disaffected colleagues you supervise, only professional courtesy keeps open insubordination at bay."

"I'm sure any member of my staff would speak directly to me if a matter of concern were to arise."

"Except for the two members of your staff who have spoken directly to me and expressed an opinion that both are better qualified than you to address the rigors and vagaries of your job."

"I'm beginning to feel a little undermined," I say to Marcia, unable to read the willful deflection in her eyes. "Undermined from above and below."

"Your feelings of ineffectuality and your denial of agency do not bolster my confidence in you," confides Marcia. "I am here to help, if you are willing to help yourself."

A nausea pit opens up inside, as expected. I try to adopt the expression of someone whose center has not dropped out. "I am not only a competent squad leader, but a cooperative team member as well, may I remind you." The quaver in my voice hits right at the midrange between offended passion and craven whimper. "I have never shirked a recommendation to help myself."

"Fine," says Marcia. "There's a training event I suggest you attend." She looks around the cafeteria and stirs coffee. She has taken not taken a single sip. "This is not an order or an official directive. I'm not advising you as a colleague and superior. I'm just putting a possibility out there, as a friend, well, an acquaintance. I'm disinterested perhaps, but not indifferent. A woman I was in school with, we've taken divergent paths. She is tops in the motivational field. She can put you in touch with an inner resource to help you stanch that flow of disrespect that streams toward you."

Just like that, I acquiesce to undergo a self-assertion seminar conducted by the superior's great college friend. It wasn't that simple. I first had to schedule a personal day off from work, which required securing Marcia White's signature approval, apply for enrollment at the Seize Your Power lecture and workshop, respond openly but strategically to an application questionnaire (How do you hope to grow from the SYP Program? How were you made aware of Raymi?), pay an exorbitant registration fee with a penalty tacked on for last-minute signup and explain to my wife why I am driving to an airport-adjacent hotel rather than to the hospital.

"It's all down to Marcia White's veiled threats, and the stealth advances on my authority by Sloan and Logan. Believe me, none of this meets my idea of a productive day."

My wife is a person who places a positive spin as a sort of deep moral imperative.

"I can think of no encouraging interpretation for this assignment," she confesses. She is a police dispatcher. She is heading out the door to her job. "If I don't get any calls about you, we'll consider the day a success."

Success. It means so much to all of us, especially to us who feel success slipping away. The universal pursuit of financial plenty and high regard among the community draws five hundred and fifty achievement-seeking customers to a hotel complex located within striking distance of the city's primary airport. The complex is complicated. An overlapping, interlocked composition of towers and remote wings and connecting corridors and retail malls and food courts is deliberately designed to be something other than readily navigable. Once I have parked the Mercedes (not top of the line, running toward the end of its lease), I have no trouble following the stream of expectant Seize Your Power attendees. We stride, most of us on heels elevated one notch above sensible, out of the parking structure into a main atrium through an interstitial courtyard and up a designated escalator to a between-spaces mezzanine, spilling into a tight lobby.

Like these eager, alert, focused women, I have arrived prudently early. We cluster three deep at a phalanx of registration tables and receive Seize Your Power lanyards from brisk, beaming, uniformly groomed women in camo-pattern sundresses. What I take to be a lieutenant in the SYP brigade presses a plastic lanyard into my palm. She says, "Seize your power." I accept her three words as an invitation, promise and command. Her squeeze of my hand and unabashed eye lock makes me feel singled out for special attention, a reaction I presume is duplicated in every woman flowing in before and after me. Now, tingling and actualized, we stand all together waiting for the auditorium doors to open. There is no avoiding bumping the shoulders of clustered and mingling Seize Your Power seekers. Coffee, I notice, is being widely consumed from ceramic mugs. I maneuver through the tightly arrayed bodies in search of the coffee's source. An audible attitude of happy expectation nearly rubs off on me.

"This is my sixth time seeing Raymi. You will not be disappointed."

"I don't know what exactly to expect. I certainly don't anticipate being disappointed."

"Did I see you at the goddess ninja business arts conference last month?"

"I was unable to get away for that one."

"It was a little off in the outskirts. Well worth the commute. I went back to work the next day and was project leader by the end of the week."

Maybe forty men are peppered in with the female crowd, less than one in ten. We keep our distance from one another and stifle gestures of acknowledgement. We would prefer the women not notice our presence.

I find my coffee just as the auditorium doors open. A smiling attendant stops me at the entry. "I'm terribly sorry, sir. No beverages are allowed within the theater."

She holds out a tray for my ceramic mug. Her camo sundress exerts its command. This coffee, I have a feeling, will be essential. I drain the cup and step through the doorway while the steaming liquid scorches my throat. Stacked seating gives the auditorium an operating theater feel. All the aisle seats are occupied. Contrary to my preference, I point at an empty seat six spaces in on row VV. I nod my head and widen my eyes in an attempt to communicate.

"Is that seat open?" I believe I have said these words. The coffee has seared my vocal cords. It might have come out as a croak.

"Did you want to sit here?" asks a woman beside the empty seat. Her blond oiled hair is pulled back so tight that her eyes appear to be lifted. She personifies incredulity. That I would want to sit next to her and that I would not vocalize that desire. She nods what I interpret as consent. I mime "pardon me" with grimaces and awkward bowing to five seated audience members that I dutifully do not step on, all openly evaluating women. I sink into the open chair like a man exhausted. It is not quite 9:00 a.m.

"I'm sorry," I explain to the woman who had granted rights to the seat. "I drank my coffee too fast." I have more to say, a full explanation.

"Oh, I get it. Is this your first time with Raymi?"

I nod yes, clutching my SYP lanyard to my heart.

"Hold onto your seat, mister." She pats my knee.

As if on cue, the room darkens. The women and I look toward the front. A still figure appears on the blank stage under a rising light and in a hush.

"Here she is," says the woman to my left. "Raymi."

The woman on stage is an age not easily determined, like my own. She wears a tailored denim jumpsuit, something a 1970s *Playboy* Playmate would have looked at home in. Cascades of blonde hair are piled like high scoops of lemon ice cream. Her face is black as moonless night. She waits out a cresting applause, which I contribute half a heart to. Her arm wipes across space, creating immediate silence. I visualize my career advancement as less precarious for me being part of this expectant hush.

"You are nobody unless your associates fear you," says Raymi in a voice so soothing I hope to hear one like it on my deathbed. Her tone assures me my future will be rich in essential commodities.

"How else can a person feel she is being taken seriously? If you sow and breed fear, you will know profit. You will know advancement and comfort. You will know a peace that transcends all understanding."

Raymi's step is buoyant in Adidas court shoes. Her voice is full of guarantees and devoid of urgency. How did I come to this place without running an Internet search on this speaker? I've been more distracted than busy. Distracted by my fear that Marcia White will discontinue my comfortable future and prosperous legacy. Looking around in the darkened auditorium for verification is not practical. Nonetheless, I'm reasonably certain Raymi is the only non-white person on premises. *It would be a cliché*, I think, *to compare Raymi's apex feline presence to a cat in the family of panther*. She purrs. "The question is not *why* make your friends fear you. What you need to know is *how* to make your friends fear you. It's not so tough to do. You simply pick the right moments to go off script. There's no reason to act crazy, violent, or extreme. It's not the travesty you do that infects your colleagues, friends and family with festering anxiety. It's the sense of the travesty you might do."

Raymi prowls the stage lip with the centered balance of an off-duty ballerina. I'm taking it that this woman is somewhat of a radical in the field of self-improvement. She continues to speak as if to confirm my assumptions. Her words come out through a smile that reaches me three-quarters of the way deep in the auditorium and disarms and warms me.

"Once people start wondering where you will draw the line, and suspecting that you will step directly across that line once you've drawn it, their unease is yours to command. You'll find that fear is easier to cultivate than respect. Fear is more readily maintained than respect."

Her voice, as if extolling the golden rule, pitches virtue and light into the auditorium. "Unleash a half-gesture, an innocent allusion. Your friends will cower as under a raised fist."

She raises her fist. Really the remarkable thing is that I do not flinch. The dissonance in Raymi's message and delivery, and the coffee, all hit me at once. I feel internal roiling and can hear my intestines gurgle. The goal of my open eyes is to conceal any sign of disquiet or alarm. This is the same unblinking contact I maintained with Marcia White in the oncology cafeteria, Marcia White who scared me into signing up for this seminar.

"Fear lasts longer than respect." An on-stage pause—and absolute silence throughout the theater—last just longer than I can hold my breath.

"Fear is a safeguard against regret. It keeps people from bonding to you and forming the attachments that are so necessary to sever to keep from being dragged down and choked off by clinging persons who do not fear you."

What at first had been comforting in Raymi's modulated sweet calm is eerie now. Her still panther gaze sees into us, all of us. "Fear leaves a bruise that persists in being felt. The mark left by fear is a switch. Flip it on. You've triggered a battered reality. People back off. You are given space, and respect."

A murmur of agreement filters through the audience. Me, the reticent listener, I suspect that I am late to the game. Is the speaker advocating for zero human connection? Was some corrosive additive dosed into the coffee? From the moment I stepped out of the car and merged with the queue, I should have suspected that I was in the wrong place, lining up with the wrong crowd. Clearly, I stand out, even sitting in the dark. This coffee is leading to a purge. If I'd been in an aisle seat, the uneasy bowel would have carried me swiftly and resolutely up the aisle and out through the lobby. Surreptitiously, I size up the five women between the exit aisle and me. They sit stolid and stoic like five applicants ahead of me on the path of career fulfillment. The momentum of fear barrels inward. Raymi is poised on her toes. "Once you learn to erect an imbalance of power upon a foundation of applied fear, friends and foes alike will understand you. They will understand you as a fearsome person not to be trifled with."

I fear that I lack the energy to carry out the rigors of Raymi's philosophy of fear. It will require sustained effort. What about blowback? The people around me won't like playing chicken every time we interact. Some will retaliate. My mind poses a question. *What do I do when everyone turns against me?* I want to raise my hand and ask the question. That will draw attention to me. There's always a catch.

A break is called, a moment too late. The stewing mess the coffee had made in my abdomen has become an internal millstone of cemented dread. I stand and carry the petrified load with me, making slow progress toward where I assume the restrooms will be. One person in a human swarm, I am diligent in not instigating physical contact or the slightest confrontation. Every attendee has been primed to do something scary, to strike fear in the fearsome, to menace any feckless outcast who represents the fearsome other. I am afraid that when I reach the bathroom, my trudge will be for nothing. A woman seems to be pacing my shuffle. It would be exaggerating to say she has joined me.

"It wasn't really my choice to come here," reveals the woman pacing me. She is at my side. There is no one else she could be talking to. She's talking to me. She's basically whispering. I lean closer. She inquires confidentially, "Does any of this seem, I don't know, completely opposite to how people should behave in the real world?"

Her lips have hooked me, with the proximity brought on by the whisper. Her brash red hair is cut in distinctive bangs. She carries her relative youth, low thirties, with an authority that I suppose comes from early-onset intellectual maturity and self-propulsion into supervisory mid-management positions.

"I have to admit," I concede under my breath, "the directives do seem incongruent with cooperative behavior geared to advancing the greater good."

"I am so relieved to find a like mind." She moves as if to touch me. I draw back, but I am wrong. According to her wan smile, she never intended any physical contact. We are still on speaking terms. "If my job didn't depend on staying through the entire presentation," she says, "I would leave now."

She has stopped at the queue for the women's restroom. I stop with her. Obviously, this woman sees me as an ally. She's earned a confidence from me.

"I'm suspecting my supervisor was unaware of the messaging we are receiving here today," I say, placing my fingers in front of my mouth to foil lip readers. "I'm very sure she, my superior, would be uncomfortable with me operating from the Raymi approach in the workplace. I certainly couldn't be comfortable if I were to apply a fear-based strategy in my outside relationships."

"I've been so surprised. Aren't you surprised?"

"You know, since the Internet is here, I really have no excuse for it. I was caught completely off guard by Raymi's appearance."

"I was too. What surprised you the most?"

"Well, look around. She's not like anyone else here."

"You never would have expected her to be Black?"

"In this context? It seems to defy expectation."

If this woman and I had both been men, or both women, our conversation might have followed into the bathroom. I linger outside, shuffling my thoughts, trying to understand what she is telling me. Is she asking for my help? Does she need to be saved? Can I be a savior? Perhaps she needs me to explain some dynamic or paradigm that is at play here. I go off to fetch a drink for her while she's in the ladies' room. I deliver the beverage as the seminar is being called back to order. She accepts the beverage, smiles and dismisses. She has moved on. She is beyond continuing our discussion. I am back in my seat six from the aisle. I have missed my chance to relieve myself in the men's room.

The auditorium lights dim. The stage lights rise, and Raymi is back. The jumpsuit has been traded for a tight black-denim mini, black leggings, stack-heeled fawn boots and an iridescent green top of some interplanetary shine with a massive intricate collar that rises to the height of Raymi's piled lemony hair. The collar apparatus acts as a pivoting backdrop, framing the depthless beneficence of Raymi's face.

"As a solution to the problem of human interaction," concedes Raymi, "fear is not perfect. If someone fears you, it does not free you of that person. I'm speaking of the workplace specifically. The same holds true in the family dynamic and in our social circles. The person you have made to fear you must be monitored. When too much fear is applied to some people, not all people, they become persons of action. Fear becomes their defining discomfort. Any presence of a fearsome entity, you for instance, is a pressing irritant. Fear of you keeps these people from concentrating on doing their best work."

I squirm. Discomfort becomes me. I try to estimate how many of the people in this conference room are here of their own volition. Are most audience members taking this course as an elective? My attention drifts from the actual words being said. My thoughts wander off to the geriatric ward. Some of my patients are consumed by terrorizing neurosis. Others, the more sentient, have become fearless, fearless at least within the bounds of any realm penetrated by my comprehension. My time of not knowing the end date of my physical reality, such as this life limit is perceived by my geriatrics, is running short, measured out in anxious, nagging twinges. Audience laughter returns me to the auditorium. A point is being made. Someone is being turned into an object lesson, an abject lesson. I recognize a brash head of red hair and pointblank bangs.

"I talked to a person at break," declaims the redhead from her seat up front. Her voice is far fuller and more in command than when it lilted in my ear. A sense of uneasiness digs in. Will I be exposed? "I won't reveal the gender," states the redhead. "This person, I verified, had been sent here at the threat of losing employment."

"You can always spot the mandatories," interjects Raymi, rocking on her heels. "So I've been told."

"You've been told correctly. Well, this mandatory was stunned that expectations could be defied."

"Of course. The mandatory is always stunned."

"And this mandatory fully underestimated the proficiency of the woman who made attendance mandatory. Of course your physical appearance was also a total shocker."

"Shock is mandatory," dictates Raymi. The stage lights rise hotter on her again. The redhead recedes into the mass. Raymi patrols the lip of the stage, half pacing, half prowling. Her words float out on a lilting cadence.

"The people you have power over have lain awake into the dawn fearing you. They go about their daily business. Full, undivided attention has been robbed from them." Raymi halts center stage and plucks her next thoughts from the aura of emerald-yellow light refracting from her hair and the collar framing it. "These troubled souls are forever sending mental tendrils on fact-finding missions into the territory of fearsome you. Your imposing frightfulness has made the fear sector of your victim's consciousness a discomfort zone. Their process of shutting down a troubling awareness sector is imprecise. Frightened, resentful efforts to mute their brain's preoccupation with your menace may over perform. Your target ends up smothering a wider range of his personal identity than an individual can sacrifice and still hope to live as an integral whole."

My mind has wandered. I don't know where it went. The scent of Sloan and Logan is in my nostrils, an olfactory hallucination. My underlings have betrayed my leniency and my good heart. They have exploited my good intentions and good faith to block me from reaching a vantage where I can do better, for me and for others. Raymi's enunciation releases mouthfuls of airy and light vibrations.

"Too long in the shadows of threat and danger," she purrs, "and the scared cat will turn and face the fear. The fear will be you." All glittering promise, Raymi's smile is a brilliant foil for words that articulate an ominous prospect. "If you're ill-defended against those who fear you, claw marks will appear down the side of your face. The burden of fear will be shifted."

The snare is honeyed. The bait is sugarcoated. The mass of the audience in the hall shifts forward. I lean away.

"It will be you who is afraid."

The mass that shifted forward has been trapped. I have not been caught. Fear, it's as if Raymi has spoken directly to me alone, has too long kept me servile and cringing. I am that tormented cat at the turning point. Raymi's cautioning scenario has pushed me around the bend. I have been released. I stand and do not crouch and step past five stunned customers to the open aisle and walk with casual, determined purpose up toward the exit sign.

Raymi's voice at my back is suddenly a lash delivering a blessing. "When you choose the path of fear," she says, "be prepared always to deliver fear. Never allow yourself to absorb it."

I reach the empty bathroom. The acoustics are precise, like thought and mortality. Some comfort time passes. No absorption of fear takes place in that tiled and stainless, super ventilated interior. Relaxed, secure, bolted into a steel stall, I check emails and texts on my phone. My wife wants to know if I will be out in time for an early dinner, early enough to treat her to a movie afterward. Will I stop at the precious butcher shop run by the nose-to-tail lesbian couple and bring home two fat lamb chops? Lamb is not among my favorite meats. The meat boutique's prices have been set to trigger financial anxiety, jacked up to keep out the low earners, a gouge that bites once and warns downwardly mobile consumers to spend your pittance elsewhere. I agree to stop for the meat. A job offer has come to my personal email account. I've interviewed with these people three times. They will provide curtailed benefits, no relocation allowance, reduced autonomy, extra layers of supervisory hierarchy and a deep salary cut compounded by no hope of performance bonus or equity incentives. Flattered, I have no choice but to stay where I am. I reply to that effect. I flush and am out of the stall. I wash my hands and pat down my hair. The Seize Your Power seminar is letting out. A rush of men, SYP lanyards swinging, mobs in through the exit, pushing me back toward the urinal wall. The men are voluble, giddy, giggling like delinquents fresh out of after-school detention.

"Buddy, we've got nothing to be afraid of," gushes a big one. "I was worried they might be onto something, but no. Guys, we are home free."

"There's no need for divisive talk." This next speaker looks like a poet. He's slight, slight beard, often been slighted. "These women are our women. These women are allies."

"Are you afraid?" counters the big fellow, whipping himself up to the urinal. "Do you feel yourself becoming more susceptible to fear?"

"Of course I don't," marvels the slighter man, sliding into the adjacent piss slot. "There's nothing scary about anyone in here."

"In here?"

"I mean out there."

"There's nothing scary about fear," proclaims another man. Before I can catch sight of him, he slams himself in behind a stall door.

"That whole fear game, no matter what side you're on, is just a waste of energy," says the first guy, the big one now at the sink not washing his hands, fingering his beard. "There's no point to even participate in it."

I push forward through the crush. The lobby and as far as I can see through the mezzanine and the escalators descending toward the outside world is abuzz in a head-bobbing, laughing, affectionately jostling stream of female humanity. I feel like eavesdropping but don't need to. A trio of women heading in my direction amplifies its discussion specifically, it seems, to facilitate me listening in.

"The point is to not partake in the fear," says a woman of forty in embroidered tunic and wedge leather clogs. "The fear is false."

"Fear is not some energy that infects us from the outside," agrees her close companion, also solidly forty and wearing intricately embroidered muslin. "We invent our own bogeymen. Our scary parts all come from within. Only the triggers are outside."

"Exactly," agrees the third lady, in a voice I've heard before. Her eyes pop slightly, projecting intensity of vision. "If you feel yourself being sucked into a fear strategy, go straight to that place where you're the cat that's been scared one fright too far. Throw that fear back where it belongs. The whole construct will crumble."

This third lady extends a palm to high-five. "Isn't that the exact truth, big fella?"

I slap skin with this woman, my familiar, my co-adept in this specialized knowledge. "So true," I say. "So very true."

"I told you to hang onto your seat, didn't I?"

I recognize her now by her oiled, pulled-back blond hair. She's the woman who'd scowled at the sight of me heading to occupy the vacant seat next to her. She regards me now as if we've been delegates at a political convention and nominated the superior candidate favored by both of us. I drift away, the idea being to walk as if I am on my own.

"This really was a silly way to spend the morning," says a woman I have never seen before. She indicates my SYP lanyard to explain our connection. "Wasn't it?"

"Silly? I don't know. I sense a general freeing of attitude has taken place."

"Okay, I'll grant you that. But what a roundabout route she took to get there."

This woman is correct in assigning a circuitous nature to the Raymi indoctrination. She may believe that statement is incorrect. The assertion of silliness may be a test. Avid agreement on my part could mark me as an apostate in need of reeducation. I am being paranoid, no doubt. Keeping quiet is key. To speak is to risk disclosing assumptions or conclusions that identify me as an outlier. In a casual, unobtrusive manner, I remove the plastic ID card and nylon cord from around my neck and slip the piece of SYP branding into my jacket pocket. Anonymity, if all goes well, will be mine.

As we walk into the parking structure, our SYP solidarity breaks up. We blend with that transient portion of the general public that is also walking toward a hotel parking lot. None of us is a stranger to being fearsome. *I may get safely away*, I think. *Twenty yards more, and I will reach my Mercedes. No actionable disclosures will have escaped my mouth.*

The redhead who betrayed my confidence skips up beside me. I flinch at the spring in her point-blank bangs. "Wow, I love the way you stay in character," she says. "I'd put in for a bonus if I were you."

She speaks as if my role at this event is to perform as fear's shell figure, as if I've been sent to SYP as a marked target. My future is here. I am a shill for making fear your friend. I am a walking avatar representing the lapsed tyranny of archaic archetypes. The crowd needs to know I am easily scared. The redhead winks. "You're doing great."

My car starts on the second try. I key the address for the butcher shop into the GPS. How much longer will I be able to pay the fancy bills that my wife takes to mean I am a good provider? Cars start up all around me. Power is being seized. So far, my Mercedes has a shot at being the first vehicle to the exit booth. Right at this moment, it's not too late to escape unscathed. It will be soon.

FEAR OF THE UNKNOWN

In the mornings, sometimes, she finds herself before sunrise between sleep and wakefulness in an undefended state where the old questions still pretend to apply.

Where is he? She is in the outer court at the Hollywood Bowl. The headliner's start time has been called. He has not called. She sits one of three people in a box for four. The open sky above with its far-off starlight illuminates nothing beyond the mystery of the moon and that one open seat. *How long have I been lying here?* She is drowsy on a rocky Sardinia beach. Grainy pebbles mold to her protrusions. Her towel has had a chance to dry since her last swim. He'd said he was going into the water, only for a moment, just a dip and he'll be back. *When did he say he would arrive to meet me?* She is in an empty house in a gated community. She ignores the realtor and stalks the polished cement floors. She pictures where her things will be stored and displayed in this home, where his place will be, the side of the bed she will choose *Am I late or am I early?* She is on a Spanish resort town pier, dressed for a half-day boat excursion to swim in remote coves and explore secret caves. Incoming small craft disgorge sunburned passengers, their hair stiff and wild from salt spray and breeze. Leather-skinned skippers pack expeditioners carrying goggles and snorkels into outgoing vessels. She can't be sure if she is meant to be coming in or going out. *When is he ever on time?* She is buying flowers at a graveyard, stalling for him to show up and wondering how she managed to forget her wallet at home. *Where does he go while the time goes elsewhere?* She suspects his sanctuary is an interior place. The wind sneaks in as drafts. It's all dark, too dark to see. There is breathing. There is the smell of breath. There is movement. Will there be touch? She passes through an exit she has been blind to. *If he is not here when I am gone*, she wonders, *where can he be?* Now the light is coming in. Now the figures form in pieces and gather into a whole. Specters cluster around her night table, behind the door of her clothes closet, under the empty half of the mattress. He is hidden somewhere in the center of these things, not him bodily, but maybe clues to why he has gone and maybe a key, not to let her in where he is, but to let her out of here.

The barking will not stop on its own. The onslaught had started as twin whimpers in the waning dark. A childproof gate blocks off the bottom of the stairwell. His two dogs press against the barrier, looking up, sniffing up, optimistic that this morning will bring him down to them again. Once more, he fails to descend. His dogs have no answers for that. His dogs only know that their feed time has come and is gone, and they haven't eaten. His dogs cannot worry about more than one thing at a time. She wills herself out of bed, retains balance on the stairs down to the kitchen and feeds the animals. In their relief of appetite, in the satisfaction of intake, the contentment of satiation, they are like humans distracted from wondering where he is and why he is not home at an hour well beyond when home is the place for him to be, at a time when even she is home.

His dogs have become accustomed to her being home and him not there.

A bowl would only slow the passage of ice cream from the carton to her mouth. A bowl would not mark the progress. She can imagine a therapist, a forensic psychologist, asking when she had begun eating ice cream in the morning. Is there an Ice Cream Anonymous? Does Ice Cream Anonymous hand out a little card with twenty questions leading toward self-diagnosis of your problem abuse of ice cream? Do you eat ice cream alone? If she'd known someone was going to show so much interest, she would have charted her fall. Ever more visible depths of cardboard inside the ice-cream carton indicate her declining levels. Declining levels of what? Expectation. Memory. Understanding. *Waiting and not knowing what you are waiting for is unhealthy for everyone*, she tells herself, *including the one who is being waited for.*

Full days slipped past, then weeks. His credit cards have been abandoned. His call number is deactivated. He left traces on the Internet, cryptic updates, empty statuses, no clues as to his location or intentions. The traces became months old, then deleted. Nothing fresh appears.

"Time to move on," she tells the dogs. She moves from the table to the sink and deposits the empty ice-cream carton in the garbage container under the kitchen counter.

Things pass through the mind and partially lodge.

Places he could be. Ensconced off-grid with an attractive and reclusive chance encounter. Traveling under the radar with a recent widow. Hidden and shielded with a reconciled ex in a remote mining town. Incognito in plain sight with an incorrigible adulteress as part of the continuous turnover at serial tourist destinations.

Places she has been. To the offices of a law firm they had until recently jointly employed. To a handful of regional bank branches. To pick up the tab at three employee birthday lunches. To an early dinner attended by a female associate of a man she had been seeing, a female associate who informed her that the man would no longer be seeing her.

Things he could be doing. Tracking down the family of origin he claimed to have never known. Avoiding the pursuit of business associates he had never allowed her to meet. Composing the memoirs, as he'd often threatened to do. Eating too much. Smoking again. Drinking like never before. Sleeping in.

Things she has done. Put her hands again and again into every pocket and run her fingers over each seam of all the garments left hanging in his closet. Crawled across the floor mats of his car, the car he claimed to love and owned outright, pinpointing a penlight under the seats, up behind the dashboard, along the headliner seams. Traced and retraced all filaments of his social media web. Changed the locks. Driven past a dozen psychic fortune-teller storefronts and pulled in at the showroom for the city's most elite home security specialists.

People he might be with. Persons who have accepted or been taken in by his new false or assumed identity. Confederates, witting and unwitting, in clandestine efforts, causes, existence. A new true love. A core of bosses, a ring of enforcers, a very discreet and efficient cleanup crew. A contingent of fresh souls in the waiting room of an afterlife indoctrination center.

People she has been with. A therapist who has been told nothing. Law enforcement representatives who have told her nothing. Insurance adjusters who proclaim powerlessness to do anything. Those few true friends who are too discreet or afraid to press her for details of what has happened. The trail of false friends demanding to be told what she imagines might be going on, with who and where.

Is some double face in the crowd waiting for him now? Maybe he has arrived. Maybe with this new person, the waiting is over for him, until next time, when the waiting becomes for someone no one at this time can know who. Not even he has picked the next one yet. Maybe he hasn't started looking. Also, he could be gone, all the way out, beyond waiting. She hadn't known everything about how he spent his days. She hadn't known he owned a gun until she found the empty case. She had been looking for something left behind that might speak to her. There are things she wants to be told, the eternal, necessary things, and practical matters as well. Is someone waiting for her? She may be one wrong step or correct stride away from being picked up, pulled aside and set straight. Does he know who might be waiting for her? She had a man waiting for her, in secret, for private purposes, not so long ago. Did he identify that last man who had waited for her? That last man is as much a ghost as is her missing man. His transitory presence, the reasons he had for being with her, are as much a mystery as the disappearance.

Some woman comes over, shows up at the door unannounced looking for him. This woman has been a friend to him and to her, although not lately. He had defined this woman as a fluid hybrid of government contractor and corporate shill, highly successful, connected and influential, a definition the woman had taken pains to never dispel. The woman was in the neighborhood. She rang the bell and asked if he was at home and could come to the door. This woman is given the news, which her whole flawless face says is old news. "But what's going on with you?" this person asks. "How are you doing?"

"You see how I'm doing."

"You look great, of course. I'd expect nothing less."

"I'm eating ice cream alone. I'm answering my own door."

"Have you been to the police?"

Of course she has been to the police.

"Good," says the woman. "It wouldn't look right for him if you hadn't been to the police."

"You intimate that you know more than you are letting on, more about me, and more about the missing person, my man."

"What did you tell the police?"

She is unable to tell the police much. "All of his people are unknown to me, as if by design. All of mine are unknown to him."

"Also, by design?"

Women can be so bitchy to other women, thinks the woman who has been left behind and doesn't know why. The drop-in visitor is escorted to the door and told goodbye with no lapse from propriety.

Alone again, more things pass through her mind and remain undefined. *Why was I in particular pulled out of nothing and brought to life? Did I do something back when I was nothing to deserve what has happened and become of me since?*

Some guy, a developer friend of his, sends a text. "I'm up. How are you?"

She types. "My surface is still. I will not say unruffled or calm." She deletes. She thinks it over for twenty minutes.

She types. "I am free to be plagued by monsters of my own creation, to be menaced, to believe and live a portion of timeless terror, of terror unbounded by time since it is a fear spawned by creations outside reality. No one I'm imagining is alive to me, and so this still waiting is not living." She hits send. She walks the dogs and checks back an hour later. No reply has come in. She rereads what she has sent. It started out making sense, like so much else.

The dead time is uncomfortable. It could go on forever. It won't. Something will happen, or something won't. One thing that happens is this guy, the developer friend of her man who is gone, is walking beside her as if they had agreed he would be. Her man's dogs are wary of this man. "I've found nothing," she says in greeting. "What should I be looking for? Gemstones? Powders? Flash drives?"

"If you don't know, you don't know."

"And what I don't know can't hurt me?"

"Well, honey, I wouldn't know about that."

"You'll admit that someday this will all be over," she says. "I'll be dead, and he will be dead. I know that."

"You may both die at the same time, say if a comet hits your house or if a tire blows out on the freeway."

"There is a likelihood that one of us will die first. Unless you're here to tell me how much longer he and I will be waiting to be in the same house or car again."

"Well, honey, like I said. I wouldn't know about that."

"Maybe you can tell me who would know."

"Maybe not." The developer laughs. "Think that one through."

In the next instant, the developer is gone. She's a little less alone, but still all on her own, thinking this situation through, out loud with his dogs. "When one of us dies, the other one will remain alive. It might be me, wondering, where did he go? Will I be going to the same place? No one can tell me. Does he know where I am now?"

Now that he is not here, she can't picture him liking what she is doing at any moment as she moves through her day. He would frown at her grocery store choices. He would disapprove of her boutique purchases. He would fault her cursory supervision of her employees. He would throw up his hands in exasperation as she idles her car and considers swooping into an open parking spot at the psychic fortuneteller's storefront. He must have at one time liked something that she did, a single time at least. Some event changed all that. Some circumstance. Some force of personality. What could it have been? What flipped his world upside down and dropped him out of hers? Will the world flip back and return him to the surface again?

A man she doesn't know but knows her although he's never met her waits for her at the next corner. Another man keeps pace following behind, stopping when she stops, walking when she walks. He knows her without having met her too, she is sure. He knows who she is and who has left her. These unknown men believe they know what happens next. She has learned that they could not be more wrong, but there's no comfort in knowing that.

FEAR OF SUCCESS

"You're not taking this seriously." She turns her wineglass upside down on the tablecloth, then right side up again. "At the end of the meeting, in front of both camera groups and the talent, he says, 'You really like to eat out, don't you?' You don't think that's weird?"

"It might be weird," replies her husband, craning his neck and failing to catch a waiter's eye. "Except here we are, sitting in this restaurant, because you love to eat out."

"He meant more than that. You know he reports to me. It's weird. It's rude. I don't know what he can expect to gain by that kind of remark."

"It's weird to me that we're seated and don't have menus."

"It took Sheela two months to land this reservation for me. You can wait a few minutes for a menu."

"What are we supposed to be doing in this dead time with no drinks, no menus?"

"Settle in? Become one with the luminous ambiance. Talk to one another. Bask in one another's affection."

He's looking around, surveying the layout. She's looking at him, surveying him. He almost passes for a young man in this light. He does pass as someone who could be with a much younger woman than she is. He stares directly at her a bit and passes as smart enough to recognize how lame going younger would be.

"There might be two women in this entire place who are almost as hot as you are," he says. "But not a single one who is hotter. And none of them likes to eat out like you like to eat out."

Meghan lets David get away with saying shit like this because he does not have a career. He has not worked since the first of the babies arrived. He has given up even the pretense of painting or any serious photography work. He has done a great job being a stay-at-home dad and house manager while his wife has generated income and managed wealth. Meghan doesn't experience any kind of emasculation issues in the family arrangement, but has been counseled that, denied the occasional display of primate male posturing, David might develop a repressed problem with appearances. Meghan counts on the arrival of the menus, which surely must be imminent, to put an end to David's brute time.

"Oh, Meg," David says in muted wonder. "Be careful looking over there. Phil and Bonnie were just seated."

"The Shapiros?" Meghan's neck twists in a subtle, rubberized snap. A very attentive staffer, she sees, is handing menus to the Shapiros. "They've got a great table," says Meghan.

"It looks like they're eating on their own. And we're eating on our own," observes David. David and his wife, up until six years back, had been frequent dining companions with the Shapiros. Even after the syndication deals, when the Shapiros became so much richer than mere multimillionaires, the couples had marked special occasions and life events with expensive meals, with Phil unobtrusively absorbing the cost, until awkwardness pushed David to push forward Meghan's small business Am Ex. The dinners became sporadic and a thing of the past. In the meantime, Bonnie Shapiro, dismissed initially as a dabbler, had opened a hot gallery where David's work has never been shown. "Isn't it weird that we're both in the same restaurant, and both on our own?"

"Maybe not," observes Meghan. "The two place settings across from them are still on the table."

"Have they seen us?" asks David. "Are they ignoring us? Why were they seated without a complete party? Wouldn't it be less awkward for them to wait at the bar?"

"You mean *more comfortable*," corrects Meghan. "And *in the lounge*."

"I've heard Bonnie might be pregnant again," says David. "When I was picking up Leaf."

"How did you hear that? They don't go to Leaf's school anymore."

"Some of Phil's showrunners' kids do. Maybe that's why they're seated in the dining room and not at the bar. Because Bonnie's pregnant. How do we know if we should say hello? It's so hard to know what to do. Leaving before they see us is going to be tricky."

"It'll take half a year to land another reservation. We're not leaving."

"Should we pretend we haven't seen them? Can we pull that off?"

"David. Pull yourself together. I can't even imagine who they're waiting to join them."

"Well, just stick in here with me, honey. You won't need to imagine anything."

"Maybe they've seen us," Meghan muses, "and they're pretending they didn't. Us being here could be just as awkward for them."

"I hope you can take some satisfaction in that," says David. "Maybe they're waiting for Jonah Hill."

The mention of Jonah Hill unites the couple in silent musing. David's musings are more poignant. The Jonah Hill incident had caused him a personal pain. Meghan and David are at this restaurant as a special occasion. Clearly, Phil and Bonnie—see how Phil rolls the dark wine in his exquisite stemware—belong to this establishment as everyday patrons. David and his wife, at some table so remote that no server bearing menus has yet to find it, stand out as persons who are able to visit but do not belong. The persons who do not belong are standouts. David, especially, stands out.

He has always been a standout, but long ago in a different way. Before the Shapiros knew they would be rich, the shared common assumption was that David would be a standout among their group. He'd made some sales to some prestige collections. He'd hung in a number of career-launching group shows on both coasts and a solo exhibition in L.A. He had missed a grip on the next rung. For a while, he'd been dangling as if by one arm. Now he's let go and nested several rungs below.

David, Meghan remembers clearly, used to be so funny. He was always the designated humorist. Even as his career stalled, his comedic view had soared. It's almost as if he could have gone into observational comedy as a fallback, or so people used to say. The Shapiros said as much a dozen times, until they had a series of dinners with Jonah Hill. They'd seen funny, retelling that series of dinners seemed to suggest, and they left the concluding half of that statement vague, open and broad. They'd gone on a promotional tour with Jonah Hill through California wine country. They've seen Jonah rise to hysteric highs when mobbed by adoring crowds. They've observed Jonah back on the tour bus sinking into his seat and an apparent abject depression. "You have no idea what this kind of emotional crash is like," Phil had assured them. David had thought maybe he did have an idea. While waiting for dessert, smiling at Bonnie Shapiro, he had brought to mind a depression the depths of which no one outside his closest allies could ever fathom and were unlikely ever to descend into, a plunge beyond the comprehension of even himself until those days he dropped into it. All his bouts of burrowing directly into the core of despair were mere surface scratches, according to the message delivered to the table by Phil's rarefied friends. That dinner, where the Shapiros had squashed his hill of beans under the weight of Jonah Hill had not been David's idea, and not the current dinner either, which also, he feared, was on the way to being derailed by the Shapiros.

Meghan sees a grave pronouncement forming behind David's fixed bemusement. She steels herself to parry it. Suddenly the Shapiros have spotted them. The waving and grinning from Bonnie and Phil is spontaneous, open and warm. It can only be genuine. Meg and Dave decide as one to rise and go to the Shapiros. Meg hesitates a second while David rises to give the illusion of following his lead.

"Don't mention Bonnie's pregnancy," Meghan whispers, "in case it's just fat."

Now that David is walking toward Phil and Bonnie, the movement seems correct and natural. He realizes the mistake he would have made if he and his wife had remained in their chairs and waved and nodded and smiled and proposed a toast with empty goblets. There was a time, several years before Jonah Hill's people would have returned their call, when the Shapiros had crossed a crowded and celebrity-studded Japanese country restaurant to connect with Dave and Meg, and another couple. *None of us had any acquaintances among any of those celebrities back then*, thinks David. Meghan, of course, now has worked with many famous people, reality stars, not really people of widely recognized accomplishment, not like Jonah Hill.

At the Shapiros' table, Bonnie attempts to stand, settles for a half rise. It becomes clear why the burden to approach was on David and Meghan. The burden is less for them. Bonnie is obviously pregnant, unless she has only gained an impossible ton of weight. Either way, she cannot be expected to waddle across this chic and trim expanse of tables. Meghan gives David the meaningful eye contact, warning him not to be the first to mention pregnancy. Her househusband has not forgotten his place.

The edit of his inner banter is a first response to David now. Not so long ago, his standing with the Shapiros was unfiltered. He could have picked out a humorous thread in Bonnie's weight gain, or in any other foible or pride of this husband and wife.

The Shapiros and the Nelsons share no common endeavors at this point and have no upcoming plans or recent joint experience. They are not current. Standing in a restaurant just as an intricate, extensive chef's menu is about to unfold is no occasion and not enough time to bring one another up to date. The four parents erupt in a frenzy of asking after one another's kids in the most general and glowing queries and replies.

"And I wonder," wonders David in mock wonder, "are you two thinking about having any more?"

The tableside shakes with laughter. Bonnie cups her belly and a wistful glow turns her face into a lump of happiness. Good feeling rises among the four and lingers. David's still got it. They've all missed one another. Is Phil about to suggest they get together, for a meal or a show?

"How about you guys?" says Phil. "You're still at the place in the Oaks? There's plenty of room for another kid up there."

But not room in the Nelson budget. Two children, it seems, is their peak number. Meghan and David have talked this one over. Many of the people they know, or have worked with—well, worked for or under—have opted for the third child, citing a much richer sibling dynamic and proven long-term life outcomes based on a foundation of multiple primary relations. Meghan's body, she feels certain, when last she and hubby discussed it, was up to the task of delivering a third offspring. Financially, the projected costs capped their wealth creation at a lower level. They had concluded that the third child, in this day and age, was a particularly unsupportable and selfish status symbol.

"I'm not sure if we're shooting for another pregnancy," says David, "or if all the bedroom action is just Meghan surrendering to the laws of attraction. It's not easy living with me, for a woman to stay off the stick."

Bonnie and Phil laughingly play along.

"I can imagine," says Bonnie. "She looks like she wants to haul you off for a private encounter right now."

There was a time when David could make the joke about being an irresistible piece of man ass, about being the man with the most male sex appeal of any man, and his friends or acquaintances or just well-meaning strangers would see the absurd humor and good-natured humility juxtaposed against the boastful straight-faced declaration. The key to the joke's success, why it was the go-to, slam-dunk joke, was David's confidence in his ability to project a stealth reality. Beneath the posturing blowhard was in fact a desirable, even potentially hot, fuck. David could afford to make a joke mocking sex appeal at his own expense because his sex appeal was obvious, though subtle. So ha-ha. A discerning audience lingers in David's memory, like moviegoers staying after to watch the credits roll. This discerning audience sees beyond the self-mockery to the truth of David's animal and intellectual appeal. That audience of discerning memory includes this couple, the Shapiros, but—it might have been wise for David to wonder as Meghan tugs his sleeve—where has the rest of the discerning audience gone?

"You know, she just made me give it to her on the way over here, in the back of the Uber," says David. He turns toward the restaurant at large as if appealing to an expanding crowd of spectators. Two people stand directly behind him, suspended smiles patient and impertinent on their lips. "When you've got it," finishes David, unable to stop the momentum, "you're obligated to give it away."

The two new people, it is clear to David and Meghan in the space of time when a laugh line might mercifully have been inserted, are the two diners that Bonnie and Phil had been waiting for. The new couple completes the Shapiro party of four. This pair, the woman a world-class beauty, obviously famous for it, both dressed wonderfully on point, regard Meghan and David with abject tolerance and guarded questions. Are this fairly hysterical man and his less-manic companion acquaintances—*friends* is too strong a word—of the Shapiros? Has a pair of TV nerds stepped forward to introduce themselves to the captive television creators, the fabulous Shapiros?

Bonnie coughs, makes the most of a pregnant pause, performs introductions all around and removes all doubt about who is who. Meghan catches the name of an Academy Award-winning script writer, which makes sense of the supermodel—whose name of course she already knew—hanging on the writer's arm and smile. Meghan is grateful to have been designated, by Bonnie, as a TV big shot. David, not so lucky, is introduced as "David Nelson, the painter. I'm sure you've heard us talk about him."

"David's work is very highly regarded," interjects Phil.

"What a great coincidence," says the screenwriter. "Now that the twins are walking, we have three kids' bedrooms that need to be done over."

"Oh, no, really," demurs David, "that is so kind."

"Are individual rooms something you do?" asks the supermodel. "Or primarily entire residences?"

"I'm not that kind of painter," says David, gently, as if speaking to a favored, developmentally stalled child.

"Of course you aren't!" exclaims the supermodel. She is effusive. She is a font of validation. "Next time we're at Bonnie's gallery, I'll insist she show us some of your work."

"David was just regaling us with stories of his extraordinary sexual ability," says Bonnie. Having completed their greeting hugs, Bonnie's screenwriter and supermodel dinner partners claim their chairs. The writer and supermodel look up at David as if from a front row orchestra pit.

"I've never been able to resist a story of extraordinary sexual ability," says the writer.

"We'd love to stay and hear one," ad libs Meghan, nimble, adroit, a natural rescuer, "but our waiter seems to be losing patience with our wandering."

The parting salvos are warm and overdone just enough. Back at their own table, Meghan and David order in a blur of deference and efficiency. David excuses himself to wash his hands. He stands at the urinal. David is thinking he might have been able to pull off the faux false modesty line of levity, to have extended the thread, pushed the stream to one more trickle of laughter. Leaving the men's room, David pauses at a full-length mirror. He notices that he is no slouch. In context of the dining room, he fades into the surrounding plumage, but moving into the foreground of taking his seat beside Meghan, he is brought to face and found satisfactory. Appetizers arrive, exquisite, delectable. David places the supermodel in the mirror frame, beside him in the men's room. Her command of the reflection is so strong that it blocks him out completely. Meghan had been right. She'd seen disaster coming, and had cut off his self-humiliation at its approach. Nothing he might have said to the writer and the supermodel, and no manner in which he might have said it, had any chance of snatching funniness from the overwhelming and apparent sadness exposed by their contrasting lives.

David spears a scallop, pops it in his mouth, sighs and hopes the depression will be even half so exquisite. "I almost told the sexiest woman in all media that I'm the sexiest man in the land."

Meghan catches David's eye. "The punch line is that you're not so bad," she says. "Not for your age."

Meghan sees an indication that her joke may have cheered David, insufficiently. Here come the entrees. "You need to be less hard on yourself."

"Obviously." David is eager to be quick to agree. "I mean, look who I'm comparing myself to."

Meghan looks over at the glamorous foursome. The couples are chatting with ease and familiarity and casual high regard. Meghan forks a pasta pillow into her mouth and grunts, a grunt of delight and resignation. "Just don't start comparing me to her," she says. "The pasta is divine."

"This risotto is like we're back on Capri." David gives a petite groan of absolute satisfaction. He means something close to the absolute opposite of that. Looking inside, savoring spice and juice, he compares himself to the scary person he should have been, if the paintings had taken off, if the photos had caught on, if the attention of the world had turned his way and bent to him.

The meal proceeds under the shadow of that fearsomely accomplished version of David. He is funny and magnanimous. He makes jokes that are generous and sweet. He slides forward his own credit card when the bill arrives. No polite notice comes back that David's card has been declined.

David puts on a bold face, perhaps a tad bolder than Meghan's. The husband and wife bid farewells in passing to the Shapiro party, who linger over cordials. The bold faces supported by Meghan and David stay in place until the valet pulls up with the Chevrolet Volt. The car is two kids and one income short of being a Tesla. Dropping into the Volt's optional luxury-like upholstery, David sinks into his shallow, mediocre despair, nothing like the deep, singular anguish of Jonah Hill. David's is the mundane despair of heading home on upgraded upholstery that the Nelsons had convinced themselves with double-checked columns of facing figures they could afford. Meghan, beside him in the driver's seat, is too close and in too deep to help pull David toward the surface.

David hands off cash to the babysitter. In the spring, he'll need to find another one. This one will be heading off to college, a better school than David had attended, a school that for many artists has been the first step in acclaimed productive careers. Meghan has removed her makeup and is applying nighttime products to her face. David turns on the TV in a room near the kitchen, what could be the bedroom for another child. He runs through the channels. Every second or third scripted show seems to have had some connection with Phil and Bonnie. David has stopped tracking every Shapiro series running in syndication. Every one of them, he notices now, contains a harbinger of the obsolete. The world has pivoted, like trends in theme song or interior design pivot, but in a vaster scope. At one time, the Shapiros had been lauded for their revolutionary entertainment packaging. That was all in the past. Their aesthetic is a little dated. In David's estimation, from the height of his awesome success, his friends have outlived their vogue.

FEAR OF FAILURE

This is a tale of measures taken to forestall premature ejaculation. It asks you to identify with some guy whose wife has kicked him out of the house. He doesn't know where she is at this moment. He suspects she is somewhere in the company of at least one other woman. He is their topic of discussion.

"Was there sex?" The wife's friends want to know. "Is it because there was no sex?"

"One of the problems," replies the wife, "is that he was always eager to instigate sex. It's a long story. Not a super long story. Long enough that I can't do it justice right now. We'll have to get together again. I'll give you all the details some other time."

Some other time is where Jane, the wife waiting for the valet, goes. Her car is brought around. Rather than return to her friends who are calling *ciao*, she drives off into the recent past, to a stretch of months when she had been concerned about her husband's health. His name is Miles. Jane had been worried about Miles's heart. She was in bed, under him. The notion came to her that her husband's circulatory system was underperforming. This is not a thought, really, that a woman wants popping up when she is being made love to. His erection, so rigid and solid at insertion, had flagged. Miles clutched parts of his wife with force, if not passion. Apparently he could not lock into her eyes. She tried to remember the first time she had noticed Miles's penile fatigability and realized it was a recurring condition. Thinking back, the malady had been evident for years. She counted them on her fingers. If his circulatory condition is a progressive one, it's had time to slip into a life-threatening stage. Clearly, Jane realized, Miles must be charting this decline. Is he unable to look at her due to embarrassment? Or is it something more, something closer to desperation? Fear of some dangerous cardiac anomaly—a clogged pulmonary artery for instance—might be preventing him from meeting her eyes at disappointing times of soft intimacy.

Jane had rolled out from under Miles, positioned him on his back, straddled him and taken up most of the physical labor in the thrusting. Looking down at his face, she saw panic creep in under the surface bliss of his eyes. His erection wavered wildly. Jane is lost to the moment, projecting into a future of heart specialists, dietary restrictions, targeted surgeries within her husband's chest cavity. Jane's attention and resources are so consumed by scheduling her husband's coming medical appointments and delivering him to them, that she only half notices when he turns her over, enters from behind, salvages a dissolving situation and delivers the climactic finish that Jane has come to anticipate as ordinary resolution of their lovemaking.

In the stillness, punctuated by Miles's huffing, Jane tries to come up with a delicate way to broach the subject of her husband's deathly infirmity. She breaks right in on his panting reverie.

"Honey, when's the last time you had a physical?"

"A physical what?"

"A check-up. I think you should have your heart checked."

"Why would you think that?"

"The sex. It's not finishing through."

"I thought it was fine."

Jane cannot come close to imagining, at least not yet, what might be going through Miles's mind. Mortality clearly has given him a poke in his chest. She lets him ruminate in quiet, while the reality seeps in. She shapes up what she needs to say next.

Miles watches his wife descend into stillness. He takes this opportunity to think things over. There's this girl, a woman actually, the new waitress at the coffee spot. She'd known he was watching her when she came out from behind the counter to tidy the tables. All the tables are low and impractical. That impracticality has its purpose, reflects Miles, just as improbably high-heeled shoes— steep ones like the coffee waitress wears—have a purpose. She'd bent at the waist to scoop a tray of cups and saucers. She'd caught his eye face on, looking out at him from above the buoyant view revealed by her hanging neckline. She turned and leaned forward to wipe down a Formica surface. She knew his eyes were still on her from behind. Her flex and her sway communicated this knowledge and complicity with it. He and the waitress had done something together, something very subtle and totally public. This coordinated effort had made an impression on Miles, an impression that had stayed throughout the day, beyond the evening commute and into the bed and under the dimmed lights with Jane. The performance at the coffee spot replayed during foreplay. It wasn't until penetration had been achieved and a rhythm set that Miles became acutely aware he was having sex with his wife and not the new girl from the coffee spot. His resolve had weakened. The rock hardness took on spongy edges. He had flipped through the day's encounters for women to spur his erotic impulse. A pair of legs he had followed on the stairs up from the metro raised his tensile angle a few effective degrees. When the angle dipped, picturing two office tarts who had played flit eye in the food court restored the bounce. Miles threaded up a loop of visual and verbal exchanges with women from the previous eighteen hours. His rigidity suffered a down jolt or two, but finishing had been a certainty, until Jane bucked him off and climbed on top.

Her shoulders, breasts, her face, the curtain of her hair closing in on his face as she leaned down to kiss him, her hips grinding somewhere down there, all of this was inescapable. Miles's attention was imprisoned, in the right now right here, directly with his wife.

His boner stalled on the verge of total internal collapse. Prohibited from wandering, his imagination and memory sat powerless in the presence of impending dick disaster. Jane, he'd seen from beneath her, had noticed the reverse surge. Her pleasure had washed out with his receding blood flow. Luckily, he'd had sufficient presence of mind and vestigial tumescence to slip and spin and take on Jane from behind. His visualizations roamed freely, as if over hill and dale, retrieving a firmness of purpose that enabled Miles to finish, lounge, catch his breath and know deep inside that all is well that ends well.

"We're still young," says Jane, circumspectly breaking the no-talking portion of the afterglow. "But Mary's brother had a heart attack. Betsey's sister-in-law too. They're both dead and were still in their forties."

"There's nothing wrong with my heart."

"How can you possibly be certain?"

"Trust me. I'm sure of it."

"You're not a doctor. Won't you get checked up, at least for my peace of mind?"

"What about my peace of mind? If you go to a doctor, they'll tell you something's wrong. They make their money convincing people something's wrong."

"You can check your heart health with three or four tests. Disregard all the rest."

"I check my heart every time I take it out for a spin. It's tiptop. I don't want to hear anything else about a doctor. I won't discuss it."

Miles walks to the kitchen. He customizes a bowl of cereal using three different cartons. Jane, alone in bed, giving herself an internal preview of being far more alone, totally alone, hears her husband's heart beating, erratic, irregular, an intermittently weakening staccato on the verge of giving out. She pictures what she takes to be her husband's most necessary and vital organ puffy, swollen, slack and strained, squeezing out one last pump and clenching in on itself, fisted in a cardiac death grip.

Miles returns to the bedroom with his bowl of tri-color cereal. Jane actualizes, her mouth ready to verbalize the picture of Miles's collapsing caverns. Miles shuts it down with a finger swipe across his lips. He turns on the TV.

Jane keeps her concerns about her husband's heart to herself. For the rest of that night and during the following morning, and on into a few coming weeks, with each passing day, pressure builds to share her anxiety. If not with Miles, with who? The topic is too dire to confide in her friends. Also, any one of them might inadvertently bring Jane's disclosure back to Miles, with something so innocent as assuring him they are all praying for his health. At a loss for anyone to turn to, Jane adheres to Miles, keeping him in sight, following him anywhere, even to the local ice rink where Miles plays in weekly ragtag hockey leagues.

In the stands, she can hardly see the ice for the cold and slippery realities skating through her mind. She and Miles have made love maybe half a dozen times since his heart disease first manifested to her. During each encounter, Miles's performance has been more faltering. In every afterglow, his refusal to address underlying issues and ramifications has been more unyielding. He is an obdurate man. His single-minded refusal of alternative views shows in the way he plays hockey. His skating is aggressive, heedless of impediments, infuriating.

Jane has company in the rink-side bleachers—one woman. Sitting to Jane's left and two planks up, the woman huddles to herself against the ice in the air. Despite her chill, this woman is one of those people who exude warmth. Every tentative glance Jane tosses up in the woman's direction meets a fleeting smile that lingers in lazy, friendly eyes. Finally, the woman removes her hands from her jacket pockets. She scooches down and joins Jane on the lower plank, closer to the ice and the action.

"Seems silly," says the woman, "us sitting separate and the only two fans in the entire gym."

The women introduce one another. Jane's new acquaintance, up close, is revealed to be a decade junior to Jane. She displays as many sophisticated tells—the simple gold bracelet, the subtle nose piercing, the denim that could only have come from a specialty plant in Japan—as are possible to flash in a rundown hockey rink. The hockey players fly past the protective Plexiglas, shouting encouragement and outrage, taunting and praising one another, slapping sticks on ice, bumping one another into the battered green boards, falling and sliding legs up, ass out across the ice. Neither woman pays attention to any of this. Jane, perhaps fancifully, believes she sees something of herself in this idly smiling woman next to her on the plank. This is someone, she senses, with whom she will have an immediate connection. This woman, whose name has already slipped Jane's mind, will listen and hear. She will understand, validate, maybe clarify a next step, and be gone and never seen again, taking with her Jane's certainty that her husband is gliding through life with a staggering, stuttering heart.

The woman, the anonymous potential confessor, turns to Jane and says, "Mine's the goalie for the guys in the green shirts. Which is yours?"

"Mine's orange," replies Jane, thinking, I am so relieved to have accurately identified a companionable soul. She waits, only for a moment, until Miles rampages into their sight line, clubbing defenders with his pumping elbows and flailing his stick like a lance.

"That one," says Jane.

"Oh, my," says the opposing goalie's girlfriend. Her love interest has just been ram-rodded into the back of the net by Miles's willfully out-of-control collision course. Miles is up already, zipping toward his next brutal encounter. "Yours is a real marauder."

"Not really," demurs Jane, edging to her opening, to open up about her husband's upcoming open-heart surgery.

"C'mon!" interjects the goalie's girl. "He must be from Viking stock. He's just out there pillaging from one end of the rink to the other. That's the kind of genetic code that rows over the uncharted oceans to America, during winter, just to keep from raping the neighbors back home into bloody pulps."

The woman is laughing. Her eyes alight. She's delighting in what she sees in Jane's man, and in how she is describing his presumed characteristics, but she is a conscious woman, alert, and sensitive to the feelings of others. With three minutes left to go in the game, and the clock turned off, she notices that Jane has gone silent, and has been speechless since the words *bloody pulps* had been blurted out. She puts a hand to Jane's forearm.

"Hey, I didn't mean to offend you," she says. "Your guy really is the most interesting player on the ice. I was only kidding about the pillaging."

"I know. I know," Jane assures her fellow spectator. "I just got quiet. I started thinking about a situation at work that is too convoluted to delve into."

This to be sure is a lie. The hockey game has ended. The players glide with purposeful lack of evident effort, trading expressions of good sportsmanship. Jane mentally puts to words the seeping suspicion that has been mulling while she sat in silence. Evidence indicates that her husband is not infirm at all. His heart, to judge by his elevated and extended activity levels, is a formidable organ, in no danger of betraying itself.

Miles skates along the side of the rink, and calls out, "Hello! Did you see any of that?"

The two spectators check in with one another, sharing a moment of open eye contact.

"Oh yes," says the other woman. "We saw it all."

"You nearly put her boyfriend into traction," says Jane. "I'm not sure, but an apology might be in order."

"I'd say tell your boyfriend I'm sorry," calls Miles. "You know he'd just take it as a taunt."

Miles isn't expecting a reply or disappointed that one is not forthcoming. The woman who had been beside Jane is taking long steps up the bleacher stairs, on wedge heels, toward the exit. Miles is perfectly content to observe her twisting balancing act, too content. He fails to catch Jane catching his calculating appraisal of those flexing, stretching strides.

In the car, Jane smells the piercing odors coming off Miles's body. He plays a Queen album at a volume that overpowers conversation and sings along, shouting the words he knows, with precision, loudly muttering the rest. Jane wonders, under the influence of his piquant scent, how she had ever mistaken Miles for a heart patient.

At home, even before he's had a chance to shower, Miles pounces on Jane. In a flash of moments, he has her skirt raised and her stomach scraping across the living-room carpet. Jane can't help letting out a laugh of excitation. This type of instant orgasmic coupling is a relic from their initial erotic adventures. Nostalgia for that reawakened primal passion is her laugh trigger. Miles is pronged like a super randy twenty-year-old. Jane spins off her back, trapping Miles's torso in her thighs and flipping him onto his ass. She sees the pride of youthful vigor in his eyes. She leans forward, directly into his field of view, exhaling into his next inhalation. She sees that look of erect triumph recede. Within her, she feels his ardor go from steel toward steamed vegetable.

"I'm trying to remember the name of the woman I was sitting next to," whispers Jane. "At hockey. Can you remember her?"

Jane feels a pulse quicken in the prick inside. Clarity comes to her like an unwelcome, long-stuffed epiphany. Miles's quick uptick just as quickly ticks down. The light goes on, illuminating what Jane has known for a long while. She is a masturbatory aid, and one that is losing its efficacy.

And now, in the row of nine weeks after her husband has ceded occupational rights to the shared house, Miles is sure that somewhere with someone, a person probably female and certainly unsympathetic to him, this aborted sexual encounter with his estranged wife, what may well turn out to be the last stab at physical intimacy between them, is being played back to dramatic effect and grave condemnation. Not that he should give a shit. Not that he doesn't have enough emotional dissonance clogging his mind to blot out any reverberations of his exiting wife telling dog tales across town.

In nine weeks, Miles has had one encounter each with two different women. Both have gone badly, as in all too briefly. His biggest fear, one of them, is that these two women will have lunch and tally up his metrics and add him to a no-fly list of chumps who pop at the mere prospect. By Miles's own accounting, he has thrust a total of six strokes in the months following his wife's forced severance, and most of those were post ejaculation.

The first encounter, anyone could have understood how he had squirted upon insertion. Understanding is not what had happened. The woman was younger, from a rising, almost adjacent generation, and enthusiastic. She had been an underling, one of his favorites. He'd been something like a mentor to her. He had exhibited characteristics of mentorship. He had edited her keynote presentations, pointed out the lines of power among the corporate officers and nominated her to spearhead increasingly critical projects. For her part, Carla had made her interest in seeing Miles outside the office, or furtively in some quiet cubby, explicit, without pushing him. When she was ready to fly off toward greater heights, Miles had given her résumé a rewrite and coached her, with role-play prep, for interviews.

In her new job, Carla had been pleased, not fully surprised, to receive Miles's private message. She had so much to tell him, about her recent promotion, about coming industry expansion. They met for a Saturday coffee, at her suggestion. When Miles admitted that he and Jane had separated, Carla emitted a sentence of condolence.

Her condolence was not particularly deep. "To tell the truth," Carla said, peeking out to see if Miles would permit her small, sly smile, "I'm not totally surprised. I mean, I'd heard you were out on your own. Also I sort of felt a split coming back when we worked together."

Miles dodged an impulse to speak of the happy days when Carla "had been working under him" and succeeded in not derailing the path of destiny that led from the Venice Boardwalk coffeehouse to a start-up condo Carla had taken possession of in the Palisades. In the foyer, Miles spends a moment calculating the massive bump that Carla's salary must have received to afford this place. She hadn't had time to fully furnish the interiors. A platform bed was in place, positioned beneath a sun-channeling skylight. Carla didn't have time to waste. Her hair appointment was at three. She cut out the preliminaries.

"I'll show you the rest of the place later," she said, flexing and smiling and tumbling on impossibly rich sheets, the same brand Miles's wife insisted upon. Solar rays played upon Carla's skin. When had she become naked? In the car? On the drive over? "But you're not really here to admire my high-end kitchen appliances, Miles, are you?"

It was like Miles had stepped into a sparkling house. Everything he saw—it was mostly all Carla—was a glittering manifestation of all his physical fantasies. The vision was gorgeous. He had no sense of how far from or close to him Carla's curves and indentations were. He stepped forward and stumbled, tripping on the elastic of his undershorts. Put him in a deposition, and honestly, he would be unable to say who had pulled down those shorts. Him or Carla? Miles has been asking himself this question since he'd slid onto those luxury sheets and been blinded by the sensation of Carla's smooth, giving, taking, shifting embrace. She was on pace to know every inch of his skin within mini-moments, merest fractions of time, each distinct and highly defined, photographic and tensile. It was an erotically all-encompassing, fully immersive experience. To be blunt, and succinct, Carla's body was hotter than anything he'd ever seen or dreamed of. She had spread and welcomed him within. It was as though Miles felt every sensation through her nerve endings, through her pleasure cells, through her mucous membranes. Miles had never been so fully in the presence of another human being. He felt so close to that other person, to Carla, that he might be a part of her. They might be extensions of one another, united at their pleasure centers, if only for a second.

"What the fuck, Miles?"

"Jesus. I had no idea that could even happen."

"Fine. At least get me a towel, will you?"

Miles hustled to the connected bathroom and hustled back in time to see Carla perched up in bed, cigarette lit, sheets and comforter pulled tight and tucked under her chin, sealing off any thought of further approach by Miles. Carla looked at him critically, unblinking. Miles's penis, he felt, would be ready to try again in forty minutes or less. Clearly, Carla was not going to stop staring. Miles's penis—he knew from the reflection in Carla's eyes—was showing no signs in that moment of vitality. He scooped his clothes from the floor, retreated to the bathroom and dressed quickly while screened from Carla's merciless gaze. When he is done, Carla stands in the living room, at the door leading outside.

"Look," he says, apologetic, "I know you have to rush, but maybe we…."

"If I'd been in that big a rush, I wouldn't have invited you up here."

She opened the door in a gesture that clearly meant to say everything that needed to be said. Miles walked to his car, attempting to feign a spring in his step. His shoulders slouched under the weight of Carla's message, a communication that he took to mean, "Next time, stick to someone closer to your own age."

Work, setting up his transitional apartment and negotiating with Jane over the removal of select furnishings and the bulk of his wardrobe occupied much of Miles's thought in the immediate aftermath of his anticlimax with Carla. He had installed his clothes racks in a downtown split-level loft, overpriced and lacking in basic services, but with wonderful rooftop city views and the airy feel of a double-story vaulted interior. A wall of tempered glass stood twice as tall as he did. With so much serious business shifting in his life, his most pressing concern was predicting the identity of the first woman who would come home to play with him in this downtown redoubt.

She turned out to be a moderate drinker less than a decade younger. He bumped into her, a perfect stranger, at a pop-up art gallery less than two blocks from home. By coincidence, further coincidence, Miles was friends with the exhibiting artist and conversant with the gallery owner herself, which seemed to inure him to his new connection.

"I've been watching you," she said, addressing him across the tilting surface of her plastic champagne glass. "I like the way you look at the art."

Miles saw that this woman, at least following a few drinks, was comfortable being forward, and had the body in reserve to back up that leading disposition. She was laughing, just under the surface, in her cheeks, in her eyes, in the mocking reserve of her set jaw and snaking lips, laughing at Miles's realization of this sudden visitation of good luck.

"I like to think I have an eye for the good stuff," he said, realizing as they fell off his hanging tongue that these were the lamest words he could have dripped out of his maw.

"I felt that," said the woman, "right away." She presented a face of feeling it again, a little deeper. "If you could take home any piece here tonight, which one would it be?"

Obviously, she was the answer. Miles unlocked the door to his split loft. His eyes followed his guest as she sauntered inside. There could have been no question, really at all. She had picked him, in essence, and that's the pick he liked best. She gravitated to the framed Gretzky jersey, inherited from a rich uncle, installed on the brick wall space separating the kitchen island from the downstairs media pit.

"Do you skate?" she asked. She turned to him, moved across the bamboo flooring toward him. Her entire being seemed to vibrate with the hope that he would respond to her double meaning. He closed in on her, a glass of wine in each hand.

"Every chance I get."

They met halfway. Her fingers were down his pants before he could offload the drinks. Her grip was expert and ardent.

"Don't think you're the only one who knows how to handle a stick," she said. She pushed out a cross between a laugh and a grunt. Miles had an intrusive wishful thought. He wished that she were snickering at that stick talk, that she would acknowledge it was ridiculous. She was serious, and seriously skilled. The mere touch of her precision handiwork brought about a state of instant tumescence. Her free hand dropped her skirt and panties to the floor and clawed Miles's jeans and shorts to his ankles. Miles kicked off his shoes and stepped out of his boxers, not wanting to be tripped up again by the waistband's encroachment upon his ankles. He pulled off his shirt in a controlled flurry and lifted his guest's sweater up over her breasts. She unloosed him so he could clear her top over her head and cast it away. The casting motion was so free and supple that all Miles's restraint chased after it, releasing a surge of blood that felt like he was beyond pulsating. He was vibrating, humming like a tuning fork. His lucky date licked the palm of her hand, spat into it. Her tongue wetted her lips and lurked, its tip poised between her set teeth. Her mouth rose toward his. Her spit-lubricated palm closed on his trilling shaft. His drooling mouth closed on empty air.

"What the fuck, dude?"

This woman, Miles didn't know her name, glared at him from across the space she had suddenly inserted between them. She held out her hand. "Look what you did."

She could not have been more outraged if he had shit on her fingers. This much he knew for sure. The woman shook her hand as if to fling the offending substance from her skin. She stomped into the kitchen. She stood naked in heels, bent over the steel sink, furiously rubbing her hands beneath the tap. Miles recognized a magnificent photogenic moment. He took no enjoyment in the image. He'd seen a vision, a frightening vision. He was more than half dressed before she turned back around.

"That was a juvenile little trick," she said, arranging her skirt around her hips. "If I wanted to give out a handjob, I'd be hanging out at the local high school, which looking around this place right now…." She pulled the sweater over her head and wrenched it into place across her torso. "I'm seeing high school fantasy bachelor pad. I'm seeing a very stunted man boy who is so scared by the open sexuality of an adult woman that he just rushes to squeeze off his little pee pee's spurt gun."

She reached the door. She was outside the apartment. She had only to close the door.

"I've heard of hair trigger," she said. "You're a fucking *air* trigger."

Leaving the door open, she was gone. Miles waited until he heard the elevator arrive, open, close and take her away. He closed the door, latched it and double-checked the second lock. His head banged softly on the enamel above the peephole. Each gentle knock failed to dislodge the picture of this avenging jerk-off woman and young Carla meeting by chance, determining him as a common acquaintance, and verifying each other's dire conclusions about him.

There are only so many women in this city. They tend to talk to one another. Miles has memories, imperfectly suppressed, of eavesdropping on Jane and previous women he had lived with talking to their girlfriends about men. The details were ruthless, precise, voluminous, always delivered with full names and identifying features. Dimensions, bodily emissions, signature moves, interior décor, no nuance was too slight to be remarked upon without mercy and interpreted as a larger sign of shoddy character and negative personal human worth. The odds of Carla knowing the woman who had just stormed out into the downtown streets are calculable. Miles knows he has a limited number of fails before dots connect and he is red flagged throughout the circuit of local woman who do sex.

Miles vows to be far more selective about his next party. Wary of being called out on a third strike, he sticks to that resolve for a month, longer. He does not move on the first prospect who happens within range, or even upon the second or third. He is looking for something specific. He needs to see a flaw, just one. For Miles to express and follow up interest, the prospect needs to possess one physical feature that Miles can find fault with. Not necessarily a deformity, but a feature that does not arouse him. His theory is that if sex starts, and his horses are bursting at the gate, so to speak, he can take a time out to concentrate fully on his partner's one non-arousing feature. His stallions will be calm, will settle into harness and pull as a coordinated, powerful, unhurried team through the blissfully uphill, joyously straining process that leads to and triggers orgasm. Holding his horses with a glance at the physical flaw will enable Miles to forestall the spill long enough to pass the threshold of acceptable elapsed time, delivering him into the pool of viable fucks.

Miles met a svelte, sandy blonde woman with a whip-smart smirk and a peculiar beauty mark. The blemish, prominent between her right ear and eye, was one of the first things he noticed about the woman. It was the differentiator that made her initially stand out in a crowd of attractive women. He'd caught sight of her in a stream of yoga proponents exiting an elite body sculpting studio and milling in the adjacent coffeehouse. Miles was at a rear table, out of general lines of observation, concluding an initial interview with a potential employer. The talks were going well, establishing interest on both sides. Miles excused himself to fetch a refill. It wasn't characteristic of him to be so bold. He'd just seen what he'd been waiting for.

Miles stepped up to the ordering counter, forthrightly, and stood next to the woman with the marked face. He wondered if she had more blemishes on her body. If so, would these further marks detract or enhance? He thought of the marks, without knowing they existed, as insurance. He smiled, said hello and within moments had learned that the woman's name was Emma and that her beauty mark had perplexing dual properties. It had caught his eye, had drawn him toward her. It also had the power to completely absorb his attention in a neutralized zone of flattened interest. Looking at the blemish at key moments, he knew, would prolong sexual intercourse indefinitely, if he wanted to go that long.

Emma was amused that he had broken off from a job interview to approach her. She took a seat at a table where she and Miles could maintain eye contact while Miles and the two venture fund scouts finished their talk. Emma sat with the birth-marked side of her face toward him and waited until his interlocutors had left. She allowed Miles to catch her as she paced herself out the door.

Emma and Miles went on three dates. They kissed after the first and fondled briskly and brusquely during the second. Both consenting adults presumed that date three would end with them in bed. Taking advantage of this foreknowledge, Miles masturbated to release before heading out to meet Emma on date three. This next fuck will be crucial. All he needs is one decent enduring screw. It will be like riding a bicycle, like a mastery that he can never forget. A full-on fuck with Emma, and he will be back in the saddle, pedaling like a natural. Clearing his excess buildup beforehand is only best practices.

During the date, while in the car with Emma's attentive eyes, poised lips, flexed thighs and pertinent posture closed in with him, Miles intermittently sneaks glances at the beauty mark, over by the passenger seat window, and verifies that it will hold his horses. Once they reach the restaurant, sitting across from Emma in a dining area that is stacked beyond all reasonable expectation with delectable women, visual stimulation floods toward Miles in the wild. He deliberately blocks out sexual arousal, well, dampens it. He sees everything, from ankles to necks, to that tender moist spot behind the ears. Only the least excitation is permitted to seep through.

When the sex comes, he is shaky on getting it up. His concentrated pleasure drifts mid-journey, something he had not felt since he'd been married. He admires Emma's smooth power thrusts. He luxuriates in the silken clasp of her thighs. He paws like a greedy bear at the honeyed apples of her breasts. Things are looking up. The thought of her birthmark, facing away from him, out of view pressed to the pillow, its existence held in abeyance, springs to mind. He doesn't feel himself faltering. He does feel himself recognizing the possibility. Faltering is something that could happen. He tries to cast the beauty mark aside. That concentrated effort heightens his awareness that the blemish is hidden on the other side of Emma's face. If she turns her head and puts him eye-to-eye with the mark, difficulties may descend. The boner could be lost. He needs to pull through and finish strong. Two insta-pops followed by a flop? He'll be a laughingstock across the worldwide ladies' network.

Seeking arousing imagery, Miles peers into that network of ladies, what he knows of it. He detaches pertinent specifics from five or six of the women he'd kept under semi-surveillance at the restaurant during the date with Emma. One, two, then three palpable attributes slide into frame. Emma, beneath him, feels the difference these visualizations make. Staunch firmness returns. Miles powers toward the point of no return. He achieves a vantage that sees one last spurt to the finish line. Still, Miles is not entirely out of the weeds. Emma's face is turning slowly, lifting the beauty mark off the pillowcase. Its dampening magic rotates toward Miles. He casts about for a final solid visualization to boost him over the edge.

He thinks of his wife. He pictures Jane, and he is afraid that all is lost.

FEAR OF THE DARK

Sliding into the passenger seat of Ben's car, Brenda slow flashes some shining skin. Patches of thigh and breast. Ben catches her eyes catching him looking. Brenda approves. Ben realizes he is grooving on a stream of self-confidence, satisfied to be the person he is, happy in the moment, anticipating rich body and soul gratification. He hasn't felt this way for the past half a year and more. Spousal rejection is an undermining calamity, especially when compounded by a financial hit and relocation into a degraded living situation. Splitting an apartment with same-sex non-romantic roommates is an arrangement Ben thought he had forever outgrown. Shared occupancy provides each morning and night with its base coat of humiliation. As partial compensation, daily contact with people who will never be more than losers occasionally pays dividends. To illustrate: At the start of this week, the less pathetic of his two male roommates had opened Ben's eyes to a reality that Ben had shuttered off.

The roommate spooned directly into his mouth from a carton of Icelandic yogurt Ben had bought. "Just check out the metrics on you," said the roommate. "You're getting paid triple the median salary for an American family of four living at the poverty line. You're banking in the top percentile for your age group."

Numbers do not lie, supposedly, but Ben is a person who resists easy encouragement. "I still can't afford my own place," he protested. "I'm check to check. There's no savings anywhere."

"You're a core employee at a startup with mad stock options."

"Do you know how many startups have shut down so far this year? With all the mad stock being worth mad nothing?"

"Ben, it's too late to bum yourself out. You already have a legacy, with all that hot dog Twitter work. How many people in this current workforce can claim they were on a *Forbes* list of the top 25 social media managers under 25?"

"Me and twenty-nine other people can claim that." The *Forbes* list had been online only and titled "Thirty Under Thirty."

"Twenty-five, twenty-nine, what's the difference? Man, 200 million Americans, right this second, I just did a poll. Wait, I'm receiving an update. Two hundred and twenty million Americans wish they had your spot on that list."

In his enthusiasm, the roommate spilled Icelandic yogurt from his mouth to the kitchen table and floor. He was right, of course. Ben's tenure as social media generator for Weiner Wag had set a digital industry standard. He had placed a staid Frankfurter company among the Internet's trending food vendors, an accomplishment leveled before he turned twenty-seven, with much of the groundwork laid while he was still twenty-five. Currently, Ben is over-achieving as primary opposition-research generator for Dis-Content, a startup that closed a splashy opening round for paid Dis-Content, a disruptive reinvention of brand-sponsored content.

Ben, looking into an empty refrigerator, knowing beyond doubt where his last Icelandic yogurt had gone, admitted that his roommate's flattery was fundamentally correct. Ben had a lot going for him. The facts added up intellectually. But he didn't bodily feel that he was in the winner's circle until Friday after work, when Brenda waited a discrete interval and followed him out of the office, slid into the front passenger seat of Ben's car and shut the door, sealing herself up inside.

Brenda's choice to travel with Ben holds significance. She is aligned with top management. The founder's direct assistant, she clearly means something more to that crowning executive. She has picked Ben. Obviously, she anticipates fast-track advancement in his career's immediate future. Also, beyond her advantageous perch in the Dis-Content hierarchy, Brenda is a Black woman, a young attractive one. Attractive, young Black women, Ivy League graduates in their twenties, don't slide into a car with just any white guy. As a desired, young Black woman, Brenda is uniquely qualified to detect some inherently chill value in Ben's personality. Manifestly she detects chill. Ben detects his chill too, reflected in the smile his passenger holds on him. Brenda has agreed to attend an improv showcase that Ben's flattering roommate will perform in.

"Ben," she says, "can we make one little tweak in the evening's plans?"

In the face of Brenda's high-watt grin, Ben has no real fight within him. He acquiesces automatically. "Whatever shot you want to call," says Ben, "just call it."

"Would it make you mad to stop at a work party on the way to the comedy, just to drop in?"

Following his immediate agreement, Ben is a little miffed. The Dis-Content founder, Ben presumes, is the party's host.

"A work event is not my favorite way to start the weekend," Brenda says, "but I'm feeling a little pressure to make an appearance."

"I'm all in," says Ben. He is all in his head displeased that the founder had not invited him personally to the party. Ben recalls three distinct one-on-one conversations with the founder in the past two days. The founder hadn't bothered to mention he was having a few key people over for light bites and cocktails. After this snub, how is Ben expected to feel that he's a core team member? Still, hearing about the gathering through Brenda, and gaining entry as her companion, is a stroke of opportunity. The founder will see the added value Ben brings to a party. Next time a guest list is compiled, Ben's name will be on the first draft and survive all cuts. Wait, here's something he should of thought of sooner. It's possible, probable perhaps, that the founder has suggested to Brenda that she bring along Ben.

If he'd been thinking about the road in front of him, instead of spinning out machinations all around him, Ben might have taken a clue from where the car has headed at Brenda's direction. Too late to wonder where he is being led, Ben drives up and down a street of tightly placed multi-family residences in dim light of lampposts, half of which are broken.

"What are we doing here?" he asks.

"Looking for a parking spot, goof." He takes a spot at Brenda's insistence, under silent protest, that leaves his back bumper intruding on a driveway. He follows Brenda from the car up a cracked cement walkway to a security door behind wrought iron bars. The smell of cat shit and weed wrenches Ben's attention away from Brenda's hips. He thinks, *This is not a founders' neighborhood.*

The door behind the metal grate opens to show two inches of light and illuminates the absence of a bulb in a fixture above the landing. Voices belt out into the cramped, dark entryway. "Brenda! Baby! You made it, and look! You brought a guest!"

"I told you she'd show up. I told you she'd be cool." The door swings wide. Brightness flashes out Ben's sight. From inside, unseen, " 'Brenda's down,' I said. 'Brenda's cool. Brenda will show up.' "

"And she's brought a guest, too, is what I said."

"Who?"

"It's Cool Hand Ben."

"No shit? The Killer Kid? The Peach Fuzz Assassin! Entering our domain?"

Brenda pushes forward. "He will if you open the door," she says, "and move out of the way."

Blinking and looking beyond Brenda, Ben can take in the entire interior of the single apartment, except for the bathroom. The two rooms—a kitchen with attached dining area and a living room—are crowded with party people dressed for festivity, with not a white face in the place, unless a white face is hiding in the bathroom. Old-school soul beats out from a record player at the border of kitchen and living room. Stepping inside, Ben recognizes two men from work. Their smiles and eyes are friendly upon him. They hadn't expected his arrival any more than Ben had expected to show up. They're less taken aback than he is.

"Hey, Malik," Ben says, proud for managing their names, despite never having been introduced in the office. "Nice to see you, Jared."

"Shit! Cool Hand Ben knows our names!" says Jared.

"But you don't know what we do, do you?" says Malik. "At the job I'm talking about."

The workspace is chopped into sections, territory blocks allotted by department. According to the floor plan, Ben judges the two guys to be in tech. Maybe user interface. Maybe site infrastructure.

"You're a creative," says Jared. "Creatives never know what the rest of us do."

Foggy on the details of Malik and Jared's job descriptions, Ben clings to his ability to tell them apart. The two friends—Ben had pegged the pair as off-campus friends and not just two minority individuals pushed up against one another in a majority-rules work environment—fit the trending Black nerd profile. Jared wears glasses. Malik does not. Ben says, "I'm assuming you're like coders. Or engineers."

"That's close enough," grants Jared, wiping the lenses of his glasses, perhaps compulsively. "You can call us the code engineers."

"We are not the lead engineers or chief coders," signifies Malik. "I'm sure you figured that out."

"We are the guys they bring in to fix all the fuck ups made by the guys who went to the prestige schools."

"The Dukes."

"And the Browns."

Ben knows that many of the tech guys are fans of Duke basketball. The founder, of course, is a Brown alumnus.

"When the Dukes and the Browns fuck up, that's when they bring in the Blacks," says Jared. His glasses are back on his face. His eyes glint behind the lenses.

"The Blacks come in, and we clean up messes made by the Dukes and the Browns."

Brenda makes a gesture with her brows. She is partially fed up. "How much longer do you guys plan to be talking about work?"

"You didn't even give this boy a drink," says a female voice coming up behind Ben. Three women who are not Brenda are in the room. They have greeted Brenda cordially. Ben senses these three hold themselves separate from her. One of the three, her hair unbridled and wild, midriff exposed, nose pierced, places a glass in Ben's hand. She is older than him, not older enough that he would be a boy to her adult. Being called *boy* by her landed like an endearment. Ben reflexively drinks and reflexively hides his reaction. It's rum. Straight rum. Maybe 151.

Jared moves in while Ben recovers from the 151 shock. "Are you Duke? Or are you Brown?"

"What set do you bang with?" clowns Malik. "That's an important question where we come from. Can be life or death."

Ben plays along. "I was supposed to, my parents wanted me to go to Harvard, like they did, but Stanford offered to pay me a seventy grand living stipend. I'm a Cardinal."

"You know Ben's bullshitting," says Malik, bordering on admiration. "Fucking with us."

"Oh, I caught that," says Jared. "It's game bullshit."

Ben went to a community college and snagged his job goofing off. High and bored, he'd created a spoof social media profile for a hot dog company, which had no digital media presence.

"With the hot dogs," Ben explains, "I saw a void, and I filled it."

"As a hot dog will do," observes Jared. "Wiener wants to fill a void."

The hot dog company, like its product, had been hidebound. Not so hidebound that its legal department didn't know how to deal with Ben once his spoof site became viral and highly trafficked. The lawyers had offered him a choice. Crippling lawsuit or gainful employment. Ben took the job. Eventually, the parties tired of each other, mostly due to contentious interactions with the lawyers who had initially approached Ben. The split came when Dis-Content was looking for a chief content generator. Timing was everything in life, Ben realized, especially in pacing out shots of 151. The replenishment of his glass seems a bit rushed.

"When you showed up," says Jared, "I said you were Duke. Malik took the Brown position."

"To be fair, I didn't want to take the Brown half of the bet. You don't act Brown."

"Which is not an insult."

"At the time, I didn't know we could go outside Brown and Duke. I still can't quite believe they did. The people who do the hiring, I'm talking about."

The woman who had handed Ben the drink lifts it from his hand, takes a lip-glistening sip, and places the glass in his hand again. "You bores are still talking about work," she remarks.

"What should we be talking about then?" say the men.

She arches her back and dips her hips as if signifying guideposts to proper topics of party conversation. The ring in her midriff, the piercing in her nostril and matching stainless-steel body adornment in places that Malik and Jared both apparently have seen become jumping off points of discussion.

A fairly even mix of voices, male and female, races through this conversation. Spikes in volume and intonation punctuate the accelerated cadences. At times, two or more people speak at once, whether as a form of affirmative chorusing or to express simultaneous and conflicting opinions is open to Ben's interpretation. He doesn't understand everything that is said. He's not bad at distinguishing context and subtext. The talk is sexually supercharged. The woman Ben has arrived with—a woman whose skin is on the dark side of the African American spectrum of flesh tones—understands every word and moves along with the flow. Ben drinks more in twenty minutes than he usually portions out over two hours. Malik and Jared seem bigger on their home court, and stronger, less predictable. In the workplace lighting, Ben had never realized that either one of the code engineers could take him in a fight, despite his years of Tai Chi.

Not only is hard liquor being consumed, clustered activity around a microwave oven in the kitchen proves to be powder cocaine being baked into base. "You look shocked, honey," says the lady supplying the rum. "Who do you expect to meet here? Upstanding citizens?"

The woman manning the microwave, tall and thin in flared jeans that heighten those aspects, puts hands on hips and cocks her chin and crotch in Ben's direction. "You look like you just figured out you gone slumming," she says.

The women mock him in a minor key. If they could see him at home, they would know better. His apartment is crappier than this one. That's not what he says. He is not a total fool, only suddenly intoxicated. He says, "You could never fit this many people in my apartment. The divorce has been brutal."

"Brenda, where's your heart? You're gaming on this boy when he needs help." The woman with the unbridled hair and pierced nostril has taken the glass of 151 from Ben's hand, as if for safekeeping, which is a relief for a second. She puts a glass pipe to his lips as if inhaling from it should be his most natural reaction in the world. Ben does puff, not having a lot of fight in him this evening. He imagines sealing off the smoke before it hits his lungs.

"The life hack sites all say don't get married until your thirties," Ben says in a rush, smoke billowing from him. "Here I am divorced already, and only twenty-eight!"

"You got it bad, honey? Like worse than this place?" This woman who has been at the microwave, Ben surmises, is the leaseholder on the apartment. He's not quite sure why she seems offended. He stops himself from arguing that his circumstances are so slummy that he would need to aim lower to be slumming. One misinterpretation of that squelched reasoning would be that he considers this apartment a low aim. Pleased with having caught that aspersion and held it back, he gives himself an inner congratulation and takes a bold drink and a real hit on the pipe. For a few moments, he is not sure if the entire world has spun and he is staying still in the middle or if the entire world is becalmed all around him while he spins at its center. He pants a dozen deep breaths and catches up with himself. The rest of the party watches his face closely, awaiting his re-arrival.

Everyone starts talking about the greatness of Larry Bird. Even the women pitch in on the merits of Larry Bird. "Larry Bird is the greatest basketball player of all time," summarizes Ben's new friend with the pierced nose.

"I don't follow basketball super close," says Ben, which is true. He knows that Bird is white and suspects his hosts are either being super polite and inclusive or straight-out baiting him.

"Bird isn't the best," says Malik, subtly combative. "That's bullshit. Steve Nash, that's the best basketball player ever."

"Maybe the best basketball player from Canada ever," says Brenda, firmly, "but you seem to be forgetting John Stockton, point guard for the Jazz of the great basketball state of Utah."

"All of you are mistaken. Kurt Rambis," says Jared. Is he pontificating? "You got to go back, and it's Rambis. The man was scrappy. He wore glasses. No more iconic NBA player, ever."

"Actually," says Ben, because he's not totally in the dark, "Jerry West was more iconic than Rambis. West was actually the model for the NBA logo."

"Shit," says Brenda. "Imagine how LeBron feels about that."

The abrupt and loaded and extended silence is, Ben imagines, awkward only for him.

A game of dominoes is proposed. "A quick one. Won't take any time."

"You can't drive off all tipsy like this anyway," says the woman on the lease. "You need to stay here until you sober up. You crash, and I am liable. Can't have that." Ben has never played dominoes. Women on either side of his chair coach him. Both ladies slip him booze whenever the level in his glass goes down.

Ben's hosts use a word that he will not allow his brain to register. They refer to him by this word. They address him as if this word is his name. When prompted by this word, Ben responds, answers back, but flat, as if he has been addressed as Bub. He cautions himself to stifle any sign of gloating at being referred to by this word. He knows he is not included in a blanket use of the word.

Jared pulls up a chair to sit face-to-face with Ben. *This could be serious*, thinks Ben. From Jared's tone, it is. "Ben, I have one thing to tell you. It's very serious. Do I have your attention?"

"Yes." Ben smiles, trying to lighten the tension.

"Are you smirking?" demands Jared. "Is that a simper on your face? Do you take this as a joke? Do I look like one of your nerd improv friends making a funny?"

"I'm not smiling. When I'm nervous, sometimes that happens. It's not a real smile."

"Well, you're right to be nervous. Really fucking nervous. If the boss finds out you've come here with his Black girl, you will be fired."

"You should know that," puts in Malik.

"But private time and private life," says Ben, "shouldn't be the founder's concern."

"This is given as friendly advice." Jared is cleaning his glasses' lenses again. The movement is somehow significant. "Maybe you're innocent of it, but *we* know how possessive white men can be with their Black women."

"Maybe you think you're more than just the man's hired hand. You are the golden boy."

"You are the golden wiener boy," clarifies Jared. "You struck gold with those wiener tweets."

"I don't know if *golden* is a fair word," protests Ben.

"Oh he is golden," says Brenda. "Let me tell you, Ben is the man with the golden wand."

The partying people laugh extensively, explosively, more than maybe this witticism merits.

"Seriously, though," says Malik, profoundly serious. "They call you the young assassin. The lead assassin. The character killer. The character killing kid."

Ben's response to this is so practiced that he doesn't feel the least bit defensive in the delivery. "It's not like I randomly pick people out and destroy their character. Opposition research is an honorable profession and has been for many decades."

"Of course it's honorable," agrees Jared, pressing his glasses to his temples. "It's your job. Your job is to ruin people's lives. You destroy businesses and dreams. You're just slicing up whomever we're paid to slice up. Whoever pays the price, that party calls the shot, not us."

"No one here's putting you down," says Malik with real assurance. "The company is in business to do hits. You're the hit man. Dis-Content may not survive, or it may thrive. That's down to you."

"We like you, Ben," explains Jared. "You are our best chance. We work for slave wages."

"We don't use that term lightly," cuts in Malik.

"But we have equity. The equity is what will bring it home. So we need Ben to do well."

"No pressure!" quips the young assassin.

"But that's some dark work you do."

"That's some soul-blackening labor."

The women seem to tire of this. There is a turn in the talk toward hair. Ben doesn't understand the words or the general gist. He might be able to ask Brenda to clarify this discussion later, when they are alone, except his grasp of the exchange is so slight that he is unable to establish verbal coordinates he can refer back to later. Brenda has told him, in private, one of the things she likes about him is that he hasn't tried to touch her hair. He hadn't really noticed her hair. Her skin had taken his full attention, once it was uncloaked and presented for contact. The touching had only been that one time, so far. In truth, he had never been a huge hair person. He has not been dating this woman long. He is leery of putting her in a position of explaining everything Black to him.

Malik and the pierced woman—they seem to be half-siblings—are talking about a cabin their extended family owns up in Big Bear. They go up there a few times every winter season, this whole crew of friends. Without fail they get snowed in.

There's a break in the music. Ben realizes Malik has been playing DJ on the compact record player. The sound of Malik pissing comes from the open door of the bathroom, streaming like a stallion. Malik returns, buckling his pants. "The only reason to get out of bed when you're snowed in is to switch beds."

"Switching beds is what keeps all that white stuff interesting," says the woman on the lease.

"You need to come up to that cabin, Ben," says Jared. "You've got the nuts to move about town with the boss's Black woman, then you've got the nuts to follow her up to the cabin."

Everybody is pretty high. Ben can feel that he cannot feel his face. He looks into the faces around him, big, intoxicated smiles. The women are grinning and laughing and batting eyes at him in a tolerant manner. Ben is clear that he has been invited to the cabin. "Ben could be cool in the mix," says the woman with the unbridled hair and piercings.

"There's one thing to remember," cautions Malik. "Do you remember what it is you'll need to remember?"

"I'll be sure to bring Brenda. I won't forget."

Brenda laughs. Is she blushing? Ben can't tell for sure. She seems unflustered. Brenda says, "I'm sure I could find my own way up there."

Brenda takes Ben's car keys. He sits for a moment failing to figure out how she dipped her hands into his pockets. "There's still time to catch the comedy," she says, "and my mother always tells me to arrive alive. So I'll be driving from here."

There is one thing, two if he's unlucky, Ben needs to do before leaving this place. He goes into the bathroom to take care of it. The light in the bathroom is out. Ben is afraid—shy—to leave the door ajar to use the living room light to see what he is doing. Malik and Jared had not exhibited this insecurity. Neither, now that Ben thinks back on it, had the women. The possibility of pissing on the seat, in the dark, or even worse on the floor, scares him. Should he sit, in the dark, and not rely on aim and fall prey to misjudged distance? He shuts the door for privacy and tries to make up his mind. It's scary in there, in the bathroom in the dark. The dark bathroom is a place that alerts Ben that actually he is afraid, but without illuminating what he is afraid of.

Ben, in the bathroom, the bathroom door shut, breathes in utter and complete darkness. Fearing piss splashes on his ass, resigned to splashed piss on his ass, he sits. His flesh hits the seat. The porcelain is dry and warm. If he were at home, in his own setting, a setting of his own, he might feel cozy. He's uneasy. Maybe queasy. It could be the booze. Maybe something else, like the drugs. How much money should he offer for the coke he smoked up? How does he even raise that subject? What can he offer? What of himself can he bring and share with these people in their snowbound cabin? Ben is surely an uncomfortable guest. Now that he is seated, alone with no lights, all by himself in the dark's embrace, he can't imagine how he will stand up again.

FEAR OF STARTING SOMETHING

This is a holiday story. The action grinds on throughout the season of jollity. Prepare to visit that happiest time of year, the two weeks of the annual fifty-two when 'tis greater to give than to receive. A gauntlet of work parties, drinks with friends, family revelry, also mandatory grinning in the rumpus room of neighbors who have been living on your block since their grown kids were first graders in the local public school. All of this running activity obscures the terminating year you currently live in as it limps toward its end date. The start of the next year, with its credible threats and diversionary promises, creeps up under cover of festive lights. Where to begin?

Everybody has been working so hard, with so little time for anything else. Finally, the winter break is upon us. Jennifer and Tyler have both left their offices midday. They've closed all open business and signed off for the duration. They're heading home in musing moods, maintaining phone silence in their individual automobiles, anticipating a little alone-time luxury at the home space while the spouse is off-site finishing out a full workday.

Tyler arrives at the house to discover Jennifer's car in the garage. He thinks he can hear its engine cooling. He uses the remote to shut the garage door and leaves his car in the driveway rather than bothering to swing out and park curbside on the street. His wife's car is blocked in. She is his. They have four hours before anyone expects them to be somewhere.

Creeping into his own home, Tyler finds Jennifer coming out of her clothes closet, half-naked. Each hand clutches a pair of shoes.

Tyler sees the surprise his presence puts in her eyes. *Caught you*, he thinks. She gives him a passing kiss, more sound than touch.

"You scared me." Jennifer steps around her husband. She intends to model the shoes in each hand, to compare and contrast their effect in a full-length mirror on the bathroom door, while in her underwear. Tyler can picture, anticipate, the way the shoes will highlight Jennifer, front and back, half-dressed. Tingling, he steps into her sphere of attention. She looks up and directly into his face, accustomed already to him being home.

"Have you noticed," she says, "the fence at the bottom of the backyard is really needing to be rebuilt? I was thinking we should use the money you're going to get from…."

He has not received that money yet. He has not begun to ruminate on the ways he would best be gratified to spend it. He can't be sure the funding will arrive. He tallies the current mandatory expenditures pursuant to maintaining and upgrading the residential property, absent the fence. The totals and the priorities baffle him. If he were to count off these issues out loud, he can't say what divisions might erupt between Jennifer and him. One thing he does know is that his erotic charge has shorted, turned inside out. His wife, in panties and a clinging T-shirt, studies the flex of her flank in the full-length mirror. Her legs are luxuriant stems set in exotic stilettos. The flesh is firm; Jennifer is staying strong through her late thirties. Tyler might as well be looking at staggered fence posts.

"Rebuilding the fence may have to wait until after Christmas," he says.

"I don't want to do it before Christmas," she replies.

Everything must wait until after Christmas. It's one thing between them that goes without saying. From now until Christmas, the Connells have a Santa's To-Do List that, eight years into their union and four years into residing at this property, both know by heart. Jennifer gives Tyler a pinched look from the bathroom door. She would like him to give her space while she critiques her body in various pairs of shoes. Deflecting the part of his mind that wishes it had a place in this house where he might masturbate in peace, Tyler silently reviews the action items that he and Jennifer need to execute between now and New Year's.

1) Buying the Tree: Erecting a fragrant, prematurely felled pine in the home should be easy enough, and rarely is. Shopping for the tree never ends in a snapshot of Tyler and Jennifer basking in mutual admiration. Every year, Jennifer loses recall of the traditional exasperation. Her singsong call to sally out and select a tree hearkens far back, to years well before she met Tyler, to childhood's joyous chorus.

It's evening, dark already because of winter. Dinner has yet to be consumed. Out on the driveway, Tyler's eyes linger on his wife while she fastens her seatbelt. Strapped in, the webbed harness bisects her breasts. Jennifer catches Tyler eying her. A flush up her neck and across her cheeks alerts him. She feels it too. If this were early in the relationship, he would have trouble keeping his attention off of her. Having her bound into the passenger seat like that, pursing her mouth to apply lipstick, would constitute a driving hazard. He starts up the sport utility vehicle, of recent European origin.

"Which lot should we roll up on?" she says. He remembers they should have decided this before they left the house. It probably wouldn't help. Two likely lots are within one-half mile of the house, in opposite directions.

"Which one worked for us last year?" he asks. He's floating a balloon with the answer printed in Magic Marker on its side.

"The sketchy one, the one that might also be fronting for drug deals. That's where we found that particular kind of tree I like. Last year."

"I agree. It felt like they were selling cartons of cigarettes there, with no tax stamps, which is more criminality than I generally want to be exposed to, but I'll head over." Tyler pulls the European station wagon into traffic and heads south.

"No," decides Jennifer. "We know I'm not pregnant. I may never be pregnant, or ever try to have a child. We need to make a decision on that soon. Not tonight, honey, but soon. All the same, if some day I do become pregnant, we'll be glad we sucked up to the charter-school fundraisers before it becomes obvious that we're sucking up."

Tyler pulls a U-turn. Last year, and the year before as well, he had watched his wife browse at the holiday tree lot operated to benefit charter-school funding. The trees being sold to support the charter school had been almost amazing last year. This evening, walking in the sudden chill and mist that descends out of nowhere, just like last year, in the muddy paths between the rows of charter school saplings, Tyler sees in a broad survey that the charter school trees are almost amazing again. Jennifer shivers. She's wrapped a scarf around her neck but hasn't brought a coat. A parent volunteer follows at a discrete distance.

"I'm really not wearing the correct shoes for this mud," Jennifer says, loud enough to be overheard by the trailing parent volunteer. "Why can't they have the trees we like? The skinny tree, you know. The branches stick out straight."

"Those branches have a lot of open space between them," says Tyler, clarifying for the trailing parent. "I know."

Jennifer picks up the thread, and why not? After all, the thread is hers. "The decorations stand out better with that tree type. Do you know I have all those decorations I've had forever? Some are from my mother. They were handed down from her mother."

Back in the sporty European auto, Tyler watches and waits while Jennifer blows her nose, extensively.

"I hope I didn't catch a cold out there." She dabs the tissue at the tip of her nose and clenches the wadded paper in her fist.

"Seatbelts, honey."

Jennifer gives Tyler a quick look, checking to see if something is wrong with his tone. She averts her face and buckles up. Driving and thinking about something else, Tyler misses the turn to the sketch lot. Jennifer lets him figure that out on his own. Even parking is sketchy at the sketch lot. The criminal types darting in and out of the camper shell that serves as office and, for all Tyler can imagine, crack den have the exact tree Jennifer craves. A lot man whose prison-made tattoos blossom up over the collar of his shirt quotes the tree's price. That tree is twice as expensive as any other tree of its size on the sketch lot. The prices are beyond comparison to costs at the charter-school venue.

"If you toss me your truck key," says the lot man, "I can tie these sticks on for you. No extra charge." The lot man looks like he's between gigs as a barker for a traveling carnival. Tyler raises the luxury SUV's key and clicks the doors unlocked from where he stands.

"I only wish they had prices on their trees." Tyler keeps his voice low, below reception of the lot man who has pulled their selected tree and is tying it to the roof of the SUV. Tyler isn't fully fond of the way the lot man's speculative eyes never leave Jennifer's body. "I feel they just pull a price out of their ass. It's always higher for people like us."

"Oh, don't be paranoid," orders Jennifer at full voice. "No one is ripping off *people like us*."

"In that case, you tip him." Tyler sees his mistake before he's finished setting it up. Jennifer tips the lot man with a five, well within the bounds of propriety. However, the extended eye contact she bestows upon the man, the muted upturn of her mocking lips, the perfected posture, and her slow mounting of the passenger seat for the lot man's study might all be argued as outside proper bestowment of a gratuity. People say communication is key to healthy couple relationships. If some slight issue bothers one person in a marriage, the false wisdom goes, that person is obligated to talk it out, preferably before the man and wife crawl into bed and go to sleep. Tyler knows better. Behind the wheel, taking the turns, he says nothing, gives no critique of Jennifer's performance for the lot man.

At home, parking is stacked up and down the street. Four houses either way, every spot is filled. Jennifer waits for Tyler's customary expletive-rich objection to neighbors installing project cars, cars not yet running, in two prime spots opposite their house. Tyler keeps the rich expletives to himself. They join the list of things that can go unsaid between them.

Tyler leaves the car in the driveway. Blocking the garage will force him to drag out of bed and move the SUV early before Jennifer heads for her daybreak yoga class. Jennifer disappears into the house, quiet and victorious, the tree an unwieldy trophy attached atop her husband's vehicle. Tyler had thought ahead and brought along a pocketknife. Tyler hacks through the twine, lifts the tree off the roof of the car, and staggers under the awkward weight. Jennifer has reappeared, silently, to act as a witness as he regains his balance. Tyler stands the tree in the enclosed courtyard. He and Jennifer walk away from it in opposite directions. She slips into the house. He tends to the scraps of twine and pine needles on the car.

2) Editing the Christmas Card List: Jennifer and Tyler sit across from one another at the dining-room table. The improvements Jennifer has made in dressing the layout of this room are on clear view. When she and Tyler had first toured the house, their real estate agent, Clarise, had said, "No, this isn't what I would call a fixer-upper. On the whole, it's good to go." If only Clarise could see what has been done since then and try to eat those words. Clarise would just choke on it.

Tyler has printed two copies of last year's Christmas Card List. He slides a copy over to Jennifer. He fans out the pages of the list on the table before him. Jennifer sneaks a look of approval in his direction. He takes that as a compliment. In fact, she's congratulating herself one more time for installing a midcentury abstract mural, Calder-lite, above the vintage bar cart, which happens to be situated behind Tyler. She interprets Tyler's look of triggered desire toward her as appreciation of her home décor.

"I don't know why we send all these cards to the WME people," she says. "You haven't worked there for three years."

"No," responds Tyler, consciously not defensive. Defense leads to offense. "But you've been out of college for fifteen years, and we're still sending cards to people you blackballed from your sorority."

"Those people have helped my career more than you could ever know."

"I do know. You've told me."

"They may help me more, in the future, more than we can possibly know right now."

"All of these WME people are ones who felt I got a raw deal there. They all offered to support me, in what happened."

"Seriously, Tyler, if that WME crowd had supported you, *at all*, during the six years you were there, we would have bought a house up in the Hollywood Hills, and not be, you know, pioneers out here where we are."

There is something he doesn't like about the way she holds her mouth when she is righteous, especially when she is righteous and wrong. "Pioneers out here where we are," he echoes, "with the brown people."

"As if that's what I mean."

"So, to your point, the brown ones, the people who were living here before us, they're all in one column here on page three. You want we should just scratch those?"

" 'You want we should just,' " says Jennifer. Her hand gestures and facial exaggerations make clear she is mocking him. "Now you're talking like some kosher gangster. Of course I don't want that we should just scratch the brown people. We have to live here."

"With them."

"Hey, Tyler, we made the bed. Okay, so it's a little wet and maybe someone peed in it. We've still got to lie in it."

Truer words, you've never said, thinks Tyler.

"Got nothing to say to that, do you, big brain?" Proud of herself, full of herself, happy with herself, Jennifer thinks, *He really does bring out the best in me.*

To block out thoughts almost opposite to Jennifer's, Tyler goes on deliberately, precisely, absolutely inking WME names off the Christmas Card List. Satisfied that the evening is going well, Jennifer fills two bowls with pasta she's had the forethought to order delivered.

3) Reviewing the Gift Strategy: Tyler learned a lesson while editing the Christmas Card List. His input during the season's gift strategy work session is to give unanimous assent to Jennifer's list of designated recipients. He does, occasionally, haggle at her assigned dollar amounts, never more than fifteen percent in either direction, and only to give the impression of being engaged.

The pasta really is quite tasty, Tyler notes. "That was a good idea," he says, "ordering the noodles ahead of time."

Jennifer had just been remarking to herself how smoothly the allotment of gift-buying funds had gone, much quicker and smoother than previous years. Maybe the difference lies in providing a delicious, nourishing meal to accompany the negotiations. She will remember this next year. Tyler has gone to the kitchen for seconds. He'd been put off from her for about a half hour there. She isn't oblivious to his moods and whims. He is in love with her again. Him wanting her goes a long way to influencing her toward wanting him.

"What a good man you are," she says.

4) Locating the Christmas Decorations: Things had been going well. With no hint from Jennifer that he should, Tyler had rinsed the few plates and utensils and stacked them in the machine. Jennifer decides to take things a little further.

"Let's pull out the Christmas decorations," she says. "We don't have to put them up tonight. It's late already. But we can have them out and ready to go."

"Aren't they in the garage?"

"You should know. I mean, you put them away, right?"

"I put away the outdoor decorations. I put those in the garage. The indoor decorations, I seem to remember you were in charge of those."

"Of course I'm in charge of them. I mean, they are mine. I like to buy two new ones every year and have been since I moved into my first apartment. Some of them have been in my family for multiple generations."

"Two generations. Generation one, and then you."

"No, three generations. My grandmother, my mother, me."

"Okay, so your family brought them over from the old world. Does that help me know where they're stored now?"

"You know what? Let's forget the decorations for tonight. We seem to be tired."

"I have plenty of energy. If you know where you've put your heirlooms, it will be no problem to pull down the boxes and stack them in the living room."

"You know what? I can picture where they are now. I have your Christmas gift hidden in there with them. So let's just drop it."

"I know where the outdoor decorations are too. I'll just wait to pull them down until your car's not in the garage and I'm ready to put everything up."

They go to bed at the same time and both sleep alone.

5) Bringing in the Tree From the Front Yard: Over the next two days, walking into and out of the front courtyard, heading to or coming from his car, which seems always to be the one stuck parked on the street during this holiday break, Tyler encounters the rich green Christmas tree ten times, interpreting the dying pine as more abandoned and forlorn with each passing. Tyler really is, if he says so himself, a sentimental person. Sentiment, and Tyler's high regard for it, factors into his ready acceptance of Jennifer's suggestion as dinner wraps up that this evening is the time to bring the tree into the house. His immediate enthusiasm, something she knows her husband has zero ability to feign, warms Jennifer to him. She follows him out to the courtyard and watches.

Tyler lifts and swings the tree as if it were a contentious dance partner. Jennifer pictures her spine curving to accommodate the arch of her husband's torso. She loves seeing Tyler in action, lost in the exuberance of physical motion, like a child or an animal, a beloved family dog. Her affection for him rises like a muffin in the oven, is how she pictures it. At the muffin image, she must laugh. He has expanded her love from matrimonial to in the neighborhood of maternal. Tyler doesn't realize that his wife is blessed out over her capacity to feel, physically feel, love for him. He has heard the deprecating laugh, and presumes she is deprecating Tyler. Did she notice that he had stubbed his heel on an irregularity in the patio paving stones? Is that funny? Had she anticipated that he would trip on the step up to the doorsill, one step up that he cannot see, obscured as it is by the tree in his embrace? Was she simply laughing at how easily he had snapped to doing her bidding? He is not so nuts as to assume the answers to these questions are *all* yes. He knows about laws of probability and percentages. It is very unlikely the answers are all no.

Two can play at this game, he thinks.

6) Dressing the Tree: After she had slept on it, Jennifer did remember where she had stowed away her precious indoor decorations, of course. She'd placed the heirlooms (clearly *heirloom* was not too strong a word) in a crawlspace behind her shoe wall. The stacks of cartons, all as light as blown glass, had been packed neatly out of the way and well within her reach. Of course they were.

She'd put them there. She took them out with almost no strain. She didn't need Tyler to bring her delicate decorations upstairs for her. She also didn't need him staring at her critically as she sorted ornaments and determined their hierarchy upon the tree. She's wearing the crop top, he notices, a garment that she seems to take entirely for granted. She puts it on as if donning a hand-me-down she has decided to wear one more time before discarding. Tyler loses his resolve to be dissatisfied with his wife. It's as if she isn't aware that this particular t-shirt makes it obvious that at thirty-seven his wife is far from leaving the prime of youth.

Once Jennifer's gotten to the actual work, as she stretches and balances and deftly accessorizes this tree, her husband's appraising observation is unnerving. He passes into reflective witness. Eyes open, spacing out, he realizes that to continually pick that t-shirt, and uncountable garments that produce a similar effect, illustrates a kind of genius in his wife. She bends to pluck a purple angel playing a golden harp. Their eyes meet. He produces a smile that communicates, in his mind, his appreciation for her Einstein-level dressing game. She half returns that smile and puts her face into the tree.

Unblinking is not a good look on him. It makes Jennifer self-conscious in a way that she does not enjoy being self-conscious. She sees beyond the surface admiration in Tyler's appraisal and presumes he is mocking her. He leaves the living room and walks to the kitchen. Jennifer's tension eases. He saunters back, cracks a beer and settles deep into the sofa, enjoying himself, looking at her as if she were a TV. She doesn't like him when he is blandly critical of her like this. She would prefer a fight. She suspects a spat is what he has been trying to arrange all along.

When all the ornaments have been hooked to the tree, Jennifer knows she is done. She stands back and takes in her work, admiring the effect. Tyler stands next to her, conspicuous in doing the same.

"Amazing," says Tyler. "Every time. I don't know how you do it. You never miss the mark."

"Thanks," she says. "That means a lot to me. It makes up for you not even helping."

"That's the effect I was going for."

They go to bed very politely and both sleep alone.

7) Putting Up the Outside Lights: From the beginning, when the Connells first moved in, installing the outdoor decorations has been a delicate process. You don't want to outdo the long-time residents, also known as your neighbors. If you put up something too fancy, you risk having it envied. Tyler is out in the front yard, visible to the street, stringing up the lights, testing the connections. The process always takes longer than he had anticipated. He is still fumbling about. Last year, Jennifer had been more involved. She had wanted a nativity scene. Tyler had purchased a nativity scene. It was not the scene Jennifer desired. She wanted a nativity scene that showed diversity. You have to take the sensibilities of the neighbors into account. She wanted a brown Jesus, a black Joseph, and a Mary who might be Salma Hayek's cousin, to judge by skin tone.

"Also, let's see if we can make the bigwigs arriving with the incense and myrrh race appropriate. Arabs, at the lightest."

"Should I try to find some gay and transgender figures as well?"

"There's no need to resort to absurdity. These people we've moved in with, LGBT issues are not at the top of their radar."

Tyler had made all that happen. He doubted that a more ethnically diverse nativity scene existed anywhere throughout the land, not even in Berkeley. He and Jennifer had sat up half the night, watching the multicultural figurines in their front yard from the living room window.

"It's like we expect someone to drop in and congratulate us for it."

"You're right," agreed Tyler. "We really should be ashamed."

"I think the thing to do is stop watching this thing and go to bed."

"I think you're right."

Tyler couldn't remember if they'd had sex that night, which meant probably they had not. It's not like he could consult with Jennifer to verify one way or another. The nativity scene was a touchy subject. Actually, in one sense, it had been a mistake to stop watching the thing. In the morning, the grouping of figures seemed off. The balance had shifted. It wasn't until she was backing out of the driveway that Jennifer noticed one of the wise men, the darkest one, with the rainbow shawl, was missing. She texted Tyler, while she was driving. He was at work when the text came in and was distracted from responding. In fact, Jennifer's text slipped his mind entirely until he arrived home. His headlights swept across the nativity gathering, and a reply to Jennifer's text popped immediately to mind. *Holy shit, Baby! Black Joseph is missing too!* That night, before they went to bed, Salma Hayek Mary went AWOL. By morning, brown Jesus was absconded too.

The lights go on across the street and on the two houses to either side. Tyler sees elements from the stylized manger he had installed last year, the one that had walked off piece by piece. The tightly grouped figures have been split up, *chopped* Tyler believes is the vernacular, like a stolen car. The three wise men, Mary Hayek, black Joseph, brown baby Jesus, the figures gaze back at him with blank, lacquered eyes, having been incorporated into the décor of one house after another all the way down the block.

8) Purchasing the Gifts: Jennifer and Tyler arrive at the most sparkling outdoor mall on the city's affluent west side. They offload the European sport vehicle with a valet. Just having someone else park the car, in contrast to the ever-wending parking travails of home, induces a mild and pleasurable culture shock. Jennifer slides the valet ticket into her purse and swells into the packed crowd promenading through the walkways that wind through store facades. Tyler notes that Jennifer moves in an extra perky motion. What could be causing her heightened buoyancy?

Jennifer puts her mouth up to Tyler's ear. The proximity of her lips, he is happy to note, continues to arouse him. "It's a little weird," she says, apparently meaning *it's a little exciting*, "that we're at a place where so many of the people pressing into us come from multiple generations of financial solvency."

"A lot of them are white," observes Tyler. "Almost all of them are white. You could just say a lot of white people are gathered here and get to the point a lot faster."

"We look just like them," says Jennifer. "But we are not, are we?"

Tyler feels as if he is a sort of gallant, a pioneer, a virile frontiersman. Jennifer observes other women in the crush of shoppers. She witnesses their gazes wander to her husband and actualize at sight of him. It's not as if they stare, Jennifer explains to herself. They manifest a triggered physical phenomenon. Tyler is different from the men they know. Although at skin level he looks like he aligns to the same tribe as them, these women sense a subcutaneous unknown about Tyler. They are intrigued. The unconscious, automatic, autonomous unyielding attraction Tyler exudes upon these affluent female strangers piques Jennifer's interest in him. Tyler is aware of being this animal center of magnetism. He is aware that Jennifer is aware that he is aware. This current of attraction is something they are sharing, without speaking about it. Both pull a charge from it.

Tyler and Jennifer have wandered into a store that sells candles, elixirs, lotions, and potions that any health- and appearance-conscious woman over thirty cannot be oversupplied with. Though adequately expensive, the store's items are simply too cliché for purchase as gifts. The aromatic interior is a soothing, centering space. The three salesgirls, Jennifer and Tyler both notice, are all women of color. Two are black. The other might be living right down the street from the Connells, at the Ortega home for instance. A surge of shoppers crowds the store. None of these shoppers appears to notice the existence, never mind the humanity, of the three shop girls. Several of the women do notice Tyler. Jennifer, for instance, notices Tyler literally wink at one of the black salesgirls, as if to communicate a shared experience of the white crowd at large. Tyler's attempted signal of solidarity, and the girl's flat-out rejection of it, take less than two seconds. Jennifer has seen enough. The spell is broken.

9) Wrapping the Gifts: Any time Tyler watches his wife concentrate on a task, he awakens anew to the power of her intelligence. This awareness has been particularly acute every year at the holiday season when she wraps Christmas presents. The way her brow holds steady and furrowed, the adept agility of her fingers, she brings everything to this task, more than the minimum requirement. *That*, he reflects, *is how Jennifer goes about life, always bringing more to the table than she could have gotten away with*. Her work with ribbons and tape inspires him. He picks up scissors and selects a roll of wrapping paper. He positions the paper along a box set of Burt Bacharach recordings. He makes a cut in the paper. The cut veers wide and irregular. His fumbling, Jennifer notices even as she calculates how to fix his error, is so cute. He wants to help. That desire is sweet to Jennifer's taste. It alerts her to how sweet she is on him.

"I think there's a way you can do that," suggests Tyler, "that would require slightly less effort and be slightly more foolproof."

Jennifer realizes she's stirred too much sugar into her coffee.

10) Scheduling the Social Obligations: Again, the Connells face off across the dining table, incoming invitations stacked between them. Many days between now and the New Year require two decisions. Some days, one event is early, and the other is in the evening. Other days, the festive occasions run simultaneously. Three invitations for the day after Christmas all overlap and are set at opposite ends of the sprawl.

Raising his eyes from the invites on the tabletop, Tyler sizes up Jennifer, attempting to be objective. The longer he gazes upon his wife, the more obvious it becomes why the couple's presence is overrequested. She is a gorgeous gem in any sparkling social setting. The WME alumni holiday party, for instance. Tyler suspects he's invited based on the assumption that Jennifer will come along. That prerequisite doesn't bother him. There is work to be done at the WME party. Jennifer's dazzle is the perfect cover for him while he gets that work done. Suddenly, Tyler realizes he has locked gazes with Jennifer, the stack of invitations inert beneath their sightline. Tyler feels as though his wife is reading his mind! Maybe he is right. Maybe she does.

"This is the year we beg off from the WME losers' luncheon," Jennifer says. "I've never felt so trotted out in my life. Last year was the last year."

Every couple, Tyler reflects, has differences in opinion and approach. It's not a conflict. It is a retreat into acceptance. Jennifer and Tyler often are not coming from the same place. They will not be going to the same places either. To prove this theory, Tyler is in bed and convincingly asleep one hour before Jennifer has turned out her dining room reading light.

11) Addressing the Cards so They Will Arrive in Time for New Years: How did the Connells let this duty slip again? What is so difficult about mailing the cards in time to arrive for Christmas?

"What can I say, baby?" says Tyler. Lunch is finished. The days off from work have stacked up into a neat pile of leisure and crammed activity. "We get carried away. We think we have more time than we do. We lose track."

"Don't we do this every year?" asks Jennifer, laughing at how obvious the answer is.

"Well, we're getting it done now," observes Tyler. "Getting it done late is better than not getting it done at all."

They forgive one another. In forgiveness, arises affection. Tyler's furrowed brow touches the folds of Jennifer's heart. He has neatly printed almost one hundred addresses, which puts him at almost halfway done. His face takes on a gratifying look of satisfaction. He is accomplishing things.

"People are probably happier with our cards arriving late," says Jennifer, in theory. "Our cards stand out from the rest. They extend the Christmas spirit beyond the imposed limit of Christmas Day."

"There's no reason to make excuses for it." Tyler sounds to Jennifer as if he blames her. "What's the point in talking up our faults like they're virtues? Next year, we address the envelopes when we go through the list deciding who's on it and who's not."

Now her husband's brow is smooth and certain.

12) Attending the Social Obligations: Tyler and Jennifer are spending the early evening in the house of a Mexican American family that lives two doors down on the same side of the street. The Ortegas are O.G. residents of the neighborhood. This is not the family that has two non-operating cars parked along prime curb space across from the Connells' residence. Both Jennifer and Tyler consciously refrain from using the term *O.G.* where the Ortegas can hear them. The Ortegas' outdoor Christmas décor includes the figurine of a brown-skinned wise man clad in a rainbow shawl.

"Oh hey, Tyler and Jennifer," says one of the Ortega daughters, this one being Theresa. She takes the Connells' proffered box of shortbread cookies. "Mom," Theresa calls into the house. "The settlers are here! They brought those white bread cookies again. The ones you really like." Theresa taps Jennifer on the sleeve. "You know these things aren't good for her diabetes. She just loves them."

Around the doorway, Jennifer and Tyler see two other white couples deep in the kitchen. These folks had settled within the past year or eighteen months, newcomers in a way. The settler couples operate on a theory that if they avoid speaking to one another, the rest of the party, all brown people, might fail to notice when they do not blend in.

"So," observes Tyler, privately, to Jennifer. "Four more people who only live here because they can't make enough money to live where the real white people live."

Theresa follows Tyler and Jennifer's sightlines and seems to follow their train of thought. "Is there anything sadder," she asks, "than being one of those white people who pretends bad tamales are delicious? Don't be shocked. My mother is known all through this neighborhood—even you know now—for making the driest, most flavor-free tamales the brown world has ever known."

Tyler extends himself and makes the acquaintance of the other two white couples. If he and Jennifer had children, as these others do, they would've met already, maybe not on the friendliest of terms, depending on which side of the public/private/charter school divide everyone fell.

Tyler's charm offensive leaves out Jennifer. The glad-handing reveals wider issues with her husband's duplicity. He is only pretending to be interested in these settlers. Jennifer detects a possibility that he only pretends to be interested in her. His contempt for the settlers is so close to the surface. She is amazed they cannot detect it. The other white guests must be willfully ignoring his clear antipathy, as Jennifer does every day and has for years. Without consulting her husband, Jennifer doles out her goodbyes to key guests and the hosts. Tyler catches up with her at the kitchen back door. She's making her break. They go out through the Ortegas' side gate at the same time. The Connells are a few steps short of being together.

13) Hosting Social Obligations: If they had resources, and energy, and access to parallel existence, the Connells would host three separate holiday parties, at minimum. They would hold one for career colleagues. That would be the one with commitment to propriety. Another would be for the neighbors, a family-friendly affair, with something for kids and something for great grandmas. This party would free flow more than the career-network bash. You could count on people from the neighborhood bringing specialty seasonal dishes. The food would have more highlights. The third party, the best, would be thrown for their friends who are and have been party people throughout the years. This crew adopted real jobs and actual responsibilities, but each individual is still capable of instigating crazy shit, especially in a mix of alcohol and ancillary chemicals.

The solution is to open the Connell home to all comers on the last Saturday evening before Christmas, throwing a wide enough net that every potential guest will fall well within the spectrum of attendees. No one will feel out of place, whether that self-regarding person is senior management or junior tagger. The catering is lavish. The booze is generous. The guests are numerous. The party's huge success is obvious almost from the outset. In the midst of this free-for-all of cross-cultural conviviality, Tyler sees a mob of frenzied celebrants circle Jennifer. Draining his drink, two beyond his limit, he recognizes something about his wife. She will never have any stray moments for him again. Her time and priorities are all consumed by people and things that are not him. A weird stoner three-way couple arrives. The two dudes are guests of the woman who had been Jennifer's friend in college. The woman had been Jennifer's special friend. The stoner three-way people spend time locked behind the bathroom door.

Sooner or later, all the guests are cleared out. Surface order is restored. Many glasses are washed and stowed. Jennifer finishes her nocturnal preparations and quits the bathroom to join Tyler in bed. He harbors trace pools of adrenaline from the party.

"You don't think it's strange," he suggests, "to have Jolie in our house, after all these years, considering that you'd been taking turns going under the covers with one another all those years ago?"

Tyler works up an image. The image goes a great deal of distance toward working for him. If Jennifer were to verify that image, the gap from potential to actual function would basically close. "Just a little weird?" he says.

"In school, everybody fools around like this."

"I never did."

"If you'd had access to 19-year-old vagina, you would have. Am I right?"

She is correct. It's not the right thing to say. College academics had been easy for Tyler. The rest of it, gaining access to vagina of any age, brings to mind lonely difficulties that he is better off sleeping away on his own side of the bed.

14) Negotiating the Christmas Day Movie: "Who will be going with us?" asks Tyler, insistent as if he is making a point. "Your parents?"

"Why would I want to go to the movies with my parents?"

"I seem to remember we did the Christmas Day movie with them last year. The year before as well, now that I think about it."

"If you think about it at all, you should know I have no interest whatsoever in going to a movie with my parents. Christmas or any other day."

"So who do you have interest in going to the movies with? The three-way stoners visiting from Seattle?"

"You keep circling back to Jolie and Jake and John."

"You told them, maybe you don't remember this, that we'd get together for more drinks Christmas Day. If these three swingers are coming with us, that sort of influences what sort of flick we'll see."

"Tyler, the overthinking is not working right here right now. Just pretend it's you and me. Suggest a movie that you and I would agree on."

I give up, he thinks. *Now she's turned it into a trick question.*

15) Buying the Christmas Day Movie Tickets: Tyler types on his phone, navigating a local theater's online interface.

Jennifer has a suggestion. "Why don't you give up with that phone and turn on the computer?"

"This fucking website is so counterintuitive. If you touch one goddamn wrong button, it cancels you. The prompts are all crammed in on top of one another."

"Do it on the computer. The screen is bigger. The credit card information is all stored. It's way, way easier for you and for those around you."

"They have a fucking clock running in the corner, taunting me with the diminishing seconds until it makes me start all over."

It's too late to start all over, Jennifer thinks.

16) Delivering Presents: Tyler parks his European SUV two residential blocks away from a home owned by the woman who had introduced him to Jennifer. Six months ago, this woman had landed a job upgrade that Tyler had been passed over for. Tyler has recovered from the disappointment, but perhaps Robin, or her new wife, have yet to rebound from a gloating state. Tyler has a suggestion. "Jennifer," he says, "I'd just as soon stay in the car. You run in and drop off the gifts."

"Great idea. Except, why don't I stay in the car? You run in. In fact, why not drop me off? I'll catch an Uber back home. You can saunter in and wander around. Take your sweet time coming back to the car."

"I'm not sure what you're asking for here. I can't decipher the instructions."

They sit parked and silent, staring through the windshield. One couple of their acquaintance, then two, forced to take parking spots even further distant, walk by the SUV and wave to them, en route to this Christmas Eve flash party. Many friends the Connells hardly ever see anymore have made time to squeeze in.

"Okay," capitulates Tyler, "we'll both run in. Don't expect me to endure it for more than twenty minutes."

Once the initial crush at the door is breeched, the burdensome gifts are deposited, and bearings are taken. The people are pleasant. The food is better than expected. Also, the sack of gifts that have been hauled in for the Connells is greater, in quantity at least, than the previous year. Awkwardly, of course, one couple that the Connells had cut from their gift strategy has this year brought a separate gift for each Connell. This is where Tyler's habit of overthinking comes into play. He excuses himself to the bathroom. When he emerges, he produces a movie-house gift certificate enclosed in a seasonal card addressed to the surprise gift couple, replete with a personalized message crafted with earnest good cheer. Jennifer admits to herself she feels a surge of admiration for her husband. Tyler catches Jennifer's eye from across the room. Apparently, husband and wife look to all the world like a couple that is madly in love.

Robin, the matchmaker, sidles up to Jennifer. "You and Tyler are so lucky," she says. "Not having kids, you can do it whenever you want."

Do what? wonders Jennifer.

17) Christmas Eve at Home: Finally, it is the hour of midnight. Man and wife nest alone in their dominion. The last obligation has been met and endured. The couple occupies a sofa facing the tree's flashing ornaments. The sofa is small, conducive to intimacy. All along their flanks, Tyler and Jennifer do not touch. Their thoughts are unshared and parallel.

Jennifer: *Here we are alone now, but who am I alone with?*

Tyler: *What is this person to me today?*

Jennifer: *It's like we're watching one another disappear on opposite horizons.*

Tyler: *I know how this distance has come between us. I could track each intervening segment being slotted in there.*

Jennifer: *I don't see a way to reach across this expanse.*

Tyler: *I don't know how to begin clearing out the dead matter that has lodged between us.*

The couple has bought one another gifts. Tyler's present for Jennifer is a very nice, thoughtful gift. It's expensive. Certainly, Jennifer has purchased some very nice and thought-out thing for him as well, and paid top dollar. There is a glow at the prospect of unwrapping these tokens of regard for one another. Surely, she feels it too. Gratitude and generosity are beautiful prompts to reach out and touch one another. The wrapping paper will come undone. The wrappings will fall open. Things will be different. Things will be nice. The New Year, and the new start inherent in it, will approach in a flush of excited, pleasant anticipation. In the meantime, before then, a text rings in.

He says, "This would be a great time to ignore that."

She says, "Why? Is something happening here? Do you have something in mind?"

He will not admit he'd hoped something might be happening here, on the sofa facing the flashing, lit tree. In denying that admission, the fact that nothing is happening asserts its presence between the pair of them. Jennifer's phone flickers and flashes. The gifts remain festively packaged and inert beneath the tree.

"That took two seconds," Jennifer says. Her phone remains balanced face up on her knee, perched for reply. Jennifer fills her lungs and expels all the air. Only frustration remains within. Jennifer fills in her husband on the text. One of her nephews has a birthday falling two days after Christmas. It will be celebrated, mandatory.

"That nephew is your sister's kid?"

"Yes." This admission seems to pain Jennifer.

"That's not the end of the world. Why so glum?"

"A week into the New Year, there's Aunt Tammy, whose birthday needs to be celebrated," says Jennifer. "Tammy's the start of all these birthdays coming up. I don't want to think about it."

Jennifer has two sisters, two nephews, three close aunts, one close uncle, a mother and a stepfather. Everybody, tradition dictates, must be feted with a birthday brunch or dinner get-together. So, eleven months out of Jennifer's year, and her own birthday making the twelfth, will be busted up with a family birthday celebration. "God, it's like I'll never go four weeks without the whole clan converging on me."

"It's a hassle," says Tyler. "But they do love you. You see the value in that."

For a second, Jennifer feels comforted. Her husband will brave the onslaught of in-laws and be at her side. His smile is less forced, and his eyes are more alive than they have been for days. As if by accident, Jennifer remembers Tyler's hyper alert posture the past few times he's been in a social setting with Gwen, the younger sister, mother of the two nephews, who is single now, having split with her husband right after the holidays two years ago. Abruptly, Jennifer feels less comforted.

"I suddenly feel so tired," she says.

"It's been a busy couple of weeks," he replies, by rote. They are exhausted. There is nothing either wants more than to pull up the covers and drift off into solitary dreamland. That's how the Connells move into the earliest hours of Christmas day.

18) Christmas Day: To start the morning, the married couple remains under covers luxuriating in a shared mood of resigned isolation and indolence. Their legs swing out from opposite sides of the bed late, after 10:00 a.m. The wife puts together a breakfast. It's a Christmas brunch culled from holiday food platters that party hostess Jennifer had deliberately overstocked. Historically, Tyler has enjoyed cleaning up on these leftover holiday staples. This Christmas, perhaps more than others, he's keeping his feelings and preferences under the vest. For the moment, Jennifer realizes she also is being purposefully non-expressive. She holds back any display of satisfaction that Tyler's appetite is hearty. The walls between them, she remembers, do come down in time, at least always have so far. A move will be made. Once they've taken their fill from the deli platters, it's close to show time.

"The fucking movie," he says.

"It's not something we can blow off," she says.

They have only an hour to shower, primp, dress. Passing in the bathroom, the hallway, the clothes closet, politely not touching, Jennifer and Tyler cannot help but see the spouse's attractive half-dressed profiles. Both refuse to regard the other straight on. Not every marriage reaches the stage where the fact that the partner is still found attractive is another thing to make you angry.

In the SUV, rushing toward the movie theater, both Connells suspect that the picture will be a stinker. Jennifer fears the film will put her in a bad mood, a worse mood. Tyler doubts the picture will raise him above his sinking ennui. The parking lot is aswirl in the predictable Christmas Day melee. Cars zip into view from everywhere. Tyler can't keep track of all the directions danger is attacking from. He does notice that Jennifer is typing on her phone. The film's screen time is tight. Competition to slot the car is furious.

"Jennifer. Maybe you could help look for a parking spot."

"I'll be happy to," she says, not looking up. First, she has news to deliver. Jennifer pockets her phone and announces that her father has made good on a threat to buy a plane ticket and will be coming to visit. "He wants to know if the neighborhood has changed enough that he would be comfortable staying with us."

"No," they say in unison, and both feel a spark of joy, together again.

FUCK FEAR (AN OLD STORY ABOUT SEX)

She's looking for a book, topless in her underwear bottoms, stretching on tiptoes and running a finger along cracked spines stacked on the shelves above the man's desk. She's slim and all legs, like a fawn. She has the eyes and coloring of a baby deer too. The man knows just where she is downy, and where her dew spot is. If he were doing better, successful to the degree of other men at his life's stage, his desk, the office part of his residence, would be housed in a room outside the bedroom. "Considering the amount of judging you do," the fawning girl says, "how can you expect to escape being judged?"

"I don't know that I do expect to escape being judged. That's the problem." He attempts pulling up a sheet to cover his body and gives up. The sheet is too far away. "Hey, what are you doing with this questioning? Are you seeking to be wise beyond your years?"

"No," she says. "Girls only do that when they're with their fathers."

"Or with their uncles?"

"But I'm not with my uncle, am I?"

Any way you look at it, this is an old guy with a young woman. The connection between them is fucking. That's why she has come over to his place at midnight. It is why she wears no clothes and the bedcovers are on the floor and the old guy is propped on a pillow against the headboard, breathing heavy. His hand rests on his heart. That organ is not resting at all. The heart was okay until they started talking.

"Why can't we go out in public and actually touch each other?" she says. It's a topic that refuses to grow old and whither away.

He wants their sexual relationship kept secret. Beyond not wanting to run the gauntlet of the girl's family (really, she is a girl), he does not want to endure the presumptuous censure of the general public. "Scorn from strangers bothers me," he says. He is a sensitive musician. He has played in bands that have opened for bands that you have loved. He cannot be defined as a guy in a band. He has scored many, many commercials and two films.

She has another question. "Are you afraid I'll be shunned for lowering myself to your level?"

On the best days in the kindest light, the age difference is unseemly. Beyond that, she exhibits personal qualities that further strain the relationship. For instance, she is ripe with ambition. Already graduated from law school and scaled the bar at twenty-two. She is the youngest in her class. He's done okay, never renowned or rich. He was smart enough never to marry. Half a year ago when his longtime live-in girlfriend gave up living in the condo they had shared, but he had owned, she was unable to clean him out. This girl, the young one he is with, a woman by any standard except when contrasted with his age, she's specializing in advocating for indigenous rights and immigration law. A gray male social justice attorney with a resume rich in landmark battles and television appearances has taken her on as junior counsel. The pay is not fantastic, a little more than her aged boyfriend's best year. It's only a matter of time before this girl, this woman, is delivering sound bites and anchoring opinion panels on cable news. The point being, she can't be seen to be dating a man older than the legend who is her boss. She needs to protect her public profile as much as the elder boyfriend needs to fret about his feelings, maybe more so. Her career is all set out before her. For him, it's too late to derail bright expectations of an excellent future.

"Let's talk about hanging out in public somewhere down the line," he says.

"It's late," she answers. "I need to go." That shelves the topic until the next time they are together.

He and the girl convene for pre-lunch at the raw juice bar where they had first met. The juice bar is her idea, but one he likes. He needs to stay thin and appear youthful and trim to retain his agent and attract clients. He needs the girl to remain on her side of the table. He wishes she were not leaning so far forward. It is not essential for her to cradle her breasts in her crossed arms and push them up toward his face. She does this for effect. He hopes none of his associates or their affiliates wanders into this raw juice bar. Juxtaposed with the girl, he realizes, his age is very apparent. "If I could land some television jobs," he says, "some residuals might roll in. The pressure would lessen."

"I've brought you here to break up with you," she announces.

God, but this girl looks sixteen more often than she looks twenty-two. It's not as if this coupling has a future that can be mapped out visually going forward into the coming decades, or even the next five years. He sees that nothing as fresh and lissome as this one will ever land in his lap again.

He leaves the raw juice bar feeling down, disconnected. He has a meeting with the ex. He had been dreading facing the ex in a pompous humble kind of dread. Thanks to hooking up with the young one, he'd avoided any withdrawal symptoms from quitting the ex. He'd feared he would be unable to hide his unwounded ego from this suffering post middle-aged woman and her tendency to cling when in pain. Now, freshly dumped by a precocious girl at an overpriced juice bar, his anxiety and dread center on the possibility he will look at the old girlfriend and beg her to reunite.

He enters a vegan buffet cafeteria, only a quarter hour late, and sees the ex. There is no need to worry about initiating a groveling reconciliation. She had warned him in a text that she had come down with a nonfatal, cosmetically disruptive disease. Bell's palsy. An Internet image search on the symptoms might have prepared him for a face that looks like a stroke survivor's.

"What the fuck is wrong?" she asks. Half of her mouth and the eye on that side remain stationary. "Does it cause you this much pain to look at me?"

"Looking at you doesn't bother me at all," he replies, in his opinion soothingly. "I just broke up with that woman I told you about."

"The girl my sister saw you with? I'm surprised you could cut the child loose." This is said not with any real cruel venom, just in recognition of how things are.

"The decision wasn't all mine."

"Now you're grappling with being alone?"

"Yes. But compounded with fear of being alone, I'm afraid that every subsequent woman showing an interest in me will wrinkle and dry in the comparison with this girl. Especially once the potential target gets close enough to see the lines around my eyes."

"Now you're an ageist? I should sympathize, I guess." Paralyzed facial muscles hamper the woman's expression of fake wonder in widened eyes and slackened lips. That's no excuse for the man missing her absolute irony.

"There's more involved than her youth, of course," the man explains. "In short, I'm afraid I've been spoiled." His biggest fear he leaves unexpressed. If the young one scrapes him off now, giving him no time to prepare, he lands helpless on his ass.

"Like a pampered child being dropped from a silver-lined bassinette into a workhouse latrine," says his ex, as if she can read him.

He excuses himself. He needs to cut the meeting short. The ex has already collected her phone in her purse and switched her eating glasses to her driving glasses.

In the middle of the night, the man calls the young one. "Okay, I'll do it. We'll do it."

"You'll meet my parents?"

"Jesus, no. That's where I have to draw the line."

"Don't be crazy. That was a joke. I don't want to deal with my parents meeting you. It's not like I'm fucking you to break their hearts."

"I'm glad you acknowledge that meeting the parents would be uncomfortable for everyone, not just me."

"When have I not been reasonable? Wait. Don't think about that. It would be fun, wouldn't it, if we went to a party or a show where all your friends are there too."

"I don't know if that would be fun."

"Of course it wouldn't. It would be like playing in a sandbox filled with old dirt."

"I was thinking, is there some way we can be public, without risk of running into people we know? We could take a little trip, as a couple. That seems like more than enough for a start."

"Enough for a start," she agrees. She names Santa Barbara, a coastal destination town no more than one hundred miles away and chooses the coming weekend. They have a two-hour drive ahead of them. The hours start out well enough. In the car on the freeway, he drives like a grandpa. She maintains physical distance. He is avuncular. She adopts a mien of propriety that allows him to stay in that role. At a Mexican restaurant for lunch, they share a booth, slouching backward in opposite ends of it. She picks at her tostada, shreds her napkin into an intricate paper blossom, and overtly ignores him, just as if they had been blood relations.

"You're afraid people will think you're a cliché," she says observationally, as if blurting out something she has just now noticed.

"And you?"

"I'm not a cliché. I'm an anomaly."

Prior to returning to the highway, he pulls into a gas station. He fills up and follows her into the quick-stop shop. Six beers dangle from one of her hands. She leans over the open freezer compartment, mulling the ice cream choices. In passing, his right hand makes a smooth swipe along the seams of her back pockets. His fingers aim to brush her denim down below the view line of the surveillance mirrors and the direct sight of the cowboy manning the cashier's booth. The fawn has anticipated that hand coming. She pivots and grabs her old fellow's crotch straight out in open sight. The cowboy rings up and bags the beers.

"No ID necessary," says the cashier.

During registration at the motel, she stays in the car. Nobody seems to be paying attention to her and her old guy. They go into their room, change into shorts and less and walk to sand and shore. At the beach, she's like a leggy baby deer attracting a lot of wolf eyes. Under that scrutiny, it seems natural to hang back from hanging on one another. Two girls on a blanket nearby, the oldest about the age of the old guy's girl, cradle one another's heads in elbow crooks and whisper with lips so close that tongues touch as a form of punctuation. One of the girls moves a naked leg to cover the other girl's bare thigh. No one up or down the shoreline shifts an eye.

"Why not us?" says the old guy's girl. "Why can't we do what they do?"

"I don't make the rules."

"I'm not challenging your reticence. I'm questioning society's caprice at accepting one preference and scorning another." She is rebellious by nature, if she says so herself, and would like to seal that defiance with a wet kiss on the sand. She knows that the opprobrium will be palpable. She likes this old guy. She doesn't want him to feel awkward and judged, to feed the presumption all around that he is a type of creep that really he is not exactly.

Walking in at dinner, they've had sex since leaving the beach and showered. They are properly groomed and cloaked. That desperate readiness to paw at one another is hardly noticeable. Touching hands while being led to their table, they take the intuitive step of being openly a couple. It's like coming out. This is a fancy restaurant. Appraisal and judgment are taken as appetizers and desserts. The young lady and the old guy steer a mixed course of moral condemnation and matter-of-fact acceptance.

The servers give away nothing while taking the dinner order. The wine is uncorked with blank aplomb. The old boyfriend remarks that he has lost track of how much water he's been drinking. His prostate has been flexed out of shape. Whatever rationale, he makes his excuses. Bold, unabashed, admitted and proud, he marches through the dining judges to the men's room. He does what he's come to do at a urinal, congratulating himself as the drizzle winds down. His stroll through the crowded, attentive dining room was a visible proclamation of his deep-set conviction that his relationship with the young woman awaiting his return to the table is correct and healthy and deserves acknowledgement and respect. He elbows his way through the men's room door into a short hallway and encounters an elderly gentleman in cashmere-soft tweed and gold-rimmed Cartier spectacles. The elderly gent stands directly in the old guy's path and treats him to the warm, friendly, terribly civilized flash of pristine dental veneers and a cultured, seasoned voice to match. "I must salute you and say that I envy you."

The old boyfriend isn't sure exactly what he is being saluted for. He has his suspicions. He says, "Why thank you."

Emboldened, the elderly gent goes on. "I don't know how to go about this." He channels all his decades of charming self-effacement into this encounter. "I would really like a chance to interview to be added to your girl's client list, if that's how things are done."

The old boyfriend has been punched in the face before. This isn't quite that. The hostility is lacking. Still the insult is absorbed. The elderly gentleman's presumption is disorienting. The aged boyfriend looks beyond the elderly gentleman's shoulder and watches his young love's face. He reads deep-set conviction and a proud demand for acknowledgement and respect in her demeanor.

"How did you know she is a professional?" asks the old guy. "What gave her away?"

The elderly gent, to his credit, mimes reluctance to disclose this information. "The woman at the next table mentioned it to her daughter. Once she'd pointed it out, of course the reality of the situation was obvious."

The old boyfriend's slow comprehension disguises the depths to which he is offended to be told that his girlfriend has been mistaken and maligned. His anger is rising, he realizes with a shock, more in outrage for the young lady than for himself. He quiets the storming emotions. To protest that his girlfriend is not an escort would mean to be caught out in the truth, to confess the ungainly fact that in his early dotage, he and this quick child have behaved as though love deserved to spark and grow between them. He takes the elderly gentleman's card, astounded that people still have cards, and places it in what he hopes will be a secret inner pocket of his jacket.

THE TRIUMPH OF THE CHICKEN

I'd taken a job in a chicken suit. It was a step down from my previous position as a caterer's helper, which in itself is a long drop from working in the field I'd trained for. This fowl-costume gig befell me because a scowling, well-oiled guy had fucked my girlfriend and refused to return her text messages. His name is Adrian Clifton. He is aggressive by default. When I was a high-school junior, he was a sophomore. His family owned new car dealerships. The girlfriend of mine who Adrian screwed and ghosted is the woman I'd brought back from the city where I attended music college and graduate school. Her name is Carly. Some day she may be widely known as a hell of an actress.

Carly and I had plans to marry until she refused to stop dolefully monitoring her text messages in my presence. She met Adrian at a party. I was at the party. The catering company had hired Carly and me as servers. Driving my mom's car to the worksite, Carly complained that she hadn't met one interesting person since moving to this dead-end town with me. "I would slice out my left ovary just to meet one person with an edge," she said.

The party setting was a beachfront residence crawling with gilded provincials being catered to by college graduates who had maintained idealistic majors. In high school, I would spot a girl. She might spot me. Our eyes would introduce us to one another. We'd chat leaning against her locker. She'd hand over her phone number. I'd be too nervous to call her that night. In the morning, I'd see her ditching class with a vape to her lips, proud and actualized in the passenger seat of Adrain Clifton's newest Camaro, fresh off his dad's car lot. I can't count how many times this scenario recurred or overstate how debilitating it is to dwell on.

Dwell on it I did while passing about platters of hors d'oeuvres to provincials beside the sand and the sea. None of the party's suburban-suave guests noted my existence behind the bacon-wrapped scallops. My fiancée Carly, conversely, captured the eye and attention of oiled community stalwart Adrian Clifton. Adrian leaped across a flaming fire pit to snatch a tuna tartare crisp off Carly's serving platter. A hand lingered where a hand should not linger. The hand was Carly's. Moments later, I menaced Adrian with a tureen of gazpacho and cautioned him not to alienate the affections of my fiancée. In the ensuing exchange of heated pejoratives, my catering career in this town pivoted to a close. As I was being escorted from the premises, Adrian identified me.

"Monty Shaw?" he said, lowering his fists. "It's you, isn't it? Monty Shaw! Where have you been all these years?" He took my number and said he'd call and we'd grab lunch. That was that. Carly was allowed to finish the catering shift. An Impala convertible bearing dealer plates delivered her home. We no longer talk.

My career curve dumped me into a chicken suit and propped me up in a teeming food court. As a man-sized fowl, I was meant to attract attention. At first, my heart wasn't into it. I worried that someone I knew and must feel superior to would come into the mall and see me in my feathered yellow costume. This town is crawling with people who have beefed with me since middle school. Being recognized by an adversary as a man in a chicken suit, I felt, might hurt. I put on the costume and did my best to be invisible. This delicacy ran contrary to the purpose of my job performance. People noticed. Halfway through my first shift, a blonde of twenty-three with a bachelor degree in comparative psychology pulled me from service. She guided me off the mall floor proper.

The blonde wore a yellow fast-food server's jumpsuit capped off by a yellow chef's hat. The words Bigg Eggs and an anthropomorphic chicken were embossed on the chef's cap. The caricatured chicken might have been mistaken as a parody of me in my chicken suit. I followed the psychology major into the dining enclosure. Budget families and despondent singles hunkered and ate at yellow plastic tables. We cut down an aisle. In my chicken suit, I was a center of attention, especially to the children. The student of psychology led me past banks of deep fryers and behind the walk-in refrigerators. She deposited me at the door to the office where the Bigg Eggs on-site management team convened and determined how to best manipulate the rest of us.

This office looks like every office you've ever seen inside a parking structure. The air is flavorful around the Bigg Eggs office. Still, to breath in felt like I was sucking exhaust in an enclosed garage. Management's bunker had windows along one side that looked out on the fry cooks. Blinds behind the windows could be shut tight and often were. When I arrived, the blinds were open. Pam, the woman of twenty-four who had presented me my chicken costume, motioned me in. The psychology major and Pam had attended the same high school I had, coincidentally, and perhaps were taught by some of the same teachers who had nurtured great potential in me eight years ahead of them.

Pam is a junior associate from personnel. She presented a pert, pleasant expression that was sympathetic to my plight. She hadn't yet heard what was troubling me.

"Go ahead, take off that chicken head," she suggested. "We can talk."

I preferred to keep the head on. I had this fear, not ridiculous if you think it through, that someone would snap a photo of my face popping out from a chicken costume, and use that image as blackmail to keep me working at menial, ill-paid jobs until my soul packed its baggage and fled in shame. I yanked the costume's beak, wrenched the head loose, and rested it in my lap, eyes directed at Pam.

"That's better?" she said.

"It is," I lied.

"Our goal is that everyone at Bigg Eggs is a success," Pam informed me. "We want to help in any way we can to remove your roadblocks to success."

"That is such a relief," I said. I'd assumed that I'd been summoned to the junior personnel associate's desk to be fired. Some thoughts on being fired: *My student loan late payment is past due. The people I'm staying with have not asked for rent. They'd be happy to see money come out of my pocket.*

"I see in your file that you have a master's degree," Pam said. My master's impressed Pam. Maybe she only pretended to be impressed to put me off my guard. She may have been trying to gauge how impressed I was by my own diploma, which I view as underperforming. My educational opportunities had been played as if the sky were the limit. I was no closer to the sky than when I'd picked up a viola in fourth grade. I'd been tested as a child, along with every kid in my class, for innate musical ability. The results had been tallied up. Barring an error in addition, I rank as some sort of supernatural prodigy.

My chicken suit is the uniform of the elite artist too rooted in an ideal career to formulate a backup plan. Four years of regular college, three years of graduate study. A student can learn a lot at the university. One thing you will never pick up, one thing the professional class employed at institutions of higher learning never teach is, "You truly are not good enough to make a living playing your instrument."

Often, a student of the arts lacks distinguishing talent. The curriculum dances around concealing that fact. No academic authority ever warned me that the competition for paid performance on the viola is fierce and rudely unfair. A wave of handsome teen prodigies is sweeping in from Asia, from Eastern Europe. They are here to claim America's creative class lifestyle, the stratum my poor parents (not literally impoverished, but truly unfortunate and disappointed) had set their sights on for me. Anyway, mine is an old story of hard work and folly climaxing in crushing debt.

"So what seems to be your problem?" said Pam the junior personnel associate. I detected a slip in her demeanor. Pam had become less than professional. Her interest remained more than casual, as if driven by personal curiosity, like off-the-record curiosity. Was this switch a ploy to win my confidence? Pam is brunette and slightly taller than tiny, with provocative proportions. In the flat lighting of that drab office her eyes were the color of wet blue topaz. Her nose and mouth were intelligently engineered to sniff out and savor sensual pleasure. All restrained and pursed, she flexed her face. Behind those aqua ice eyes, she truly expected me to blurt out every personal complaint that flitted across my mind.

"My problem?" My problem is I never enrolled in a computer science curriculum. I avoided any LSTAT preparation intensive. Basic bookkeeping classes eluded my consideration. As a result of pooh-poohing all sensible precautions, I was working at a mall in the hokey town where I grew up with my parents. I'm too old at thirty-plus to be visible on the front lines of retail. Doggedness haunts my eyes and lines my mouth. No one wants to be served by canine desperation at an accessories counter. My face is admissible to the retail workforce only when veiled within the feathers of a human-scale fowl.

"I'd prefer to be paid to play the viola," I said. "That is my only problem."

Pam slapped both hands on her desktop. "Your job is to be a chicken," she declared, as if I were playing dumb. She stopped herself, I will bet on it, from telling me I was a big silly. *Pam is someone who might be sort of cool to hang with*, I thought. I asked myself to imagine Pam dressed to her own preferences rather than in the yellow slacks and blazer of a junior personnel associate. I couldn't picture it. I wanted to. "I suggest you get along with the business of being a chicken," she concluded.

Taking her advice to heart, I went about the job of being a chicken. What I was afraid would happen did happen. I strutted all convivial and bold and feathered among milling mall patrons, a tout for Bigg Eggs. Almost immediately a person of my acquaintance whom I desperately needed to feel superior to pushed up into my beak. His name is Adrian Clifton. He is aggressive by default.

"Yo, chicken," hissed the ghosting fucker. "There's something you can do for me."

"Hello," I answered, playing a talking chicken, "let me invite you to step inside the Bigg Eggs dining enclosure! Please fill up on cholesterol and fried fowl!" Several yellow tabletops were open.

"Not today," said Adrian. "Maybe never. Show me a back way out of this shitty mall."

"You're right," I said. "I am able to help you." I walked him to a little-noticed staircase blended into the wall beside a freight elevator. Hidden within my chicken persona, I cautioned the ghosting prick not to trip across my big claw feet in his haste to depart.

"You all come back when you have time for eggs and thighs," I said.

I spoke to Adrian at volume. He failed to realize he knew me. Passing as a chicken, my individual humanity undetected, led to an important discovery. My voice was coming out of the mascot headpiece altered beyond recognition. The fowl disguise appeared to be impenetrable.

Two minutes later, my ex-girlfriend Carly rushed up, frantic. She'd never warmed to his town and claimed to have left it. Her abrupt presence took me by surprise. I bit my cheek to keep from calling out *Carly!* She clasped onto me, a presumed stranger, with more fervor than she had mustered during the last fourteen months we were together. The explanation is that people trust a man in a chicken suit. Put it down to sports mascots. Everyone who roots for a sports team places some degree of faith in a sports mascot. In times of stress or trauma, transference of that trust occurs. A jilted woman puts her heart in the hands of an unknown quantity dressed like a big chicken.

"Can you help me?" she asked. "I'm looking for a guy. He has this look like the wind has recently been in his hair."

"I know exactly how to overtake your prey."

I mapped out a shortcut that would intercept Adrian in mid-escape. With every blurt out of my mouth, I expected Carly to hush me and launch some variation on, "Oh, Monty! It's you! In a chicken suit! How did this indignity entrap you? Did I play a role in your expulsion from the realm of pride? In what way possible can I make up this injustice? Say the word! Any word! I'm ready to start working off my karmic debt this very instant!"

None of that happened. My ex-fiancée's only lingering with me was to double-check the route that would ambush oily ghost Adrian. She strode off toward the express escalator at a brisk pace. I stood regarding my outsize claw feet. I accepted to the bottom of my toes that this woman would never stride back to me. Casually (using that term relative to being an adult in a chicken suit surrounded by taunting adolescents in a food court), I walked to a railing overlooking an escalator bank and observed as my boned and blown-off girlfriend caught up with her fleeing cad. Naturally, the couple burst into tears at the sight of one another. Adrian and Carly clasped, shook with sobs and melded.

I pictured the isolation and misery that my girlfriend and this dolt had locked into. Their future trickled forward in a grim procession of dampened expectations and expanding body shame concerning self and partner. By my calculations, they had three kids on the way, dumb, glum ones.

Feeling for the first time that some good might come to me through this chicken job, I went back to the food-court crush and steered hungry cheapskates toward Bigg Eggs. My attitude improved. I looked forward to encountering people I knew. Personnel associate Pam cruised out from the Bigg Eggs dining enclosure and complimented my upgraded outlook.

"I'm pleased you are pleased," I responded. "I'd like to play viola for you."

"Is this you luring me up to your hutch?"

"Bunnies have hutches," I said. "Chickens live in coops. But hutch or coop is beside the point. I have so many roommates. I will need to bring my instrument to your crib."

Pam's nostrils and mouth expanded and flexed as if detecting sensual stimuli. "We could meet somewhere in between," she said.

We agreed to do that. We met at 8:00 p.m. on the shoreline promenade that ends at the town's unfinished pleasure pier. Half the shop fronts down there are closed or vacant. It's still a fun place. Enough people are loitering and lurking on the walkway that no one feels they're about to be singled out for assault. Pam stood in the light of a lemonade stand. She had dressed all in yellow with a red beret and red trainer shoes. Not wearing her personnel attire, she was unrecognizable. I mistook her for a random nut. She was eating a hot dog on a stick and finished it before shouting, "Hey, master's degree, where's your chicken suit?" I placed her by her voice. "I thought we'd dress as a pair," she said.

I felt a little bad. I'd been hoping she would take this meeting seriously. Turning my back, I unpacked my viola, tucked it to my chin and drew the bow. The bad I was feeling found its way down into the strings. The viola case lay open at my feet. I shut my eyes, and I made nine bucks. My playing brought Pam to tears. My playing brought me back to her place and into her bed. The sex might have been less than everything Pam was hoping for. She put a good face on it. "You are an amazing musician," she said. What did she know? "It is a travesty that you are working as a chicken."

Playing viola for Pam led to discovering that she had an admirer. The admirer was the 29-year-old senior personnel associate at our Bigg Eggs outlet, Pam's direct supervisor in the chain of command. His name is Josh. Josh maintained a rigid conception of hierarchy and a perfect Windsor knot in his expansive collection of ties. He had a different tie for each day of the week. As long as I worked at Bigg Eggs, he never varied their succession. He had come to our town as a young adult looking for new opportunities. Imagine the deep desolation buried in that move.

The morning after playing viola along the strand, I punched in at Bigg Eggs an hour before my shift was due, arriving at Pam's scheduled start time. It looked as though she and I were synchronized in our movements. Josh and his knotted tie stood in the doorway of the mascot changing room. I pulled the components of my chicken ensemble from the room's one locker. Josh is tall, blond, handsome and clean. I'll give him that. Also shut down emotionally in a way that disguises his cunning. Josh, he didn't need to tell me, had sensed the afterglow of my alone time with Pam. He had become an instant nonfan of me. Having dashed his hopes that Pam's virginity would arrive to him intact, I became subject to his close study. I zipped up the chicken body and stepped into the clawed feet. A brainstorm came to Josh. I prepared to pop the chicken head into place. He stopped me.

"Guess what?" he said. "I'm converting the mascot changing room into a Bigg Eggs employee-of-the-month lounge."

He watched the ramifications roll over my face. "Eliminating the changing room will force me to arrive at the job dressed for work," I said.

"Correct."

I was due on the mall floor proper. I stood and watched Josh rip out the changing room's sole locker with his bare hands. I thought,

This is the day I begin wearing my chicken suit home and on the way to work. Josh's intention was to inflict humiliation. I do not fault him. I had been through what he was going through. Adrian Clifton and his Camaros and Corvettes had dashed my hopes many times. If back in high school I'd had the power to make Adrian flounce about town dressed like a big bird deprived of flight, you would have seen zero hesitation.

I waded into the pre-lunch crush of food-court patrons. Kindness and its lack were on my mind. Most of the crowd stood no taller than the white meat of my chicken belly. Kids roved all over like they owned the place. I wondered where all the parents had gone. The next thought was recognizing my mother walking along the food court rim. Overdressed, critical, her hair adroitly captured and colored, she peered into one food outlet after another, reading menus posted above the order counters, trying to determine her least objectionable dining option. My mother had succumbed to wearing glasses full time. Obviously, she was not a regular at the food court. Obviously, I had not told my parents I was shilling as a chicken at the mall. I was drawn to this finicky, natty old woman. She was the crockpot where I'd stewed while becoming a person.

"Hello, miss," I said. "It's wonderful to see you at the food court today."

The purpose of a large, bumbling, vocal chicken mystified my mother temporarily. Within seconds, she adopted the common understanding of animal mascots as saviors. "Maybe you can help me," she said.

"I bet I can. I bet you're looking for a lunch option that is flavorful and health-conscious, with few to no empty calories."

"Me and how many others?" she said, always ready to diminish my insights.

"Go with the chicken place," I said.

"As if someone with a job in a chicken suit is someone with an opinion I should take seriously," answered my mother. "I do enjoy chicken. I'll give your Bigg Eggs a shot. Just to be clear, not on your say-so."

The blonde with the psychology degree led my mother toward a cleared yellow table and entered her order on an electronic tablet. In the time it took for payment to clear, the meal had arrived at the table. Mom thanked the scholar of psychology, and gave the younger woman's yellow jumpsuit and cap a scathing once over. I went in to sit with Mom while she ate, which is not strictly within Bigg Eggs protocol.

"Normally while I dine," she said, looking across the plastic tabletop into the yellow feathers covering my face, "I do not tolerate being hounded by an underachiever dressed as a very dumb animal. Today, it's nice not to be alone." At this moment, a batch of finger-licking kids swarmed within the restaurant. Toddlers, infants, preschoolers, they were all gaga at my presence. For my mother, it was like sitting adjacent to a celebrity. The admiration of bugging goo-goo eyes and gaping pie holes overflowed onto her. She enjoyed splashing around in it.

"Being in the midst of all these wonderful children is so refreshing," she said. "I'd forgotten the infectious optimism a crowd of children can bring to an adult outlook. I used to be a schoolteacher, you know."

Oh, I knew. "Teaching is a wonderful calling." I nodded, urging her to go on.

"I've always been interested in children. In preparing them for what life brings, the joys and the challenges."

She sensed even through the feathers that I was predisposed to be sympathetic. "My husband doesn't share this outlook. He's more what might be called a fatalist. Kids either turn out okay or they won't. That's his view. He was very good with our son though." Behind the lenses of her glasses, emotion floated on a liquid swell.

"You must be very proud of your son," I said. "I see a lot of love expressing itself."

"Do you mind if I confide in you? I'm worried about my boy. He's very accomplished in his field of study. He has two diplomas. He was engaged to a wonderful girl, also an intellectual. Now, the wedding is off. I'm on better speaking terms with the jilted fiancée than I am to my boy. He hasn't even mentioned they've broken up. What could that secrecy mean?"

Here again was a woman bereft putting her heart in the hands of an animal mascot. Advice, obviously, is something I have no qualification to deliver. I shot for understanding. "Maybe he's not being secret," I offered. "Maybe he's sad that he's disappointed you."

"I am not disappointed," scoffed my mother. She had powered through her Bigg Eggs Twin Thighs Super Plate. "My only concern is that he should be happy."

"He must know that," I conceded, "down below. My guess? He's trying to find a soft way to bring this situation to you and to his father. My sense is he wants to cause the least amount of discomfort and pain as possible."

My mother wiped her fingers and licked her lips. For her, satisfaction is expressed in a series of precise unconscious motions.

"Thank you for those kind words," she said, standing. She raised her hand to wave at the swarm of happy kids. She drew back her arm to abort that motion. "I'm off to replenish my supply of body lotions."

Standing on the mall floor, my mother stared at her surroundings as if she were a creature of habitual wonder. She strode forward in the opposite direction of the body lotion store. I could have stepped out and corrected my mother's course. It's better for her to come around and discover her destination on her own power. That's how she'd felt it was supposed to work for me.

That evening after work I headed home without changing out of the fowl costume. Wearing the outfit in public was not the worst thing that ever happened to me. The costume's outsize, awkward claw feet were a hazard, of course. I took the precaution of carrying them under my wing. I stood alone at the bus bench in full costume including the head. I pictured the bus driver seeing a full-on chicken standing at the stop, and driving on by. Should I take off the head? Showing my human face might increase the chances of the bus driver pulling over for me to board. On the other hand, popping my face out from the chicken torso exposed me to all acquaintances in passing cars as a college-educated adult forced to ride the bus and compelled to wear a demeaning costume. Keep the head on. No brainer. Two satchel-toting young men representing the digital economy joined me at the bench. The bus pulled over with no hesitation.

I climbed on and transferred my bus tokens from the hidden slit under my wing. This bus driver had seen much bizarreness during his long day and was unfazed by a compliant six-foot-tall chicken. I wrapped a wing around a pole adjacent to the back exit door and set about minding my own business.

Stepping down at my destination, I was feeling not so bad, admiring the memory of my mother, sort of. I was hungry. A new Burger Squat had been erected between the bus stop and the apartment where I was being allowed to stay. Burger Squat fits my means and appetite. The feathered costume's anonymity eased the abject humiliation of showing my face in a fast-food outlet. Identity hidden within a bulky, hot, itchy disguise, I ordered the food to be taken away, retreated to my coop, shucked the chicken suit, binged on burger and nested the night away.

In the rush to don the chicken suit before heading off in the morning, I missed my allotted bathroom shot and hit work with a dire bladder. Josh cornered me within the closet that housed the employee toilet. I desired only to finish and zipper my cock into my chicken body. Josh smiled. What handsome, clean teeth he had. "Were you the chicken in the Burger Squat?"

"What are you implying? Is it a crime to eat at a Burger Squat?"

"The way you did it? Maybe."

"Where I grab my sack of cheap, flawed nourishment is nobody's business."

"Dinner at Burger Squat makes for depressing social-media status updates, until the Bigg Eggs chicken steps in. That was your mistake. You went viral. Corporate has seen it. Corporate is pissed. I'm in charge of the internal investigation."

"Josh, I feel that you're accusing me of some infraction here. You need to be transparent about what the charges are. You have given me no indication of what my rights are. If you choose to continue addressing me in this tone, I want an advocate present. Maybe not all the way up to a lawyer, but someone with some juice on my side."

"I'll take that as a confession," said Josh.

I pushed past him and zipped my behind into yellow feathers. "Take it as a suppository," I said.

Beyond vindictive certainty, Josh had nothing actionable on me, which was no solace to Pam. I suggested we meet that night down by the abandoned pleasure pier. She begged off. "Come to my place," she whispered. "Make sure no one sees you."

I snuck over there around nine, dressed as a millennial. Josh's corporate sanctioned witch-hunt had put Pam in a false position. She faced away from me in her clothes closet, stacking, folding, and hanging garments that were already stacked, folded and hung. "I know you were the chicken at that Burger Squat," she said. "It makes me ill to think about what they are trying to do to you."

I suspected she was sickened by the professional necessity of ratting me out. I sat at Pam's makeup table. Thirty-plus years of false position looked back from the vanity mirror. "Go ahead and tell on me," I said. "In the long run, we both know you'll be doing me a favor."

She stepped out of the closet. Her face joined mine in her vanity mirror. "Oh, Monty. That doesn't change that I'd be tattling."

"You don't want to be a rat?"

She wrinkled her nose and pulled her upper lip back, protruding her two front teeth. "Not like that," she said. I rolled on my back and played a sad song on my viola. She took off her clothes, sprawled atop me on the bed and wept sweet tears into my neck.

The next morning being a workday, I put on my best face—the one with yellow feathers, wattles, beak—and set about the business of herding the food court's undecided diners toward Bigg Eggs. Pam emerged from the rapidly filling dining enclosure. She stood upon the talons of my big chicken feet, facing me. "I'm here to conduct a snap inspection of your costume." She winked, whipped out her smartphone and held the screen up to my eyeholes. "Check out this cool meme stream."

"I see pictures of a fake chicken in a real hamburger store," I said.

"Look closer, silly. Do you recognize the chicken?"

"Of course I do." The chicken was me. I recognized the awkward claw feet beneath a wing. I recognized the garish Burger Squat color scheme on the walls and dining tables in the background. I recognized the stolid eaters mechanically inserting burger slabs into pie holes.

"Read the words," said Pam.

I had work to do. Feckless masses were awaiting my slight motivational push toward Bigg Eggs. To humor Pam, I focused on the taglines superimposed upon the images of chicken man in hamburger stand: "Me doing something I know I'll regret in 20 minutes. Bigg Eggs Gets You." "Me just before 10 minutes of guilty consumption and 8 hours of gastric payback. Bigg Eggs Gets You." "Me right after I thought, *I wonder how it feels not to like myself?* Bigg Eggs Gets You."

The train of thought whistled right past me. "I don't understand what any of this is supposed to mean," I said to Pam.

"It means the Bigg Eggs social-media team has taken the 'to tattle or not to tattle' decision out of my wheelhouse. You're cleared. Even if they find out the chicken is you, you're a promotional asset!"

"That's all it took to save me? A clutch of half-nonsense catch phrases slapped across a social-media feed?"

"The social-media team couldn't have done it without your raw content!" Pam had never gushed like this for my viola playing. "There'd be no campaign without your shenanigans!"

Pam intimated there was a chance I could transfer to the social-media team, which the personnel associate within her characterized as "an elite force in the Bigg Eggs army."

"I bet they are nerds and twits and sexist pencil dicks," I countered.

"You've never met them. You might like them." The social-media team is housed at corporate HQ. Pam had visited for a time-management seminar. She had been presented to the social-media team and watched it in collaboration. "The social team is encouraged to wear whatever they want to work. You have never seen so many cool t-shirts in one set of cubicles, or chiller sneaks."

"If you're telling me joining social media is the right thing to do," I said, "I will think about grabbing at the chance." Actually, I would not. The chicken suit had grown on me. Wearing the thing in public? I'm not insane. I realized it was absurd. My street time in the suit was minimal, very minimal. But wearing the full camouflage while on the job had psychological benefits. Trading in the suit to pull on a cool hoodie and post snark on the Internet seemed like a demotion. Pam returned to the dining enclosure less elevated than when she had come to me and stood on my feet.

Against all expectations, my mother returned to the mall. I spotted her making a beeline toward Bigg Eggs. I hustled across court to greet her. Mom breezed past as though we had no history, gave me the full-on snub. That's the way it is. No one wants to reveal a relationship with a big chicken. I sat across from her at a yellow table. While polishing the lenses of her glasses, she apologized for not having noticed me. "A distraction has beset my mind," my mother confessed. Her boy's ex-fiancée, Carly, was sick. *Gravely ill* and *hospitalized* were two terms my mother used. Mom was consumed with worry, I could see. Worry did not dampen her ability to sock away a Twin Thighs Super Plate.

My mother wiped her fingers and licked her lips. "I don't know what will become of my boy if his fiancée passes on and he has not reconciled with her."

"Perhaps your boy will relent and visit this woman in her hospital room."

"That's no good," said Mom. "The poor girl is in an induced coma. If the brain fever doesn't break, the doctors say there's no use bringing her out of it."

Thoughts of Carly bedridden by a degenerative condition with little hope of reversal kept me cruel company the rest of my shift. After work, hanging out with Pam at her place, my emotions were not in the room with us.

"I don't think we will be doing this anymore," she said. "We want different things."

"That means I want you, but you don't want me." I played the viola, willing all the emptiness I feared into my bow. Pam listened. How could she not? We were in her bedroom. The music overflowed the space. There was no escaping the vibrations. Pam's mind seemed to be busy somewhere else. I finished the movement, awed by the composition. "You don't seem very sad about it ending," I said.

"Why should I be?" she asked. "We are stopping while we are still friends."

"Of course I wonder if we have ever been friends."

"It is the chicken's nature to remember nothing of importance."

No one would be taking off any clothes in that room on that evening. Pam didn't want any further music from my instrument. I packed up the viola and left her to her own edification.

The next day was my day off. I broke a personal rule and put on the chicken suit specifically to venture out in public. The agreement I had with myself was to wear the feathers only to and from work. I might stop off for groceries or a burger while chickened up. Technically I was en route. I had drawn a line at donning the feathers and heading out anywhere that was not the job.

Bending the guidelines empowered me to visit gravely ill Carly in the hospital while not being seen. I didn't want my presence as the rudely dumped ex to distress any family members who had traveled at vast distance and expense to hold vigil at Carly's side. Making any situation awkward is anathema to me. Also, I didn't want the success profile of Carly's boyfriend, Adrian, to dwarf my career standing.

In costume, I announced at the hospital's front desk that I represented a Bigg Eggs corporate responsibility program to visit cancer ward kids. If you're an animal mascot, you're welcomed. A patient-relations advocate latched onto my right wing. She marched me through a round of make-a-wish visits with sickly, bald children living in confinement. At the sight of my bulky yellow disguise, their faces brightened but did not blush. I toddled through their ward. Half a dozen chemo kids escaped their beds and encircled me. Kids hung from my shoulders and neck, practically weightless, proclaiming their love for Bigg Eggs tenders and fries. I apologized like a dumb cluck for not bringing samples. I promised fistfuls of free meal coupons once they were outside again, in the malls where they belonged. The grave children acted as though this assurance of future treats meant a lot to them. Feeling so sorry for myself partially shielded me from the incoming grief sticking to these kids like napalm, but so many chipper interactions with precociously terminal patients hobbled my morale. I am the wrong kind of narcissist for delivering cheer to the doomed.

No one questioned or stopped me as my claw feet shuffled about the wards completing my tour of childhood mortality. Medical professionals assume any animal willingly visiting a hospital is on a humanitarian mission. Before long, I found Carly's floor and stood outside her room. I looked beyond a drawn curtain at Carly hooked up on tubes, electrical wiring, monitors, a ventilator. Adrian sat bedside, his back to where I lurked. I angled my costume around until I captured a partial view of his face. He'd traveled to an emotional outpost that no new car would bring him back from. *Get out before Adrian sees you*, I told myself. *That's the only precaution you need to take.* I stared into Carly's open, dull eyes. Walking away was impossible. I hadn't felt enough yet. To my horror, I sniffled. Adrian turned toward the doorway. He realized the presence of a grown man in a chicken costume. "Do you have permission to be here?" he asked, demanding but not super loud. "Were you summoned?"

"No," I replied. "I am only here as a sympathetic character, in the sense that I am a character full of sympathy."

Over Adrian's shoulder, I saw comprehension flicker like light in Carly's eyes. She had recognized me. Well, not me, but the image I inhabited, the big helpful chicken from the mall. She shook her head no. "No one here wants your sympathy," said Adrian. "You're wasting your time here."

Adrian's assumption that time is more wasted in one place than any other can be readily refuted by a man who passes the productive hours of any given day tottering across the floor of a shopping-mall food court on false talons. I set myself to argue the point with Adrian. Carly's stricken mother, big sister and a younger brother huffed forward like a red-eyed herd. I cut short the impulse to debate.

"My thoughts are with you," I said, shuffling off stage, "and with your loved one."

For the first time since I'd known him, Adrian looked like he might age worse than I would. He pointed at the chicken head but fell short of rising from his chair. "Hey, chicken," said Adrian, "you can't do any good here."

How wrong he could be. A photo had been captured of happy hairless children frolicking on my feathery lap and climbing upon my winged shoulders. There's nothing to be done with a picture like that except spread it out along the Internet. Again, social media had captured and amplified me in my fowl guise. I arrived at the mall to be informed that the Bigg Eggs' online content managers had put the image of me with the bald kids to good use, raising $220,000 in ten hours of a matching-contribution campaign for the Children's Leukemia Society. Pam the junior personnel associate arranged to congratulate me privately within the employee-of-the-month lounge.

"Our chicken mascot is kind of a big hero," she said. "You did a great thing at the hospital. You really did a really great thing."

Since we were alone, I tilted up the chicken head. "I was hoping you'd see it that way."

"Don't get your hopes up about us." She shoved the fowl headpiece back down over my face. "I haven't changed my mind about no longer meeting you off premises."

"But you still care."

"I'll always care."

I saw the situation suddenly and clearly. "You're seeing someone else."

"Whether or not I'm seeing someone else, seriously, has no bearing on...."

"Whether or not? That means yes." *Fucking Josh*, I thought. The out-of-town Romeo always blindsides the homegrown Juliet.

Pam pressed me as hard as a person can press another person without any physical contact. "Monty, take your shot. Join the Bigg Eggs social-media elite team."

"Why should I try out for social media? Because everyone on the team has fancy graduate degrees?"

"You'll have the opportunity to apply musical scores to the goofy videos that the Bigg Eggs Twitter account is renowned for. You'll be paid for playing viola!" Pam's imagined golden opportunity contradicted my Bigg Eggs trajectory. My claw toes were scratching toward a dead end. I dragged my chicken-suited self to the mall floor proper and did more of what I did best. Work went well until Josh pulled me into the employee-of-the-month lounge.

"This is only the second time I've been invited into the lounge," I said, "since it was repurposed."

"You need to be less useless," Josh said. "Can you do simple tasks?"

He had me there. Fifteen minutes later, I'd been taught how to clean the employee toilet and change the fat in the deep fryers. The dirty old fat was to be carried in a bucket to a reclamation tub. The fat cooled quicker than I would have expected. I slopped it in with the semi-congealed fat already in the tub. The dirty fat was a fluid and flowed from the pail. Under Josh's inspection, something was always wrong with the way I transferred the old fat. He had it in for me.

The time frame blurs for me here. It might have been the next day, maybe a week later. Pam came out of the employee toilet and caught me waiting outside to clean it. "If I'd known you were in there," I said, "I would be somewhere else."

"If you don't apply for the social-media promotion," Pam warned, "Josh has the okay to fire you. You're like a wild card. You're like a loose cannon."

"Like, I'm a chicken with its head cut off?" *Is this what she and Josh talk about late at night? While waiting out Josh's refractory period, do they craft similes to describe my unhinged incompetence?* Pam was eager to put distance between herself and the toilet. Her urgency pushed right past me.

Wondering why the rush, I followed Pam's rapid low heels past the management bunker, the walk-in freezer and the deep fryers. I dropped back. She sallied into the dining enclosure. Oily, dark Adrian Clifton stood in there, beside the receptionist podium. It was like a page out of the book of revelations! Pam had fallen for the hometown cad, not Josh the smooth interloper. Adrian looked all suffering and noble, like a community-theater depiction of noble suffering. Playing to the house, Pam put both hands into Adrian Clifton's paws. They allowed a meaningful physical charge to jolt through one another's arms for what seemed like minutes beyond impropriety. They took a table. Tears flowed from Pam's eyes. Mist brimmed in Adrian's gaze. The thing about two people in love is it just spills out all over. So do the waterworks.

I pictured Carly fresh and groggy out of her coma at the hospital being told she will make an almost complete recovery, "but it will require a lot of work from you and from everyone you love." Carly, had she been a party to this mushy handholding in the Bigg Eggs dining enclosure, would have busted a cry too.

There was an action I could take against Adrian to avenge this betrayal of Carly and of myself, one courageous move available to me. Josh had taught me what to do. Though dressed as a chicken, I would not cower. I collected my bucket. I drew off a load of liquid grease from the deep fryer reclamation tub. I carried the slopping bucket almost blindly toward the dining enclosure. Pam and Adrian sat melting into one another across yellow plastic. The fryer juice cooled, as I've said, faster than expected. Still, it was fluid and redolent. Adrian saw me but failed to place me. He did register alarm on Pam's face. Pam recognized me animating the chicken suit. She saw slop in the bucket and sensed my intention. Who knows if I would have actually gone through with it? The closer I approached Adrian, the clearer the second thoughts: *Do you really want to do this? Your chicken head will be torn from your body. Your identity will be exposed. Accountability will pounce upon you like a set of four-point restraints. You may face criminal charges. You will definitely be the butt of social ostracism. This town will no longer be big enough for itself and you.*

Bucket clutched, I reached the brink of making up my mind. Keen-eyed Josh stepped into my trajectory. Walking in the opposite direction, he hit me with a handsome wink and a distracting grin. You might have read anything into the grin, other than sympathy or affinity. I closed in on my verdict (*So is it yes or no?*) and Adrian. Josh kicked his wingtip into my lifted ankle, catching my back hock in the air. My big, clawed chicken feet tangled in one another and tripped me. I stumbled face first, free-falling, and tossed the bucket of molten fat forward. My head descended toward an urgent meeting with the concrete flooring. On the way down, I tracked the bucket's foul contents cascading hot but not scalding on top of oily Adrian, drenching his head, face and shoulders. I heard and felt the clunk of my skull cracking on the floor beneath Adrian's chair.

I might have been unconscious, only for a second. My chicken head was askew. The eyeholes didn't match up. Someone stepped on my arm and apologized. The chicken head was wrenched left and right. I put up my hands to steady the neckline. Two sets of hands were working at the throat. A concerted effort was being made to reveal me. I prepared to meet the face of open hostility. The head was one twist from falling away. I released my grip on the collar, and it came loose.

"That's Monty Shaw! You've got to be kidding me!" Adrian's drenched head was dripping slime. Pam, peering down at me over his shoulder, had caught some fatty splash across her blazer and blouse. "What the fuck is Monty Shaw doing inside a chicken suit?"

"Monty!" Pam said. "Can you move? Can you speak? How many fingers am I holding up?"

I guessed one. You know which one. That was a mistaken guess. It was two or three. My vision had gone all awash. I'd come to a realization that took the sense out of every visible thing. These two people, defiled by my design, clung to a first belief that I had fallen inadvertently, through not paying attention or due to a construction flaw in my costume. Their immediate concern was to determine the extent of my injuries and help me. Also, they were angry, to be certain. Once no need for an ambulance was determined, Adrian Clifton insisted as a wronged customer that I be fired from Bigg Eggs and wages withheld to cover his dry-cleaning expenses. Josh, believe it or not, robustly seconded this customer's demands.

Outside of Josh's deliberate trip, taking advantage of my foolhardy valor, the whole wet mess was an accident based on a misconception. It really was. Josh wasted less than fifteen seconds terminating my employment. I handed my claw feet and my fowl head and my feathered yellow body to him. He dropped the lot of it at his feet. "Sorry, not sorry," said Josh, radiant like a bride. I left the mall out a back service entrance. No matter what great quantity of events and circumstances are wrong in this world, one blond, handsome, shut-down man of my acquaintance was happy with what he had done, if only for that moment.

Deprived of the protection of my chicken suit, I walked outside exposed like any other person. Spring is over. Summer is over. Fall's finished. Winter is almost done. I'm the only man on the bus carrying a viola case. What's so special about that? All the nuts are drawn to it. I jump off at my stop. I had tensed for conflict. Off the bus, I'm relieved of that burden. The rain has blown out. The sun is long gone for the day. A fat, bright full moon backlights the clouds. This will be one of those brilliant, clear nights that offer no place to hide.

I unpack my viola and play beneath the window of a person who says she is nothing more to me than a former coworker. I presume I will have coworkers again, perhaps ones I sentimentalize as much as this one. She once believed I played wonderfully. What does she know? It's all in the song. I'm playing a wonderful song someone else composed. I can't play this song forever. Before long, Pam will have to ask me in, or she can wait it out until someone else calls the cops.

TIME APPEARS TO BE RUNNING OUT

You're in the car, driving toward a certain and happily anticipated destination, sure of yourself behind the wheel, admitting the possibility of sex happening in the place you are headed toward, and suddenly needing to shit. This need starts out as a pained contraction deep in the bowels. There has been no gradual buildup. Intestinal movement is all in one direction. It will not be reversed. This you know as fact. The motion pushes forward at a speed all its own. You may be able to slow the progress, for a short while. The pang in your gut is a disturbing insistence. You will be powerless to impede the outcome. Traffic is going nowhere. You are not alone in the car. The presence of this other person sitting in the passenger seat makes you more isolated in the global dismay of your gastric helplessness than if you accompanied only yourself. Your face twists. Your jaw clenches. The last thing you want is a witness.

The other person, the passenger in your car, is asking about your comfort. "Are you okay? What happened? What's happening?" *Solicitous* is the word. He really is a good man. He exhibits hallmarks of being a good man. He is present and wholly attentive without presuming to touch you physically. His eyes communicate a desire to understand what he does not know. His mind operates within a box of decency. His mind contains no thoughts so base in nature as to explain your sweating, sudden-onset panic.

You've shared a very nice meal. Half an hour ago, he picked up the check with a grace that had no strings attached. Glancing eye contact extended just the correct range of feelers. The effortless companionability had started with the marking of the date. You'd met up with an extended group of friends for an afternoon concert on a museum lawn. He'd been known and liked among these extended friends. In fact, as he'd reminded you although you had needed no reminder, you'd met him twice before: One time at a gallery, another time at a wedding. He'd been unfazed by you wanting to take your own car on this first date. When driving your own car, you have control and the sense of not depending on someone else's proficiency and mercy. Autonomy is important to you early on, in the getting-to-know-one-another stages. You hadn't needed to explain yourself. He'd said, "Sure. Where would you like to pick me up?" He hadn't presumed that he would come over to your place and leave his car parked there as an assurance that you two would be coming back together alone to your apartment, where the bedroom is never more than one doorway distant. Also, he had avoided suggesting a noncommittal meet-up at the restaurant, with the presumption of eating, chatting and motoring off on your own ways. He had recognized and held firm to the principle that real intimacy can incubate during the drives to and from. Once in the car, with the doors locked against outside intrusion, his scent had been clean, no additives. You sniffed out that he might have had a cigarette, and a hit of weed, recently, inhaled somewhere outdoors. You took turns looking into one another's profiles as you alternately peered forward through the windshield. You failed to contain an irrepressible smile of pleasure at being appreciated on the sly from the side. So did he. He spotted the parking space, was just the right degree impressed by your parallel parking skills, and handled the meter. He was kind to the servers, both of them female and trim, with no lapse in his attentiveness to you. Ordering the meal had been a collaborative anticipation in sensory delight. The dishes had arrived, been devoured, and their charms dissected. He'd wanted to know more about you. He had not pried. You had divulged. Guards were down. The ease of being together with this man had lulled you outside your gastronomical comfort zone. You'd eaten something you knew not to eat. Deep-fried, battered and delicious revealed a sinful interior richness. At first, your stomach indicated you'd gotten away with it. Placid inside, tingling on the outside, you hooded your eyes and looked into this man's frank, pleased appraisal across the table. You had suggested dessert and coffee at your place. You had entered the car confident, solid within.

A few blocks later, you'd taken the freeway onramp, locked into bumper-tight traffic stretching out beyond where you can see. The good man has noticed mounting distress. "Can you tell me," he asks, "whether the problem is physical or emotional? I can't know if you don't tell me."

Only you can know. The message of this physical and mental and fully existential crisis is that everyone else must not know. The self-awareness is about to become more than you can handle. Your gastric system has betrayed you. The breach, when it culminates, will separate you more fully than at any previous living moment from any person near you. This catastrophe has hit you before. You know how it ends.

"Get out of the car," you tell him.

"You aren't even pulled over."

Your car is pinched in immobile traffic. "We're not going anywhere," you insist. "Get out while you can."

If you had been driving alone, you would throw the transmission into park, run from the car and head toward a row of bushes on the horizon. Shit would roll down the backs of your legs. You would not look back. You had left a boyfriend one time sitting in the driver seat bewildered as you squatted between two parked cars in a residential district. A father and two young daughters had been walking a dog on the sidewalk across the street. Your boyfriend had never encountered anything quite like this, not from you, not from anyone. "I'm not a fan of close calls," he had told you, as if anyone is. Humiliated, not breaking up, but receding from talks about moving in together, you'd been motivated to do something, to find help. You'd consulted a specialist and followed her prescribed dietary regimen at great cost and commitment. You'd worked so hard on your nutrition. The results had been palpable. You'd thought this precipitous, violent, gushing voidance was all behind you. Fucking shit, how many more of these battles can you afford to lose? You flip open the car's door locks.

"You must get out," you tell this good man. "I insist." You tell him, "I will be back for you." You are crying. You tell him, "You must trust me." The seconds have ticked down as far as they will tick down. With every tock, a pang in your gut tightens one last twist.

Because he cares, because he is a good person and is concerned for you, this man locks the door, in effect bolting himself in the passenger compartment. He looks at you with unwavering resolution and says, "I'm staying."

Cars behind you honk. Traffic is moving. You take your foot off the brake.

YOU SEEM TO BE ALL ALONE HERE

All the emotions of his eventful life visit the father of the bride at the wedding of his only child, even those feelings attached to events he has missed. Being a family man, the father of the bride reflects, means forfeiting so much else. Not that he would trade any parallel life over being the bride's father at this wedding, a wedding staged on a grand scale. The ceremony is being staged within the city's cavernous museum of natural history. The father imagines the cost of renting a museum of natural history. This edifice had been the groom's venue choice, its vast vaulted interiors, its lifelike dioramas of extinct peoples and beasts, its panoramic windowed ceilings, all paid for from the groom's bankroll.

In the unreal hour preceding the ceremony, while his daughter is fitted into her princess dress, the father wanders from the glad-handing and candid photos at the colonnade entranceway to stroll alone among towering dinosaur skeletons. Contemplative and deliberate, he walks the length of three massive halls, humbled and awed by the presence of ancient and colossal bones. *The world is so much bigger and persisting than any of us, than even the most important among us ever bear in mind*, the father thinks, *yet all this vastness perishes*. This thought and others of its ilk should prepare him for any course human events may take during the coming few minutes.

The father rejoins the thickening crowd in the grand entrance hall. Almost two hundred people gathered in comradely good finery. The majority are work associates of the groom's in the peak power of their earning lives. Many of these people are accustomed to being the center of attention. In this brash, colorful, voluble swirl, the bride's father instantly spots Chloë Sevigny standing chic and casual at the center of the marble floor. One of the single male guests has brought this amiable figure of easy elegance as his plus one. No one had told the father of the bride that Chloë Sevigny might pop in at his daughter's wedding. He's not cool. He plays it cool. On the face of it, he handles the sanguine presence of Chloë Sevigny with unfazed aplomb.

Next, the father of the bride catches sight of his older brother. Shane has shown up after all. That blip in the course of human events throws the bride's father. The brother stands aloof at crowd's edge, freshly shaved no more than two days ago, hair formally greased, smirk dialing between obsequious and sneering. He wears a glowing white dress shirt, skinny red-silk tie and black-leather blazer. The blazer is vintage, lovingly preserved and vulva soft. The bride's father had handed the blazer off to Shane a decade and a half back. After so much time, walking toward that jacket unlooses a slew of feelings and emotions. The bride's father stops those feelings before they arrive at concrete memories and missed events. He and Shane meet halfway, in the middle of the guests. No hug. No handshake or clasp.

As a greeting, the father's brother wants to know, in a confidential whisper, "How is this actress Chloë Sevigny a guest at a wedding for someone in our family? I mean, look who we are. Look where we come from. Remember our old man?"

Shane's attendance, in its way, is more of a shock than Chloë Sevigny's. "You could have RSVPed," says the bride's father. "We're happy to have you here, of course."

"I thought I for sure sent that thing in. To be honest, I couldn't be certain I'd be able to make it." Shane's eyes do that trick where they smile warmly, scout the perimeter and act like they see through every secret you're trying to keep hidden, all while evading direct contact. "Work is crazy," he says.

"Work? What's work these days?"

"You don't want to get into it here, trust me. The demands are not like a normal job."

"You seem to have shown up all alone. Aren't you remarried? That phone call, last year? Two years ago? You were about to remarry."

"Seriously, what's the draw for Chloë Sevigny? Is this joint being sponsored by Target?"

"The groom works in showbiz. Behind the scenes."

"When my kid finds out, she'll wish she had been on talking terms with me. She's missed out on a selfie with Chloë Sevigny. She'll die."

"Wren was wishing Breeze could be here. They were close as kids."

"Wren isn't missing anything with Breeze not being here. Breeze is off the rails. Breeze is not in the same class as Wren. Breeze doesn't do well around free booze."

"Hey, just to be clear, Shane. No photos with any guests you don't already know. Don't go asking Chloë Sevigny for a photo, like some rube."

"Don't worry about me being the one that's the rube, pal. Have you looked at us lately?"

Between these brothers, the bride's father is the obvious stunner. His gray has come in as though air brushed. The nose, the brows and the jaw are all clean and symmetrical, rugged in a very refined way. The eyes and the mouth always seem full of strength and empty of malice. Shoulders straight, posture erect, silhouette trim and tall, the bride's father is a handsome addition to any collection of very good-looking men. His brother looks okay. Shane is complicated. He's feral and domesticated. Shane is older, but thinner. The leather blazer suits him. The jacket drapes well, hangs appealingly sinister on hard angles. The parents are gone. There's an older sister in another country. She's agoraphobic while she's at home. The big brother is all that's left, really. "You're looking good," says the bride's father. "It's really good to see you. It's time to go in and sit. Come on, I'll show you where."

A little acoustic combo has set up its instruments in the main hall, to the side of where the vows will be exchanged. Under the surveillance of a fully reassembled tyrannosaurus, the four musicians play delicate, string-suspended versions of "Lotta Love," "With a Little Love," "Love Will Keep Us Together," gently drowning the sounds of guests filling their seats.

"You know who that guy is with the shades and playing the acoustic guitar?" asks Shane. "Don't you?"

The bride's father doesn't know the guitarist's precise identity. He is sure the band is made up of working musicians. "One of them," Shane tells him, "has won a Grammy. You seem uptight. You've got Chloë Sevigny and a Grammy winner on your team. What can you be 'plexed about?"

"I'm not 'plexed. It's time to walk in Wren."

Stepping away from his older brother, the bride's father is purposeful, overflowing confidence. He's smiling. He presses flesh and says "thank you for being here" to every friend and stranger in his path, twice to Chloë Sevigny. The bride's father stands exactly where he's supposed to stand, precisely when the team putting finishing touches on Wren needs him on that mark. The bride's father is 'plexed. His daughter steps forward, veiled in lace. He summons enough presence of mind to tell her, "A more beautiful bride has never been seen." For a quarter of a minute, he's free to take in the miracle his girl has become. He trusts someone is taking photos. He will never remember this moment on his own. A speech is in order, from the father of the bride. He will be called upon to deliver it within the hour. That prospect couldn't be more perplexing if he were to be shot afterward.

Moving up the center aisle under the bones of a monumental, extinct reptile, the father matches his pace to his daughter's. To either side of him, a congregation rises in unison. Late afternoon sunlight frames their placid faces. A recurrent speech impediment lurks in the father's back-story, eclipsing the lightness of the passing seconds. Guitar strung notes of "Here Comes the Sun" expand crystalline and momentary in the loving acoustics of the museum's vault. The father identifies the song but loses the melody in a cacophony of trepidation around the impending speech. He puts the odds of his throat clamping during the speech and his brain shutting wordless in an aphasic seizure at thirty percent, but then he has always been an optimist. A squat, bearded film director of multiple features and many commercials, someone the groom hopes to work more with in the future, is officiating the wedding. The director permits the dearly gathered to be seated. The father of the bride takes his place next to his wife, the bride's mother. He moves to take her hand and misses it. Potential disastrous results of the obligatory speech nag in the father's inner conversation, and nag throughout the exchange of vows.

Man and woman have been proclaimed husband and wife. The bride's father hunches over a men's room sink splashing water upon his face. Shane appears beside the sink like a man who has located his lost little brother after searching all the neighborhood.

"You were hardly even there," observes Shane, handing over paper towels and mopping moisture from the father of the bride's face. "Don't make me worry about you."

"You're not here to worry about me." The father of the bride drops paper towels to the floor, blind to their utility. "We'll just take a few photos with the families and the newlyweds. Then it'll be time to eat. Dancing, drinking, everybody goes home happy."

"You already took the photos," says Shane. "This is what I'm talking about. Why do you think your eyes are so blown out?"

"I don't know. I haven't thought about it."

"Flash bulbs, fucker. You just stared into fifty, sixty flash bulbs like some acid burnout gazing into the sun. What's wrong with you? You need to maintain."

"You always said that when Mom came home from work. Maintain."

"Was it ever bad advice? Pull it together, lightweight. This shit coming up now with the daughter and the new in-laws? No one will give you a do-over on this shit."

"You know," answers the bride's father, reason filtering back into his gaze, "this is crazy, but I could smell that jacket from across the room. The leather. I'd recognize it with my eyes closed."

"You had a panic attack," explains Shane. "It's over. It's the old man's fault. He taught you how to panic at the dinner table. It's a wonder you can talk at all."

"I don't need to make excuses blaming the old man."

"He's not here now. He's gone."

The bride's father has closed his eyes. He takes a deep breath, inspecting every particle of incoming air for the scent of soft black leather. "You could have said something. You could have helped me. Not when you were little, when you were bigger. But you left."

"I'm here now. I'll be right in front of you. He won't."

Shane places a hand on the father of the bride's shoulder and walks him out of the men's room. It's like the brothers take assurance from moving in relation to one another. They steady one another like shared history and enter the reception hall solid and self-possessed. To say they're a team might be a step too far.

The caterer's people have stocked the buffet trays. The deejay has set up his sound system. The guests are ready to eat. They're all waiting for that first speech to be over.

"Ladies and gentlemen," announces the deejay, "I give you the father of the bride."

The bride's father steps forward alone. His brother's hand no longer grounds him. He takes hold of the microphone. The guests, two hundred and change, have found their table numbers and located their positions. The bride's father tracks the gradations of status in the faces turned toward him from the ranks of tables. He sees the film director who had officiated sitting among a daunting caliber of sophisticates. Flanking out from the director's table, the father sees well-fed cheeks and expensive dentistry and boutique apparel. He sees Chloë Sevigny waiting attentive and expectant. He feels more than sees a suffocating vision of how far in he is over his head. He spots Shane.

Shane sits at the father of the bride's table, in the father of the bride's chair, next to the mother of the bride. The brother clasps one of the wife's hands in his own, prohibiting it from being withdrawn. Shane. Always the imposter. Older and less mature. Shane, who had not been there for his own daughter's birth or graduation, certainly not any wedding, looks up with his familiar boldness, always adjacent to a wince. Shane had never finished anything that required completion. Millions of promises, boasts, easy assurances that the future holds splendid days ahead, that's the shit Shane is full of. The father of the bride had been present for his daughter. He had finished what he started. His actions backed his word. He inhabited the world as the person he was, no more and no less. He looked at Shane over the course of five or six seconds. The differences between him and his older brother buoyed him toward self-certainty. Nothing was morally wrong with Shane. The older brother had chosen a sketchy path. That's all. The father of the bride stood confident and grounded, as a good man should.

"I want to welcome and thank everybody who is here to celebrate the wedding of Wren and Jacob," says the father of the bride, speaking directly down to his older brother. The voice is clear. The words clip smoothly, filling the space and reaching the most distant listener. "My wife and I are prouder of our daughter, Wren, every day that we know her. We are full of admiration for the woman she has become. We are excited to see what new levels of achievement, adventure and kindness she will reach." Feeling brave with the ease of his opening sentences, the father of the bride makes unhurried, solid eye contact throughout the room. His scan stops short of Chloë Sevigny. His view moves back toward Shane. "Wren knows that she is loved to the depths of our souls. How could we not? Wren is the most loving person I have ever met. Now her love has expanded to include Jacob." The bride's father is no fool. Of course he had prepared a statement. The rehearsed pitch has proceeded so well, without his throat collapsing and his brain blanking, that the father of the bride, taking a look at his craven, lowly brother as a confidence booster, decides to venture off script. "Which brings us to the question of what's so special about Jacob. How has Jacob won the heart of this amazing, giving and gifted woman? Is he just some incredibly lucky mug who stepped into the affection of Wren through no virtue of his own? Was Jacob simply in the right place and right time to capture a sort of sympathy devotion? Is the secret to Wren and Jacob matching up just dumb luck?" The bride's father pauses his unfaltering delivery here in case the guests care to release a friendly chuckle. They give it to him. Shane, he sees, is not seeing what he expected to see. Shane is mystified. *From where,* Shane is wondering, *did this public speaking dynamo emerge? How did I underestimate him so fully?*

"Dumb luck would be fine by us if it were true," continues the bride's father. "It's not dumb luck. Jacob recognizes Wren's one-of-a-kind soul. She is a woman who looks at life as a lifelong growth opportunity. Jacob, as all of you who know him will attest, has the persistence, the passion, and the compassion to grow with her every stage of the way. Wren's mother and I are so full of gratitude and high anticipation today. Wren has met her match. And Jacob has met his. Congratulations to the new husband and wife. And now, let me hand off this baton to my son-in-law, Jacob Pastor."

Applause accompanies the bride's father back to the family table. His brother stands and cedes the father's seat. Assured that his speech has landed well, the father is able to eat. He has expressed his love for his daughter. His son-in-law, Jacob, is talking now, extolling the virtues of extending and melding families. The bride's father listens to himself again describing his daughter as gifted and giving. The best man, handed the microphone by the groom, launches into chatty praise of groom and bride that is bawdy where expected and mawkish at other places. He is a professional comic. The crowd's emotions move where the comic wants them to move, other than the emotions of the father of the bride, which are moved by his own recent elucidation of the love he and his wife share for this proud, kind, amazing woman—their little girl.

In a quiet moment, the father of the bride notices that everyone at his table has finished their food. The maid of honor, the final presenter before the cake will be cut, speaks of Wren, a wild, fun, adventurous young lady who has become a brave young woman. The bride's father had missed citing his daughter's courage. Her power to overcome obstacles had featured in his prepared statement, abandoned. The maid of honor finishes up. The father of the bride addresses his plate of food, replaying the loving details of his speech for his daughter as he chews. By the time the last of the rabbit is pulled off the bone, he is eating alone. Where has everyone from his table gone?

They've stood and grouped up and paired off throughout the hall. The father of the bride is pleased to see the guests so garrulous and intimate with one another. He sees his brother corner Chloë Sevigny. This looks like trouble. Shane looms over the actress, one arm on her chair back, bent and angular. His jaw hinges smooth and sure. Chloë Sevigny smiles up at Shane, for all appearances engaged, laughing to the cues of his sharp gestures. The bride's father sees two groomsmen introduce themselves to his brother and convivially lead him toward the deejay. Chloë Sevigny walks from her table into the milling crowd.

The bride's father looks for a grouping of guests to break in on. Finding no easy openings, he heads to the bar, a default, no-fault destination. He orders a Chivas and leans on the bar waiting for relief. Chloë Sevigny leans on the bar beside him. "Congratulates on your daughter's marriage," she says, "and your speech. It was impressive and moving."

"Thanks. I'm glad you liked it. By the way, let me apologize for my brother."

"Who's your brother?"

"The guy with the red tie who had you pinned down over there a few minutes ago."

"Oh, come on. Don't be sorry. Your brother is a total character. I really dig his jacket. He was a perfect gentleman, as they say. But look, even if he'd been something more interesting than that, the right blazer gives a man a lot of leeway."

The bride's father, in mid-sip of Chivas, tries to formulate a sentence that will inform Chloë Sevigny that the jacket she admires, it once belonged to him. He almost has the words to express this casual gift of black-leather character.

"I want a picture. I need a picture." The back of his own jacket is being tugged. The bride's father turns to see a girlfriend of his wife, frumpy, plain, connected since middle school. Her voice is high and pitched and directed at Chloë Sevigny. "Don't worry! You can be in the picture too!"

The girlfriend of the wife turns her phone camera sideways and holds an expression of squinting expertise on her face. The father of the bride and Chloë Sevigny place arms over one another's shoulders. The father of the bride suspects that his wife's friend, taking the photos, is unaware of Chloë Sevigny as a cultural touchstone. He has a thought. *Chloë Sevigny has seen a thousand black-leather jackets with better character than Shane's.*

"Did you get the shot?" asks Chloë Sevigny. She smiles and dashes. The black-leather blazer, the father of the bride reflects, has been a weary cliché for a decade. Chloë Sevigny's praise of it was either a gracious wedding guest playing nice, or mockery. In retrospect, he's glad not to have said anything about the leather once belonging to him.

The cake has been cut. Slices are being passed on paper plates. The dancing is approaching a sugared frenzy. The bass drops. The frenzy drops to a molasses crawl. Who are these musicians being spun by the deejay? The father of the bride has no clue. Even the genre of music is unknown to him. He is accustomed to the white wedding where Wild Cherry and Aerosmith workhorses are trotted out. On second thought, Chloë Sevigny has surely heard hundreds of speeches more impressive and moving than his. In praising him, she had employed a sliding scale. He was a fool for sucking in the smoke she'd blown. Still, she hadn't needed to give him any warm words at all. That she did was a graceful act. The father of the bride searches the room for her, not with any intent, and locates the actress in deep comradely conversation with a cluster of people outside his acquaintance. They all inhabit a world fully separated from where he lives. Suddenly, the father of the bride is aware that his older brother is the center of Chloë Sevigny's tight-knit group. The brother is talking. His hands move like he thinks he's conducting an orchestra. The older brother's eyes are on fire, alternately fierce and friendly as he assumes various roles in the tale he's telling. Shane has been drinking. His listeners appear spellbound. Perhaps he has dealt drugs to them all. Chloë Sevigny punches him in the shoulder with hard hilarity. The older brother's story delivers its climax. The festive group embraces him as one of its own.

The father stalls between bar and dance floor, unaccompanied. Alone feels like a natural state of fatherhood. Waiting for the kid to come home while the wife sleeps. Sitting up with a book wondering what he will say or do if the kid once more fails to meet her curfew. Driving the streets, with no passenger, looking for familiar cars and teens that might lead to his daughter's friends, to the ones who might know where she has been for the past five days and might pass along the message that she is welcome to come back home. On those nights, he had thought he had never been more alone and would never be so alone again.

He sinks into an empty chair at an abandoned table. His wife is across the room speaking with a childless couple. The childless couple has recently come back from Europe for the second time this year. The wife of a man who pays too much attention to the mother of the bride settles into a chair directly beside the father of the bride. Her scent is loud and floral. Her lipstick is rich, bright and thick. She has styled her hair, again, in a conspicuously young manner. Her vintage matches the age of the father of the bride. She has taken better care of her physical package. She shifts the legs of her chair and effectively corners him. Their thighs make contact all along the outside. She is someone he is never in the mood to talk to.

"I have only one lament this night," says this woman, her face close, pores taut, breath clean. "You and I never seem to see each other despite having many common interests." She waits for the father of the bride to indicate he shares this lament. After that, she waits while the father of the bride watches her husband join the grouping with the childless couple. She waits while the mother of the bride and her husband trade kisses to the cheek, kisses that from this distance seem to linger. "I suggest we should see each other more in the upcoming months," says this woman to the father of the bride. "We are both available now. We could set up a scheduled lunch, like weekly."

The father is pinned in. Feeling the need to be rescued, he looks around for a savior. Will no one break in and dislodge this person? No. All the guests are grouped up. The groupings are tight, insular, none of them summoning the bride's father to break away and break in upon them. His big brother, so often an unwelcome interloper, accepts a request for help in his little brother's eyes and turns away. This woman, the wife of his wife's male friend, presses the father of the bride, thigh along thigh. "Wouldn't it be nice to check in weekly?"

A good familiar song comes on. It's from the early 1980s, and the father once knew its name. The dance floor is crowded again. Plenty of dancers are dancing in groups or singly. "I can't hear you," the father tells the woman. He mouths the words as if to a non-English speaker. "The music is too loud. Don't you agree?"

He stands abruptly, skirts the woman and lurches forward as if intending to address volume issues with the deejay. Three quick steps later he veers as if under an impromptu influence onto the square of floor crowded with dancers. Dance partners, as far as the bride's father can see, are random and interchangeable. Everyone seems to be taking turns dancing with everyone else. Making a leap of faith, the father becomes one of those dancers. He has a few moves. He is not without rhythmic resources. By now, after that speech, he shouldn't be a stranger to anyone on the floor. He's known some of these people since his daughter was a girl. A few of the older, dumpier specimens were friends before Wren was born. Many of the bobbing shoulders and twisting hips rubbing his own belong to people he has met only one time, for the first time, tonight.

The deejay calls for hands to be thrown in the air like you just don't care. The father of the bride flings his arms skyward and looks up. Long dead raptors, gone for thousands of years, hang from the distant ceiling, leering down upon them all. The father brings his limbs and his attention back to ground level. His daughter sways and dips within arm's reach. She holds her phone camera sideways as she dances and records happiness on the faces of all who look upon her. She holds her camera on her father for an extended, sweet moment, and moves along. Her husband is a little further away, behind her father, standing outside the periphery of dancers, tapping his foot to the music. The groom holds a phone to his ear and speaks rapidly and at length into the device. He looks out upon the revelry. His eyes have that diffused intensity of being focused somewhere else. The celebration is at its peak, thinks the father of the bride. The groom knows he must soon move on to the next thing. The groom has already left the wedding. The father remains here, in a moment that has passed already, on his own. He dances in the midst of everyone else. He knows he is behind the beat. The song is crashing to an end. He catches up with the fear that he will be forever out of step.

THE USEFUL COWARD

The theme of today's cross-generational advisory is Do Not Meet Trouble Halfway. Attendance for Mark is mandatory. He sits in the backseat of his mother's Tesla, silent and fully charged, just like the sleek and futuristic automobile's electric motor. A recent laceration has been inflicted beneath Mark's left eye. He is the type of thin teenager who is coiled and tight even when relaxed. He's not relaxed. He feels the welt on his cheekbone becoming more swollen as the car hums along.

"I hope you're listening to this," says Mark's mother. Everything about her that she has any control over is perfect: Undetectable cosmetics and chestnut streaked hair, proud posture, conscious composure. She's piloting the vehicle. The "this" she refers to is the halting spiel of her latest boyfriend. *Latest boyfriend* isn't a totally fair characterization. Jacks is the first serious male companion Mark's mom has entertained since her husband, Mark's father, left. That honorable and tolerant man died almost three years ago. In the meantime, Mom cannot be accused of dating in any manic or deliberate way. For one thing, the widow is busy. She's always been busy beyond the hours in any day. Overbooked is her comfort zone. As a younger boy, Mark had set up a system of Google news alerts to keep him apprised of his mother's activities in her world of corporate social responsibility.

Jacks is flipping his hair in the Tesla's front passenger seat. Jacks is in the car because Mom, whose name is Muriel, believes that Mark might take "the talk" more seriously if the talk is delivered by a man. Jacks isn't entirely on board with his role in this plan. Mark, who is sensitive to the awkward realities navigated by others, can understand the older man's reticence. Jacks has two children pushing thirty who rarely find any reason to speak to him and, from a much younger second wife, two kids in preschool who a custody agreement prohibits Jacks from talking to. He and Muriel had met backstage at a concert benefiting climate change refugees. Jacks had been way down on the bill as a solo act and was charmed that Muriel recognized him and had name checked the two songs Jacks's band had rested its slight renown upon. Muriel is the kind of woman who is emerging from middle age and inspires beautiful girls in their twenties to tell one another they hope to look like Muriel if they ever get old. Jacks has great hair and takes obvious pleasure in sifting it through alternating hands, a surface self-satisfaction that is not lost on Mark, who is more systematic in his judgments than the average adolescent. Exhibiting a sensual pride in your hair, in Mark's estimation, is a girlish trait and in a man may indicate a deep and undermining narcissism. Then again, Mark's disapproval of the affection between Jacks's hands and his hair may stem from a son's allegiance to his dead father, a kind, attentive, slow-paced man who never had great hair and had lost most of it prior to his mourned departure.

Mark decides to say something to show he has been listening. "I'm afraid I missed that last part, Jacks. Or maybe it was the first part. I'm a little distracted back here, what with the recent trauma of arrest and incarceration."

"I only said one part, Mark." Jacks squeezes his temples in the span of a single hand. "I said, 'Don't meet trouble halfway.' "

"I'm sorry. My attention wandered," says Mark. "Are you saying that trouble will overpower my ability to cope with consequences at an abruptly attained midpoint? And am I now in your estimation approaching the halfway mark on a downward spiral of no return?"

"You're halfway to being enrolled in public school," says Muriel. Her deep-set hazel eyes are bright points of challenge and intelligence. Usually, she keeps scorn out of them. She makes an exception now. "When you take a moment outside the downward spiral, maybe thank me for negotiating your expulsion down to a two-day suspension, with home study privileges."

"Jacks went to public school," points out Mark. The son's eyes are darker than his mother's, also deep set, every bit as bright and challenging, and much more apt to glint with mockery.

In the front seat, Jacks is aware that the back of his head is fully exposed to Mark's dissecting gaze. That business with his fingers stroking through his hair is a motion triggered by anxiety, which is afflicting Jacks twofold. Fold One: After more than half a century on the planet, he hadn't anticipated the queasy surge that had flushed his bowels upon stepping into a police station. He was certain of no active warrants for his detention. His business with law-enforcement was solely to accompany his lady friend while she accepted custody of her minor son, Mark. Fold Two: The upcoming man-to-man talk with a precocious, emotionally guarded, rightfully angry and obdurate 16-year-old had been totally unforeseen when Jacks first encountered Muriel's recognition of him as a minor cultural reference point and potential dinner partner. Her figure (grief starved, but Jacks could not have known that) and the depth of feeling in her eyes and smile had ignited a set of emotions he had been keeping below simmer lately. Her age, roughly in range of his, offered an assurance that she would be considered, considerate and stable. In the ensuing four months, Muriel has followed through on all these promises and revealed untold enticements to spare. Still, she needs to be out of the car before Jacks fully turns and goes eye-to-eye with Mark. How to remove the encircling, managing mother from the conversational loop? It is a puzzler, and puzzlement is of course the next step toward consternation, which is where Mom's boyfriend's presence of mind currently flutters.

Mark speaks up from the backseat, his tone indicating a desire only to clarify the situation: "What's telling here is that no one has even asked me what happened."

"The sergeant showed us the tape, the phone footage," says his mother. "We saw what happened. You attacked a teacher."

The video showed no physical threat, thinks Jacks, just a teacher sitting behind a desk, maybe smug and complacent, as a boy rails at him with vitriolic zeal.

"For all we know," continues Muriel, "that video is already viral, with your name, my name, and links to all our social media profiles. Go ahead. Check your phone. Tell me I'm wrong."

Berating the implacable teacher, Mark had wielded a colorful, precise, vicious vocabulary, Jacks noted, and a remarkable lack of profanity. Jacks has enough sense not to quibble aloud with Muriel about piddling details. So does Mark, although the boy is compelled to lodge some form of protest. "There's a bullying situation at school," he begins.

"In fifteen minutes," responds Muriel, "I have a meeting with a project director from the U.N. whose name I still need to learn to pronounce." Mom pauses the Tesla next to a gray vintage Citroen, an impractical relic of Jacks's improbable heyday. The French sedan is parked in the lot of the café where Jacks and Muriel had rendezvoused before heading to pluck Mark from the clutches of the police state.

The Tesla purrs into the flow of traffic and out of sight. Jacks and Mark stand in an area between the Citroen and the door to the Canyon Diner and delay looking at one another. Mark shifts his backpack. "On the positive note," he says, "you and my mom can rest easy that no drugs were to be found among my belongings."

Truth to tell, Jacks wouldn't mind locating a drug or two in that satchel. He's left his travel stash at home, a prudence inspired by knowing he would have physical contact with cops. He says, "You must be famished after the hunger strike I know you organized inside."

Father and son, but not to one another, they enter the diner ahead of the dinner rush, smile to servers who know them, and take an open table that they both prefer. It's near the front, but not so close that the outside atmosphere hits them every time some tourist opens the door. No need for menus, a waitress takes their order and leaves her curiosity about what happened to Mark's face unexpressed. The table affords views of the main dining area, the server station, the cooks, and the counter. Beyond that, Jacks is also in excellent position to monitor anyone coming in or going out the front door. He says, "The positive note here is that you knew not to give the cops the name of who cut you."

"How do we know that?"

"The desk sergeant was begging your mother to pressure you to rat."

"To rat. Nice use of the vernacular, Jacks. It illustrates your extensive travel in the underworld." Jacks gives Mark a look of disappointment that holds truly sad and dashed feelings. The kid immediately feels sorry. "I mean, I told them I didn't see who did it. Maybe take my word on that. And don't ask if I would *rat* if I knew who to rat on. I don't know if I would rat or not."

"That is some advance-placement denial, Mark. No wonder you're already at college-level logic."

"I don't follow you."

"You've wrapped your denial in an extra layer of false speculation. When you wonder if you would rat or not, it's a double lie. You do know who cut you. You didn't rat. That's important to know."

"I have a different conclusion: You haven't known my mother very long; still, you are fully aware the no-ratting conversation is not the talk she was hoping you'd give me. I appreciate that."

The food arrives. Despite previous practice, the waitress reverses Mark's and Jacks's orders. The diners, cooperating all man-to-man, smoothly right the plates.

"I could say some slick shit about the slippery slope," says Jacks, "but I won't say shit. You don't want to hear the shit I have to say."

"Thanks for that string of appetizing phrases."

The Canyon Diner sits halfway between Jacks's Beachwood tree house and Muriel's Lake Hollywood midcentury multilevel. Beyond the convenience, the food's passable. Jacks and Mark are always happy to land here. Muriel feels a little too fancy at the diner. The meal is eaten mostly in silence.

"You know you're locatable on the Internet, Jacks. Fine. Don't react. When my mother told me the band you were in, the band you fronted, I found that photo of you at the Saint Patrick's Day Massacre. You've seen the picture?"

"I think I know the one." Elk's Lodge, MacArthur Park, downtown Los Angeles, March 17, 1979. "I was a kid."

"My age now? A little older? The riot cops charging across the MacArthur Park lawn. All those naïve little punk rockers cowering like possums in headlights."

"You and the Internet can set a vivid scene."

"Young Jackson Porter, lead singer of the Worst, standing tall and stick thin on an upturned trashcan, giving two middle fingers as tear gas swirls and nightsticks rise."

"You're telling me storm trooper cops overran the Harvard Westlake campus, and you caught a badge across the face? That's what happened to you?"

"All I'm saying is that you were once a person who met trouble halfway. Standing on that trash can, you might have caught a rubber bullet in the face. A tear gas canister might have ripped off half your skull. You were out there meeting those projectiles halfway."

"Look, Mark, I only jumped up on that trash can because I wanted to look cool. I was afraid the girls would see me as a coward."

"Yet you advise me to opt for looking like a coward? Not cool."

"If you don't want to look like a coward, keep an eye out for incoming trouble. Avoid it before it hits. Split. Remove yourself before other people see you backing away. If you wait until trouble arrives, that's when opting out may look like cowardice."

"This atom splitting is maybe too high level for a youngster like me to grasp."

The waitress drifts within range. Jacks orders a round of coffees for the table. He could use a double bowl and a whisky. Jacks leans forward, props his chin on his gripped fingers. "Let me ask you something, Mark. You're the kid who was dragged out of class by cops and taken to a holding cell. But you're wearing the battered face of an innocent victim. How does that happen?"

"What happened is, I wasn't worried about not looking like a coward? I was worried about not being a coward?"

"There's always a middle way. You could have made some brave move short of grandstanding in front of two dozen cell phone cameras."

"Someone needed to step up. What was I supposed to do?" The kid seems to really want to know. "Should I have called a cop?"

"Not that," responds Jacks. "Police make all things worse."

Mom's boyfriend is not a man to lodge a brutality complaint with law enforcement brass. Mark slides into confiding mode. "I didn't rat on who hit me because it was a cop who hit me. I mean, obviously. Who else would it be?"

Jacks chews and thinks. Both those activities play out on his face. He says, "You must have been talking to the cop who hit you."

"Me talking to a cop explains how I got my busted eye, to your satisfaction?"

"Removes all doubt, thank you. What about dessert?"

"Don't you need to run out to your car and get lit?"

"I do, but I'm not in a terrible rush for it."

Dessert is decided against. Jacks ferries Mark in the Citroen up the steep, twisted approach to Muriel's trophy home with its jewel-like facets opening on 300 degrees of elevated Los Angeles views. Coming into the driveway, a typical house cat jolts across the car's trajectory. Jacks brakes the Citroen. The feline scoots into the underbrush.

"The coyotes will eat that cat at sunset," says Jacks. "Unless you step up and save it."

"I will," says Mark, stepping out of the car, "if you'll stand by and document the rescue on my iPhone."

The Citroen coasts down the bluff and crosses Beachwood into a realm of more humble, hidden homes. By the time Jacks turns off the car and unlocks his front door, telephone footage of Mark and his biology teacher and one other student has been loaded to the Internet and reached maximum viral velocity.

Part Two

Jacks has been ejected from his comfort zone. He sits squinting behind the wheel of Muriel's Tesla, driving in thick, erratic sundowner's traffic toward the city center. He should have pushed harder with Muriel that they travel tonight in separate cars. Chances are he will be ready to leave, will need to flee the premises, while she is still basking in collegiality. The dinner party they are heading to, hosted in what Muriel characterizes as "a ridiculously art-damaged loft by just stupidly progressive and absurdly educated people," will be a sort of unveiling of Jacks to a gathering of Muriel's closest friends.

The past forty years have prepared Jacks to grin like a champ through dinner parties. Jacks works as the institutional memory at a pesky weekly paper that was swept up in the consolidation plans of a media conglomerate. The job keeps him in limited intimacy with a crew of cosmetically bright content creators. Not one of them is too old to be Jacks's kid. Jacks fits in well enough. The best way to get along with people outside his social demographic, Jacks has determined, is to keep his opinions, alliances and telling observations under the vest. Any closely held belief that makes the heart stir should be contained secret and secure within that organ.

Muriel hasn't tired of saying that she loves when she and Jacks sit quiet together. Neither feels the necessity to make conversation. Pleasant as that may be, Jacks feels he should say something here in the car. "I wish we would have paced ourselves to show up a half hour sooner," he says. Jacks had argued for an early arrival. Muriel had professed to know better, a mannerism her quiet new man is coming to expect. He doesn't know how much he likes it.

"If you're in the loft as other guests arrive," Muriel explains again, while Jacks drives her car, "your attention will be toggled back and forth, in I don't know how many directions. Every time a new guest arrives, you'll be jumping from background to foreground, stepping out from behind the host's function as primary greeter to be introduced to the new arrival. You'll do a little gush on the new arrival, then you'll step back behind the cover of the host's function.

"It's better if we show up when everyone else is settled in. You can adopt a one-size-fits-all graciousness and greet the assembled guests one after another. It'll function like a receiving line. I expect everyone will be presented in order of ascending importance." This hashing out consumes three passing freeway exits.

"I want you to understand my reasoning on this decision," Muriel says. "I'm not imposing an arbitrary preference. Plus, if we're there more than half an hour before the food hits the table, the amount of alcohol forced on us could make for a rocky, rocky evening. It's easier for you and me to get along if you know what I'm thinking, don't you think?"

Jacks agrees. Transparency does help. He opts to not disclose the THC-medicated edible he had popped into his mouth before knocking on Muriel's door, about an hour and fifteen minutes ago.

Muriel watches her official boyfriend's profile with critical disquiet. Jacks steers her Tesla across four lanes of the 101 Freeway to the sudden and tricky Broadway off ramp and swings sharply left into a hidden freight alley. Muriel admits out loud that forcing Jacks to confront this group of eight core acquaintances (three couples and two wild cards) as a mass is too many tricky introductions at once. "But my schedule is so crammed," she explains. "To present my people in manageable clumps might take a year, maybe two. Who knows if you and I will be a thing that long?"

She laughs with sophisticated gusto and genteel lust and places a hand high on Jacks's thigh. A squeeze communicates that of course she is joking. It's been a congested crawl from the Hollywood Hills to Downtown. The Tesla turns in at an opening in chain-link and razor-wire fencing that encloses a grouping of cars belonging to, Jacks presumes, the other dinner guests. The valet is weather beaten and ill suited, like a homeless man in a vest. Could the valet be an imposter? Jacks pushes against the urge to grab back the Tesla's key fob.

Muriel latches onto her boyfriend's arm. "All set?"

Jacks sucks in the Downtown air. He locates the smell of homeless encampments that line the alleys in the darkness beyond the fenced-in automobiles. Jacks wonders if the guy who took custody of the Tesla was brought in from the encampment outside the video-monitored gate.

"It looks like we are the last to arrive," says Jacks.

"It's all part of a plan," says Muriel, with a comforting touch. She notices Jacks turn to her in the evening light and note again the prize package containing his new companion. Jacks follows Muriel climbing single file up ten steps of repurposed fire escape. His THC-medication had been coming on during the drive, and is in full effect.

The metal laddering accesses an iron door that is open on steel tracks. "Remind me not to be too bombed on the way down from here," Jacks says. Muriel knows that Jacks drinks very little. She has even surmised, out loud one evening when Jacks had become perfectly content to drift off to sleep, that Jacks might not drink at all except under the pressure of social exigencies. *She really is a thoughtful and considerate companion*, Jacks recognizes. He also knows that she has no idea how often he is lit. Not to exaggerate, he is usually a little short of full baked, at times barely short of full, when visiting Muriel's house. Her boy Mark's knowing looks and keen comments have indicated a precise sense of Jacks's THC intake. Mark has kept these observations private from his mother, which goes a long way toward explaining Jacks's ease around the son.

"You're going to do fine," says Muriel. "Don't feel like there's any need to perform. They're just some people I know."

Jacks's contemplation of his ease around Mark, a kid with huge asshole potential, predisposes him to relax and be nimble and open to a universe outside his own. In this other world, the one he's moving into right this moment, it is reasonable to anticipate positive interactions with newly encountered human beings. He follows Muriel closely through an entryway. In the mid-vast distance, a sunken living room seems to spill out through ceiling-to-floor glass into the middle of the Downtown skyline. Glittering towers cross the horizon like massive saw teeth, all glossy and purple in the aftermath of what must have been an apocalyptic sunset.

The names and the handshakes and excellent displays of restorative dentistry come at Jacks in a casual, convivial and truly interested sequence of warmth and curiosity. The new man feels disarmed, off guard and secure, smiling, eager to know more about these people, as people. He warms to the promise of impending human-to-human connections, which almost smoothes over the cringing awareness that he has failed to catch and hold a single one of their names.

Some of the guests make it obvious. Clearly there has been an opportunity to be briefed beforehand on Jacks's background. Conversely, Muriel had withheld the identities and positions of her friends. "I don't want you putting their names into Google," she had explained, a week back when the idea of this party had been broached, "and judging before you even meet them."

"You don't want me going in as the righteous underdog," said Jacks. He assumed they all own or run endeavors that make vital contributions to the community and the culture. Muriel does not maintain purposeless acquaintances in her personal database.

Now that he is among these mindful-achievers and passion-led investors, maybe it is the weed, maybe it is the friendliness, maybe it is the universal democratic process of time rolling forward, but fundamentally Jacks feels on equal footing with everyone he's just met, no matter how irreproachably driven they might be as individuals in the political, business, entertainment, academic worlds. Age is a common among them. There is no need to speak of what the years have brought and taken away from each one. The very fact of being out of bed and at a social occasion is an acknowledgement of snatching and savoring small victories from the certain defeat in the common, larger battle.

"I remember the Worst," says one guest. She has gray hair that is big and wild but not untamed. Her pantsuit gives a loose sense of being form-fitting, incorporates all the colors of the rainforest, and no doubt owes a debt to some peoples indigenous and distant, perhaps in Central America, maybe on the African continent. "That band was known for being real to the scene and a curse to all poseurs."

"The ultimate pejorative," agrees Jacks. "*Poseur*. Everything we did we did so we wouldn't be called poseurs. It was our entire guiding principle. We were very worried about that. We were all such poseurs."

"Right." The defiantly gray guest grips Jacks, perhaps only to hold him in place as she moves on toward a different guest. "Great catching up."

Two women stand openly appraising Jacks beside Muriel. Jacks marvels at how natural his lady friend looks as she accepts a cocktail off a tray from a young Latin American woman (early thirties) in a sleek black tube dress.

"Jacks is considering bringing his band back together to open for X during X's residency at the Roxy," confides Muriel to the pair of appraising women at her side, and to everyone else with ears between her and the windows and the darkening skyline. The sleek Latin American woman in the black tube dress pops up unobtrusive and solid at Jacks's side, offering a frosted martini glass brimming with clear spirits. Her presentation is so skilled that Jacks's acceptance seems long practiced. *Maybe I am*, he thinks, *after all meant to be a part of the liberal white ruling class*. A sip of the alcohol emboldens him.

"The X thing, it's a long way from being certain," he says, launching the preamble to an extensive demur.

Muriel interrupts. "Of course Jacks is weighing all the pluses and minuses of performing in a support role."

Objectively, Jacks can't reason how any of these people would be impressed by his prospect of playing an opening set for a senior citizens nostalgia act, but a general coo goes through the gathering, which seems to cue everyone to take their seats at the long, gleaming, single plank dining table.

"Punk's spirit is so democratic though," says a woman taking the chair at Jacks's left. Her hair, in the decorous loft light, is streaked with a tinge of blue. "The distinction between headliner and supporting act is mostly superfluous in the punk context," she states.

"You're right," agrees Jacks. "I'll ask if they'd like to change positions in the lineup on alternating nights."

"Oh, no," says the woman. "I don't suspect they would agree to that, after all—"

"Jacks is joking," explains the fey man on Jacks's right. His hair and mustache are waxed and dyed. Over a shocking white T-shirt, he wears a vest color-coordinated with the indigenous rain forest motif of the woman with the defiant gray hair. He reaches across Jacks and taps a wrist of the woman with the blue streak. "Your leg has just been pulled, Juliet. Lucky for you, it is such a shapely leg." In a lower voice, the man continues ostensibly for Jacks's benefit, "So now you know her name is Juliet. I was tagged at birth, unfortunately, Reginald. Everyone calls me Reg. That gives you two names, in case you lost track as you came in under the fusillade of full scrutiny."

Jacks thanks Reg for the help, and enquires, "Is it out of place to ask you for a rundown of the table?"

"Nothing could be more out of place," juts in Juliet.

"Total breach of protocol," agrees Reg.

"I'll start," insists Juliet. "Reg here is in charge of picking what paintings you see when you step inside that big museum downtown that really needs to have his family name stamped on the front."

"You're a curator?" asks Jacks, immediately self critical at dropping a lapsed buzzword.

"I'm a director, officially," says Reg, lowering his eyes to soften the blow. "Of community outreach for underrepresented and underserved populations." Jacks notices that a bowl of soup has been set down before him, and a bowl before everyone else. He wonders, *What else am I missing until after it happens?* Juliet is a self-confessed "cliché." While amassing resources and allies to complete production of her first feature film, she's keeping her skin in the game as a casting director "on projects that really, really speak to who I am." Reg puts in, that if casting directors were to be acknowledged by the Academy, as rightfully they should be, Jacks "would have seen Juliet claiming her stout little statue at least three times in the past seven years, providing you were a religious viewer of the Academy Awards broadcast. Imagine how impressed you would be to be sitting next to dear Juliet." Jacks confesses that he is already very impressed to be seated next to Juliet, although he never watches the Oscars. Reg concedes there is no harm no foul in him not doing that.

The other four guests include Georgeanne, an obvious yoga enthusiast sheathed in exquisitely appropriate Isabel Marant. She's a professor of constitutional law with a celebrated history of human rights advocacy. At her side, her long-time date Jeremy, a double Ph. D. in biochemistry and math, whispers into her ear. Jeremy is a pharmaceutical corporate responsibility officer. "He would have been shortlisted for a Nobel twice, if they gave one for CROs," says Reg.

Bo, apologetically finishing up urgent business on his phone across from Reg, is a compliance officer in the financial sector. Bo is on track to become one of the state's most effective grassroots political power brokers. Bo's wife, Cheyenne, an ex-model Internet fashion magnate, is modestly stunning to Reg's right. Their hosts, Richard and Glenda, split the head and tail of the table. Glenda, of the defiant gray mane and rainforest indigenous pantsuit, is a philanthropist in a major way. ("We won't even tell you her maiden name. It's just straight out a blunt instrument.") Richard isn't quite a partner in the biggest conglomerated talent agency in this company town, but his influence there purchased, renovated and maintains this loft without dipping into Glenda's money. The soup is finished. Salads slide into place, delivered by a fresh duo of Latin American women in sleek black tube dresses.

Muriel, really the most attractive woman in the entire room to Jacks's eyes, is seated across the table and two places away from him. She's not close enough to squeeze his hand. She has watched her two friends break down the names and thumbnail biographies of the bodies around the table. In the dim light, Jacks can't see if Muriel's face is supporting him, keeping a neutral expression in deference to the other guests, or maintaining a blank façade to shield Jacks from her disappointment. Or maybe she is simply enjoying the kale and *jicama*. Once the salad is gone, the separate conversations as determined by seating chart expand to become general and table wide.

Glenda, the philanthropist, proclaims it marvelous that Muriel's son, Mark, has assumed a place of prominence in championing the rights of students whose abilities are variants on the norm.

"I can't tell you what a fucking relief that full video was," bursts out Muriel. "At the police station, all Jacks and I saw was the last couple of minutes, before the police burst into the classroom. Stripped of context, Mark had all the appearance of being the bully."

Juliet, as casting director, offers a professional assessment. "The video, as I first saw it, really was an excellent call to action. You're sitting there, watching that poor kid who obviously is doing her best to overcome a crippling stutter, with the teacher hovering over her, rocking back and forth like an angry metronome. That mockery was just so unfathomably cruel. About a minute in, and you—along with an audience of now millions—are just crying out for somebody to step up and do something."

"That somebody shows up, and it's your son," puts in Richard, squinting in a way that communicates his eye for talent. "I've watched the clip a dozen times. That surge when Mark steps up is stronger with every pass."

"It was punk rock," opines artful Reg. "Don't you agree, Jacks? Shouting down the teacher like that was a punk rock thing to do."

"Sometimes you need to step into the line of fire," says Richard.

"Totally punk rock," agrees Jacks, with no undue emotion.

"I'll tell you, Muriel," says Richard, musing out loud, "if Mark had a good agent, and I can think of three off the top of my head who would be very good, we could readily establish him as a spokesperson. He speaks well. We've all heard him. I'm not saying he's a ham. He does know how to work an audience."

"That's a fact," agrees Jacks, with an uptick in enthusiasm. A serving of affection for Mark catches him unaware.

Muriel taps knife to wineglass, assuming the position of table moderator. "I'm reining back on my son's public appearances," she says. "I am allowing his social-media interactions, and the personal site he's set up for blogs and video statements. I'm sure you know we politely declined *The View*. The teacher went public, on two of the news networks, to plead his case after being fired. We all saw how badly the backlash has gone for him. Mark doesn't need to be on TV or become the face of something."

Muriel cedes the floor to Cheyenne, the online magnate. "No one's suggesting Mark should attempt to profit," Cheyenne suggests. "It's not like he had anything to do with initially posting the video."

"Of course not," agrees Muriel, quickly. "But six very good colleges have already contacted him offering early acceptance, based on this video's reach and reception. That may be as much water as we need to draw from this particular well. Jacks is driving up to the Bay Area next week with Mark, to scout campuses. I'll be in Davos, unfortunately."

Glenda, fully vested in extending positive influence, appears to have been struck by a blunt-force thought. "Muriel, you must be so happy that Mark is adopting the invested activist role. This ownership is at the core, as I recall it, of the punk ethos. It's a beautiful synchronicity to have Jacks as a mentor to that spirit."

"I'll just be driving the car," says Jacks with unfeigned humility. "We'll each have our ear buds in."

Cheyenne, the model of Internet magnetism, jumps the topic to a favorite theme. "Activism really is today's prime marketing differentiator. Brands that don't offer a double bottom line, that don't contribute a measurable metric to the pressing issues uppermost in consumer concerns, are destined to forfeit relevance and fade."

"The entire system of mindful capitalism is revitalizing right now," says Bo, the financier political fixer, "from the top and at the bottom."

The lofty Downtown conversation redirects to dissatisfaction with the current presidential administration, potential candidates for the next round of elections and strategies for amplifying voter interest at the working-class level. Usually, Jacks is quiet when the talk turns to politics, not from some desire to avoid confrontation and keep the peace. He is happy for people to suspect that he knows better and is above their level of discussion and cannot deign to lower himself to their stream of simple-minded, uninformed chatter. This party, he sees, is made up of entirely informed insiders. None of them mistakenly suspect that Jacks is keeping silent in deference to knowing better than they do. The table talk circles again and again to answering the call when the call comes to step up and do something.

Jacks sits quiet. The table discussion unspools without his full attention. Barely following the thread, Jacks tracks his perspective as running contrary and unwelcome to the party's accepted direction. Bo and Glenda are mystified that the base electorate refuses to rush to the polls. Cheyenne and scientifically grounded Jeremy attribute the deficit in electoral fervor to educational lapses and bottom-fed media diets. Jacks debates within. Should he share his dissenting point of view? He opts to keep it to himself. The certainty of that decision displays on his face as conclusive finality, which Richard, being a professional watcher of faces, catches and misinterprets.

"Jacks, you haven't said a word. But I just saw you come to a solid conclusion."

"My boyfriend is a man of disciplined quiet," says Muriel, who has heard him talk.

"I appreciate the controlled, silent type, believe me, with the logorrhea I go through every day," says Richard. "But everybody, layman to lobbyist, has an idea for how to activate the non-voting masses."

Jacks feeling forced to speak isn't the problem. The risk is that once he commits to voicing words, he somehow is compelled to say what he actually thinks. This flaw, he recognizes as he opens his mouth, has been the cause of downfall after downfall throughout his life. Luckily, he has never climbed so high as to be more than winded in the drop, so here goes, "I don't like to admit out loud that I've despaired of democracy in America. People tend to take it personally, like I'm rejecting some sensitive religious belief."

"Actually, no offense taken," says law professor Georgeanne. "How can you be held accountable for having ascended to some rarefied height of surrender and irony? That's punk too, as I remember it."

"I feel more like I've been dropped than I've placed myself above the political process," quibbles Jacks. "When half the electorate doesn't vote, it's actively voting no. It's been left behind and sees no value in catching up. Maybe they've recognized the political system as a wing of a fully ineffectual industrial entertainment complex that is not interested in bringing substantive improvements to vast swaths of the electorate. Voting is like being a complicit participant in the process of defrauding yourself."

"You don't feel that your belief is somehow, I don't know, irresponsible?" This is the fashion maven talking. Jacks senses she is taking the lead so that Glenda, in the constrained role of hostess, isn't forced to find objection with a guest while that guest is under the protection of her zinc-tile ceiling.

"What I'm saying is an observation," argues Jacks. "I don't know how an observation equates to a renunciation of responsibility.

I mean, come on, you people are in a privileged position to see what the actual democracy sausage is made of and how it works out for the general populace."

"I'm not saying what you say has no relevance," cautions Richard. "That kind of talking in slogans is a jaded way of saying it. Dangerously jaded."

"Well, I've said it this way since I was eighteen, nineteen." Jacks speaks with a side of pondering, as though he is reflecting. Muriel knows his reflection pantomime is a charade. She assumes everyone else at the table recognizes the stratagem as pompous and pretentious. "So I've been jaded a long time," Jacks says. "Since I was just a naïve sprout."

"How eighties," says Juliet.

"Early eighties," sighs Reg.

Jacks is missing the eighties reference. His is not the place to ask for clarification. A quick scan of faces around the table reveals that disapproval of Jacks seems unanimous. Rejection's open display lasts only a moment. On the surface, no one's expression admits that an argument has transpired, but the friends all agree they will never arrange to share Jacks's company again. Dessert is served. After dinner drinks are declined. Jacks has a feeling that the party is breaking up faster and earlier than might otherwise be expected. As hasty departures are made and clipped goodbyes exchanged, some of the group opts to smile at Jacks. Others opt to meet his eyes. No one is doing both, certainly not Muriel.

Muriel accepts the key to the Tesla and hands the valet a shockingly received twenty. She neither smiles nor looks in the direction of Jacks. He waits for her to unlock the passenger door. Once in the car, moving along the access road toward the freeway entrance, neither of them find anything to say about the encampments of tent people pitched along the sidewalks lining the route. This is a high-density population area. Driving through it generally elicits a remark. Jacks stops himself from making what in normal conditions would be a subconscious cough, used to announce an oncoming statement. He is acutely aware in the passenger seat of Muriel's Tesla that she regrets having allowed him to drive her car. She wouldn't mind having a little more personal space in the interior of the vehicle, such as if for instance Jacks had never entered and seated himself.

"I told you we should have brought two cars," says Jacks.

"I wish you'd stop doing that with your hair," she replies.

"I didn't realize I was doing anything with my hair."

Muriel joins the jammed flow of molten red taillights heading north on the 101. It's like the world is an endless stream of flashing crimson cop lights, at least to Jacks it's like that. With so many police in this life, it's impossible to avoid and deflect them all. Jacks remembers exactly where he ran afoul of Muriel's friends. What could he have said differently? He wonders how far the evening's fallout will go and how Muriel will explain it to her son, but only for a second. He visits another nagging question and breaks the silence in the car.

"You know," says Jacks, "I'm not convinced that Mark isn't the person who posted that complete video onto the Internet. The version that starts with the teacher mocking the student."

Muriel's eyes are not at all concerned with being empty of scorn. "So what if he did? The video only shows what really happened."

"I'm not saying the events were completely staged. The teacher certainly didn't rehearse or pre-approve the part he played. But it's not crazy to wonder if there was a coordinated setup arranged by the girl with the stutter, whatever kid was filming, who knew to be filming, and the hero stepping in at the prime dramatic cue point."

"You can't believe that," says Muriel.

"Believe what?"

"That Mark is capable of ..."

"Oh he's capable of mastering the logistics and of hatching the plan. We both know that. What we're questioning, if you want to ask the questions, is his will to attack and take down and leave some working person to suffer the consequences of job loss and public shaming."

"You're telling me this is what my son did?"

"You know him better than I do. Like you say, so what if he did?"

This new silence that Muriel brings into the car won't tolerate any words being spoken out loud. Jacks wonders if this suspended communication means he is relieved of taking Mark up to the Bay Area to look at schools.

"Fuck," says Muriel, jolting the car to a stop. Jacks's head snaps back. He looks up and out. The Tesla is three-quarters up the twisting ascent to Muriel's home, the house she and the dead husband had hoped to age together gracefully in. It is not unusual to see coyote or deer or raccoon on the road. The car has cornered tight around a curve and narrowly stopped from climbing the back of a lone male pedestrian, also not unusual, striding purposefully up the roadway. The man, as Muriel lurches past, is seen to be wearing tattered clothes that give off an essence of something other than cleanliness. The man seems familiar to Jacks, maybe because of the encampments they had passed on the way to the freeway. Homeless people this high up in the prosperity hills, that is unusual.

Driving the final twists of road to her place, Muriel maintains mute poise. She pulls into the driveway and makes no move to hit the remote that will open the door to the garage that grants access to the house. Jacks's French car is alone at the curb, vintage and three-quarters restored, not a complete aberration to the neighborhood, but out of place. "This is where I get out, then?" says Jacks.

Muriel still won't look at him. Her gaze is interested in, not distracted by, a line of sight that she tracks in the Tesla's rearview mirror. "If you don't mind," she says, "when you get to your car, can you not take off right away? We've had a lot of mail theft and auto break-ins up here lately. Can you wait to go until you're sure this guy walking up the hill passes by the house?"

The pedestrian has come into view. He's tall, slumped. His face is downcast. His pace is glacial.

"Are you actually worried about this guy?" asks Jacks.

"Not all the way. It's just, since my husband's been gone, not having a man around the house, it's made me cautious."

The man and woman lean toward each other, make slight sounds with their lips, and agree to miss landing the actual kiss. Jacks steps from the car into the night. A queasy block of angst drops into his stomach. The sliding garage door rumbles upward, admits Muriel and the Tesla, and swallows them. Jacks walks to his Citroen and openly watches the shambling male pedestrian advance. The general familiarity of any disenfranchised wanderer approaches specific identification. Jacks recognizes the drawn features as one of the city's most consistently working film composers. That acclaimed face is demanding to know what the fuck business Jacks and his ratty old French car have in this neighborhood.

Part Three

Later, in the light of a new morning, the Citroen looks less out of place in the visitor parking area for the Disney rehearsal halls. The Disney music complex is clean and corporate. Access to it has been granted to the band X as a favor. Jacks knows about the favor because the guy who granted it also owed Jacks a favor. This guy did the favor of telling Jacks that X had yet to decide on an opening act for its reunion at the Roxy. The guy offered to make an intro.

"I mean, I imagine you knew John and Exene back in the day," the guy clarified. "I can bring you and the Worst into the conversation, then you come in and talk for yourself, or send a rep."

"I'll go in and talk for myself," Jacks had opted. "Just let them know I'm willing to come in, and let me know when's a good day."

Jacks had ignored the instinct to keep this upcoming meeting to himself. He'd told Muriel about possibly being offered the opening slot. This gig supporting one of the city's most beloved punk originators might raise his band to the legacy it deserved. The Worst rank, in Jacks's estimation, not among the top tier of L.A. bands, but at a meaningful level, where real, lasting contributions were made. This telling Muriel had happened back before the disastrous dinner, on a day when he believed there might be value in revealing to her the workings within his mind, seeking her views on the things he thought should be thoroughly considered. Muriel had played along. "It can't hurt to check with your guys," she'd said. "Call and see if they'd be interested. No harm in gauging desire."

On Muriel's recommendation, Jacks had called two guys from the Worst, the best two guys, the guitarist and the drummer. The bass on these songs was so basic that even Jacks could play it. At his age, the instrument might function as a good stage prop, giving him an object to wield axe-like while hiding his stomach. The guitarist and drummer, one now a teacher the other a retired cop, were accustomed to hearing from Jacks every two or three years, never with any interest in playing their songs. They both jammed together, with a pickup bass player, every three weeks or so in a garage studio the cop's kids had set up and abandoned. Jacks had listened to the guitarist and the drummer describing these sessions and had never floated the idea of joining in.

"This is not the normal Jacks call," Jacks had told each. "This time, tell me, how would you feel about getting together and playing maybe ten of the old songs?"

"Like in front of people?" asked the guitarist.

"Opening for X." There. It was out. "For a week of shows."

"We would have very limited time to rehearse," pointed out the drummer.

"All the songs are basically the same song," reasoned Jacks.

"No we had two songs," countered his Worst band mates. "Several variations on two song templates."

"All the same," conceded Jacks, conceding nothing, "three days practice, and we'll be better than we ever were. That's with taking long lunches. Two days, and we'd match our peak. One day would work for adequate proficiency."

The drummer and the guitar player are all in. They are down. Before ringing off, they each reminded Jacks that he should have known they would be agreeable to play. The only one holding back has always been him. And so, prodded by Muriel, with the expectations of friends backing him, and on the strength of a second-hand invitation, Jacks has driven the Citroen to the Disney rehearsal hall, marveling along the way that a band of X's stature, amid the chaos and stresses that go into reforming for a week at the Roxy, is open to showcasing an act from the early scene, an act like the Worst. Fueled by optimism and a sprightly sativa hybrid, having outlined a discussion of duet possibilities with John and Exene, he breezes to the rehearsal hall door and finds it locked. He presses a button, a click sounds, and he enters a quiet, stark white, deeply air-conditioned room. A composed young lady at a reception pod eats from a bag of chips and looks ready for lunch. It's as if she and Jacks are on a sci-fi set. Impenetrable security doors with crosshatched safety glass close off what Jacks imagines as sterile corridors spoking off from the central control hub. It is ten a.m. Which corridor will lead him to the X practice space?

"Jacks Porter here to see X," says Jacks, announcing himself.

"That's you, Jacks Porter?"

"Of course."

"To see X? I know nothing about it."

"They're rehearsing here, for a show coming up, a series of secret reunion shows."

"Oh, I know all about that." A door has opened behind Jacks. He senses humans moving up to his rear. "Just have a seat, Mr. Porter. I'll figure everything out."

The receptionist is not chewing gum. That's one nice thing Jacks is willing to say about her. He sits and notes the proficiency with which she clicks three groups of A&R people, technicians and musicians in through three separate doors into three diverging hallways. None of these people strikes Jacks as associates of X. He stands and walks to the desk.

"Can you tell me if X is here already?"

"I'm sorry, Mr. Porter. Studio policy prohibits disclosure of client names or presence."

"I'll just sit back down."

The receptionist picks up a phone and turns to face away from Jacks as she punches numbers and deals with it. She turns back toward him. She is ready with an expression brimming with gracious expectation. The receptionist bypasses Jacks's eager eye contact and settles her attention on a computer screen directly in her work sphere. Jacks stands, takes a few steps and peers to see what he can discern through the safety glass of the security door nearest him.

"Mr. Porter. I need to ask you to remain seated. I'm sorry. Security is a priority at Disney."

Jacks sits, sullen inside, convinced he is still fresh to look at. He remembers a time when he would have brought a book to a place like this. There are, he notes, no magazines and no other reading material or décor in the holding room. Anther batch of entertainment agents, clerks and musician aides enters. A few of these are Jacks's age, old, and are recognized as types by Jacks. The receptionist swiftly dispatches each fresh arrival to his or her appropriate hallway. She raises her head to register Jacks standing at her window. Her expression convinces Jacks she is warm and open.

"Do they know I'm here?" asks Jacks.

"Your name has been accepted and recognized. Beyond that status, I have no other information I can give you."

"You have no other information? Or none you can give me?"

"Accepted and recognized, Mr. Porter. It's all I got." The smile she gives him is too good. He feels the vibration of a message coming in on his phone in his pants pocket, and reflexively reaches in and fishes out his device.

"Oops, sorry again, Mr. Porter."

"No phone?"

"You'll need to keep it in your pocket. No pictures or social media check-ins are allowed from this area."

"What about once I'm back there with the band?"

Her smile, as impossible as it might seem, comes at him even better. Jacks calculates. He has been in the reception hub, its lone occupant, for thirty-five minutes. He waits another hour in which he imagines his accepted-and-recognized name slipping down the line of priorities, then checks with the receptionist that it is okay to do so and steps out to the parking lot to call work and tell them he will be later than he had anticipated. He checks all incoming messages on the off chance an update has come in from the man who had owed him a favor and had arranged this audience with X. No such luck. Mark has sent a text confirming departure time for the drive to the Bay Area. Muriel has emailed reservation numbers for prepaid rental car and overnight lodging up north. That excursion, apparently, is still on.

The front man of the Worst takes a deep, resigned breath, puts on an optimistic front and returns to the reception area. The receptionist greets him warmly but silently. A tilt of her chin shifts his attention away from her. A guy stands there, smiling, extending no hand to shake. The guy is burly, well-fed from birth, the product of several decades of professional maintenance in teeth, skin, nutrition and exercise. The man's overall effect in faded denim jeans and a silky marine-blue dress shirt is so sleek and burnished that he is a version of ageless. He might be ten years older or ten years younger than Jacks. Either way, Jacks's virile stack of hair clearly bests this man's greased thinning mop. *Buddy*, thinks Jacks, staking the high ground, *you should have worn a hat.*

"Hey, Jacks," says the guy, as if they have known one another for thirty years and just had breakfast a week ago. "Thanks for coming down."

"Good to see you," says Jacks. He can play any game anyone else plays. "Are they ready for me to come back there now?"

"Not quite. There's some band business being straightened out. The management asked me to come out and determine the purpose of your visit."

"You mean like to see if I'm selling encyclopedias?"

"C'mon, you're Jacks from the Worst. You'll never take a job like that."

"Listen, I guess we can cut to it. I heard the band was asking about having the Worst open for them during the Roxy stand."

The burnished fellow knots his brow as if stumped by a brain puzzle. "First I've heard of it."

"Kind of awkward me being the one to break it to you."

"Especially awkward because I'm the one who would be making that ask. But not to worry, I do have a request ready for you. It's not for the full band though."

"Really? I'm not sure how you expect me to tell Slug and Jeremy that they won't be backing me." Jacks knows exactly how he will break the news to his guitarist and drummer. What he doesn't understand is how this guy talking to him does not have a gold chain glimmering at the open neck of the marine blue dress shirt. Did the galoot figure out to ditch the gold links himself? Did a hired stylist provide that pro tip?

"Jesus," the guy sighs, "we've had so many misunderstandings in such a short period of time. Our request, Jacks, is to be able to use the photo of the punk rocker on the trashcan at the Elks Lodge Massacre."

"Why ask me? It's not my copyright."

"X wants to leave the identity of the guy on the trashcan open."

At this point, Jacks is so uncomfortable that he is aware of being uncomfortable. He steers this large, healthy weasel out toward the parking lot. The receptionist sings out *bye-bye*. It's all Jacks can do not to trill *see you later* back at her. Outdoors, he corners the weasel up against the wall, positioned so that the sun is in the man's eyes. The man squints down at Jacks.

"What's your concept?" asks Jacks. "You want to print up an X concert poster on my photo so people think it's John on the can?"

"Or maybe Billy or Don. No, seriously, we want to have the poster sit as an everyman. The ideal of L.A. punk."

"Why are you even talking to me about this?"

"We know how much the presentation and the preservation of the scene matters to you. We know you would want to be on board with this contribution."

"You want to make sure that I won't start yelling on social media and to whoever will listen that I'm the man in that picture. That the Worst is the band that played in the face of the LAPD. You want me to stand down from a legacy that belongs to the Worst."

Under the influence of the sun, the grease in the burly man's sparse hair melts and runs. The tracking smarm creates furrows that are ridiculous to look at, but do nothing to undermine the man's confidence in his position.

"Acting out the butt hurt artiste role is one option you could exercise," he concedes. "If that's the legacy you want, after all these years. You could play the OG street protester card. Then you'll have people coming out of the woodwork swearing they saw you slip off the flank of the incoming wave of cops, swearing they saw you sitting in the window of Union Grill Chophouse, eating a porterhouse and baked potato and watching kids the scene really mattered to getting their faces bashed in going head-on against Chief Parker's finest."

"You have people lined up to attack my credibility?"

"They haven't formed a line yet. They are in the woodwork, Jacks. The woodwork is full of them. They'll be coming out of the woodwork. Look at the bright side. This poster is going to be iconic. It'll fire up whole spectrums of symbolism in everyone who looks at it, young and old. The image will stay forever young. You contributed some element to it. Isn't that the story of the Worst? Can you really think of a better story for the Worst?"

Jacks turns and walks away from this gleaming bush-league Machiavelli. The bitter reality, to Jacks's mind, is that he *had* thought of, and been telling himself, a better story for the Worst.

Part Four

Two days after leaving the Disney studios, in the early a.m., Jacks imagines alternate outcomes in the back of a taxi, being delivered to the car rental place. It's going to be a long drive, and the Citroen is staying at home. Everything at the counter is in order. The transaction goes smoother than any experience he has ever had at a car rental outlet, a smoothness Jacks attributes to Muriel's extraordinary credit rating and purchase power.

In the rented Lexus hybrid, Jacks thinks of the smoother route his life might have taken if he'd made only a few disciplined, mainstreamed decisions. He arrives at Muriel's. Mark is waiting on the lawn, a backpack hanging from one shoulder, a satchel of electronic devices hanging from the other.

"My mom's on a rampage. She found some weed. I thought I'd spare you the fallout. Plus she's late to catch her plane to Switzerland. You don't want to experience her late for a plane."

"Was it my weed she found?"

"It might have been at one point. But I had taken over possession. Your name never came up."

Jacks and Mark mull over separate visions of Muriel as the Lexus makes smooth work of the descent to the freeway and the first few miles north. A junction is coming up fast. Muriel's son and her sidelined lover debate which route to take: The direct Interstate 5 expressway that slices boring as a concrete ribbon across flat scrubland and agricultural parcels? Or veer to the occasionally daunting coastal highway with its cliff-side hairpins and marine blue horizons of far-off eternity? Driver and passenger argue solely in favor of the coastal highway. Jacks turns off at a canyon pass that shoots them across the Santa Monica Mountains to the ocean road. He has the Lexus. He has the time. Why not make it a mystical traveling experience?

Mark inserts a pair of ear buds, appears to occupy himself in deep thought, and drifts into sleep. Snoring like a sock puppet, he misses the unspectacular traffic in the expanse of residential territory above Malibu. Beyond Oxnard and Ventura, four lanes of northbound congestion pass through Santa Barbara. The Lexus exits the mountain tunnel after the rest stop above Refugio State Beach. Two clear driving lanes open, and Jacks pushes the car to the outside speed limits. The smooth highway cuts through lush rows of wine grapes. Mountains range in the eastern near distance. Clouds stack above. Hawks circle in the rising heat. A good car, as has often been noted, is all any man really needs to trigger a spiritual experience. Mark comes awake. Jacks recognizes a massive marijuana half-life hangover.

"Get on your phone," suggests Jacks. "Find a place for lunch."

The handheld mobile device commands Mark's attention for nearly sixty miles of roadway. Jacks admires the boy's concentration and focus. Mark is obviously deep into a research groove, on a topic thread of his own devising. He comes up with no restaurant suggestion. Jacks eases off the accelerator and allows the

Lexus to coast into the parking lot of a taco temple north of Morro Bay. He's had good luck here in years past.

While eating, Mark peppers the meal with interrogative conversational sallies. Primarily, Mark's chatter presses observations about Jacks's manner of dress. "Your need for non-alliance extends to your clothes," observes Mark, perhaps casually. "Expensive but sturdy, designed equally for form and function, never ostentatious. Everything you have on could pass for work gear, except I know the prices. You wear no badges or visible branding, which makes your presentation more personal, more individual, your own creation."

The guacamole is as chunky and the tortilla chips are as fresh in their sheen of hot grease as Jacks recalled. "You know," he says, his mouth burning, "I never really plan out my wardrobe. The way I dress is not a conscious strategy. You're giving it more thought right now than I ever have."

"But you do concede that you dress to defy easy classification?"

"For the sake of speeding up this meal and keeping the car moving northward, sure, I'll agree to that."

Mark takes a bite of taquito and gazes at the shredded beef protruding from the crisp, tightly rolled corn tortilla. It is a cue to wonder. "Does this conviction that your clothing expresses your unique individuality remain unshaken even while walking headlong into a stream of people whose wardrobe appears to have been cloned from the same template as yours?"

Jacks has a notion this is not the first time Mark has proffered some variant of this precise statement. "Do you and your mother discuss me?"

Mark's lifted eyebrows admit everything other than culpability. "I know what you're objecting to, Jacks. Seems weird. Her talking to me about you, it means she's really hooked on you somehow. Trust me, she's not looking to me for advice or input. You can relax on that front."

They do relax, motoring the picturesque highway, which slips into gorgeous mode in the approach to Big Sur. With water and sun glistening to their left and ranchland resplendent to the right, driver and passenger talk in general ways about sundry subjects. For instance, fishing. Neither of them is a fisherman. Both have caught a few fish. Neither had a father who avidly fished. That, they conclude, explains that. Between them, Jacks and Mark know several surfers. Neither has ever popped up on a board. Two topics in, Jacks realizes that Mark's after-lunch retreat to the taco stand bathroom had been an occasion for THC replenishment. Muriel had not confiscated the boy's entire stash. Jacks allows one hand to rove lazily through his hair, judged by Mark's bloodshot eyes and default smirk. Out of parental-adjacent consideration for Mark, Jacks has gone mobile without a travel supply, all weed products left at home. There's a friend across the Bay from where they'll be staying who's always in pocket with sweet product. Jacks can drop in on her, if he truly feels pressed for relief. He debates asking Mark for a share of the stash, pictures how that request might play out, and the highway becomes truly hazardous as it does to any driver not paying absolute attention. In a coherent and cogent soliloquy, Mark dissects the self-preservationist imperatives implicit in a fear of heights. Jacks agrees to take his fingers out of his hair and keep two hands on the steering wheel. Mark marvels at the diamond patterns of sun reflecting on the peaks and troughs of tossing ocean surfaces. He asks Jacks, "Are you listening? Like to the actual individual words, or just enduring the stream of talk as a rhythmic background drone?"

A black pickup truck shoots past the Lexus on the left, terrorizing the oncoming traffic and adding menace to the precipitous drop to the ocean below. The truck's doublewide back tires squeal around the next set of bends, and the black pickup flicks out of sight. Mark expresses his dumbfounded wonder that fans of drag racing exist when Gran Prix rallies are held almost every day, to judge by how many classic runs are available on YouTube. "What do people admire more," he asks, clear that he will not wait for an answer, "skill or brute force?" As an aside, he notes that a car cannot tumble off a cliff in the movies without coming to rest in an explosive ball of flame.

They hit congestion. Mark runs out of next things to say. Cars move one by one at a stop-and-go pace, backed up a quarter mile. The Lexus reaches the head of the impasse and pauses at an accident scene. Two cars are piled up. A black pickup truck is upside down, having skidded fifty yards on the roof of its cab. Someone appears to be pinned within the squashed pickup. Jacks looks at Mark, to gauge whether or not the boy is up for whatever adult responsibility they might encounter. He pulls the Lexus to the side of the road in the midst of the wreckage.

"Get in the road and make sure those cars keep moving," Jacks orders Mark. "We need traffic flow so the ambulances can reach us."

From where Mark stands on the asphalt, urging rubbernecked drivers to keep moving forward, he sees his mother's boyfriend become something more active than a bystander. On his belly, Jacks crawls up inside the crushed window frame of the pickup truck. He appears to be talking to the person inside, keeping the person company. Ambulances and police have yet to arrive. Mark feels that the situation is in hand. Help has arrived. That help is Jacks. This embrace of inconvenient involvement by Jacks clashes with Mark's conception of Jacks as a person of inaction. It does not automatically make the boy approve of Jacks. He ponders what to make of this disconnect. A slap on the shoulder brings him out of it.

"I said, 'Let's go, Mark,' " says Jacks. "Get in the car."

"But the cops are still on the way."

"We're done here."

Inside the Lexus, a possible reality dawns on the twilight of Mark's high. "Are you saying the guy in the truck is dead?"

"He was the driver. He was in there alone. Yeah, he's gone."

Looking for signs of some drastic change in his mother's boyfriend, or any change at all, Mark peers into Jacks's face. The eyes are focused and alert. The mouth is relaxed. The expression is placid. Is there, perhaps, a greater depth of feeling below the surface than Mark had guessed at before? No, not as far as the eye can see. "You were talking to him while he was dying. What were you saying?"

"I told him everything was going to be all right."

Mark guffaws. He thinks, *incredulous*. He thinks, *absurd*. "How could you say that?"

No ripple of doubt or distress betrays Jacks's calm. "It's what I believe. Nothing happened in that truck to suggest I'm wrong."

Blood is on Jacks's hands, and on the cuff of his shirt. It isn't a lot of blood. It's enough to focus Mark and hold him in silent contemplation until they reach the Bay Area hotel prepaid for them by his mother. During dinner, the boy still hasn't come up with much to say. Jacks begs off dessert. Citing the long day and a need to sleep, he takes to his room, leaving Mark alone with the realization he too is exhausted.

Part Five

In the overcast and windswept morning, crossing the parking lot to the Lexus after separate breakfasts, Mark searches Jacks's face surreptitiously, discovers no fresh clues and wonders how anyone can possibly find any solace in the fiction that everything will be all right.

At the university, they meet and greet with an administrator connection of Muriel's, and a third-year political-science student takes two hours to promenade them around campus. In light of the bully-takedown video, the school representatives view Mark as a minor celebrity and future thought leader. The interactions go well. Jacks, however, is withdrawn in his manner and stilted in his responses. When they are alone in the dining hall, Mark calls out Jacks. "You didn't make any attempt to engage."

"We're meeting these people so they can be interviewed by you," says Jacks.

"Of course, but if someone tosses you a conversational softball, you could give it a little tap. No one's asking for a homerun. Just dribble out something that the infield can make a play with."

"I'm not a ball player."

"Would it kill you to take a swing?"

"Everyone seemed super smart enough without me hitting pop ups."

"It's got nothing to do with seeming super smart."

"True," says Jacks, "if by *nothing* you mean *everything*. You're at a college. People you interact with here will want to be seen as smart. Stature is derived from giving the impression of intelligence. These people want everyone within earshot to admire their depth of specialized knowledge."

Mark makes a face. He is choking on the words he has just heard. It is as if language and the very function of his voice have failed him. This, of course, is only an affectation. He quickly recovers. "You are one of these people who wants to appear omniscient, Jacks, although you are not the type who announces your all-encompassing understanding of all things. You are the quiet knows-best type."

"You know, a man died in my hands yesterday, Mark. I'd rather not argue geopolitical circumstances with some low level university regent, and debate the efficacy of local election initiatives with an undergraduate political science major."

Jacks adopts the projection of silent omniscience. In that quiet place, he's protected from having his point of view questioned. People, Mark for instance, can't pin him to one side or another. Mark is unable to define Jacks's political orientation. No group can claim that Jacks is one of them, or not one of them, or one of any particular rival group. His allegiances are beyond fault. Jacks's silence, he suggests without saying as much, is profound. He is a person of deep beliefs, of core convictions, which he will defend to his last exasperated breath. That defense may occur only within the commentary running inside his head.

"Politics comes into this," insists Mark. "Politics comes into everything. You were in a band, the front person. You're still recognized. It's not like you're as important as Bono. You have some lingering, minor prominence. I won't go so far as to say you have a responsibility. You have an opportunity to reach people, as few as those people may be."

"I'm recognized by grandmothers who saw me play when we were twenty. We're tired now. We're all looking forward to that one thing at the end, what I saw and felt in my hands yesterday."

"What if I were to tell you," says Mark, "that now, at present, you are an accidental attendee at a college campus where a spontaneous political rally has been called to disrupt a scheduled speaking event?"

"I'd say that's an accident I'm not here to make," says Jacks.

Under cover of going out for dinner, Jacks takes public transit across the Bay to hunt down a more personal, self-involved pursuit, cloaking his true motive even from himself. He has a friend, from the past, who has suggested he should drop in. She's not home. She is the same age as his oldest daughter. If Jacks were to follow that thought out, he would remember that he'd met this woman through his daughter. Maybe knowing Jacks is on his way, his friend has stepped out for beer or wine or delicacies, to bring back to her apartment and share with him. Or she has needed to re-up. A picture of her back is tacked up in a place within Jacks where he displays visions he wants to never forget. Her back is shapely, smooth, burnished brown like a prized violin, with sound points that quiver to the touch. Jacks holds that picture for fifteen minutes in the hallway outside her door. She has yet to return, which puts her a quarter hour closer to coming back. Jacks goes with the obvious plan. He shoots a text to tell his friend he is nearby and is leaning toward dropping in. He'll wander off for a coffee, and circle back on his way to the public transit.

At a coffee store, when a barista asks for Jacks's name, he always gives his real name, on the off chance it will spur pleased recognition. It's not that he says "Jacks" and waits to see if recognition comes. He orders a coffee, gives his name, takes out his phone and, waiting for his quad-shot latte, camps on social media. He's not one to pimp his past on Instagram. No response yet from his friend who always has such sensuous weed. His fingers roam freely in his hair.

A woman, young and tan, calls, "Jacks!"

He quick steps to the pickup counter, wraps a hand around his coffee fix. The young, tan woman hangs onto the cup, refuses to let it go. Jacks meets her eyes. She releases his drink. "The Worst?" she says.

He is recognized, up here hundreds of miles from home. Life is full of delightful possibilities beyond anticipation. The hardware in the young, tan woman's nostrils is delicate and precious. Her hair is dreaded. Her eyes are china blue. Her scent is fresh and not at all virginal.

"Are you up here for the demonstrations?" she asks. Her smile is like someone asking him to prom.

"That depends. What are you going to be demonstrating?" he asks. She looks at him as if he's being a wise ass, like someone's wise-ass dad. He realizes the stupid depths of his reply. She moves toward the next cups of coffee, toward the next customers in line.

"No," he calls after her. He's apologetic, as apologetic as he has ever heard himself be. "I'm up here on another matter, a family obligation."

"Oh, that's cool," says the young, tan woman, perceptibly cooler than she had been a moment earlier. "I saw your name on a handbill for a climate change benefit. I thought, oh wow. Old Jack is still passing as woke."

"But," Jacks demurs, "the Worst were never woke. It was a different time. It was an unwoke time in a fuck you world."

The young woman returns to the job now. Any more from Jacks is just more work to her. She gives him the incontrovertible, "You have a good day, sir." He has no comeback for that.

Out on the sidewalk, where no one has witnessed the exchange in the coffee shop, Jacks tastes a long drag of his coffee. The brew is delicious and potent too, obviously. Jacks doesn't anticipate catching a positive buzz from the stuff. He'd felt a lot better walking into the shop, anticipating a reunion with his friend whose back is akin to a priceless violin. The drop from that emotional high has come down because Jacks failed to realize that a political demonstration is the weekend's big attraction.

Without really trying, his steps arrive at the door of his friend, the one who always has the best pot, with the undying regard for him, with the back like a priceless musical instrument. His knock on her door echoes through an empty apartment. The only sounds of life are coming from him. He decides to not leave a text trail or a quavering voice message begging for his friend's location. Yesterday, on the side of the Pacific Coast Highway, he had been given a glimpse into the wonder of existence. He has opened the question of whether there is more to existence than life. Who can say if anything is real? Success and achievement are relative, beyond relative. Accomplishment and the lack of it and the space in between those two states are no more real than the arbitrary line between life and individual existence. The need to be a self, the need to be human, the need to be alive: We don't really need any of it. It's all very nice to have, to experience. We don't truly possess a breath. Experience is transitory when it is even noticed at all. Existence is not ours. We belong to existence. The world of atoms and molecules and decomposition knows and owns us to a far greater extent than we know or own ourselves. "I feel pretty good," he concludes, stepping from the apartment hallway into the sunlight and cloudy blue canopy, "for an old guy."

He goes abstract on the train back across the Bay, absorbed in redeemable thoughts of death and decay. His mind is distant as if wrapped in bunting. Moving from the Bart station toward his lodgings, a good distance for a brisk walk, he notices more homeless than he'd seen on the way out. Men and women who exude the quality of no fixed address, this is strange, are retreating from the sidewalks, melting into passageways and spaces between buildings, taking up defensive positions in the recessed doorways of closed businesses. From looking at the homeless, Jacks's attention extends wide, taking in an escalating agitation all around him. Stalled traffic fills the street. Pedestrians stroll between the cars, heading with a purposeful pace all in the same direction, toward the university campus. Drivers and passengers slip out of the blocked-in cars, lock the doors and attempt to walk against the stream of excited youths pouring forward. A block further along, the commotion is impossible to dismiss as some passing or arbitrary thing. Even if he had been baked, Jacks would have known to be on high alert. *Something is happening here*, he sings inside his head, *and I don't know exactly what it is.*

Onlookers gawk. Small groups of confederates roll and wrap dampened bandanas around necks and foreheads, fully halting progress on the sidewalk. Jacks steps down into the boulevard. None of these cars are going anywhere. Within yards of forward motion, Jacks is shoulder-to-shoulder and ass-to-pelvis with a roving mass that is, he estimates, one inciting incident away from being classified a mob. Many in the crowd carry signs or banners or unfurl and wave flags. Jacks refrains from staring closely enough at the printed slogans to read the individual words. He doesn't want to give the appearance of not knowing where he is. Furthermore, the marching masses in front of and behind him have closed off the option of pulling back for a wider view. Being trampled beneath the boots and sneakers of this young, eager push of righteous congestion isn't uppermost in his mind. Nevertheless, dying, or severe bruising, if the herd were to stampede is a possibility. Anyway, he doesn't need to read what the slogans say. He has a good idea from the invective crackling through the crisp air.

"No free speech for Nazi scum!"

This outcry draws Jacks's attention to a grouping of five men, mid-twenties to early-thirties, dressed with an impeccable lack of imagination, almost as though they are regimented. If asked, Jacks would have been hard-pressed to single out what visual cues differentiated these five from the dozens of agitated young people surrounding them. The opponents have no trouble identifying one another. The tallest of the five beleaguered antagonists responds as if to a child he doesn't care for: "Free speech is nonnegotiable, snowflake. Free speech is my inalienable right."

The surge of rebuttal is a physical shove, passing through Jacks like a wave at a sporting event. Aghast, against his will, Jacks feels himself jostling the pack of provocateurs. Over his shoulders, a torrent of righteousness streams by on both sides of his face. *"Fuck you and your fucking fascist hate speech!"*

The five from the dissenting side respond as one multi-headed fount of preening mockery. "Love your love! Love the way your love trumps hate! Love your love of intellectual debate!"

The factions split off and join comrades of each ilk held behind separate cordons, like contestants waiting to be called into play in a massive game of full-contact dodge ball. A wedge of cops splits the flow into the designated holding areas. The lead cop at the wedge's point catches Jacks in the eye. His look asks, *Do you know where you are, old fellow?* "Left or right," says the cop.

It's a little late for Jacks to stop and explain that he has never been involved in this taking of sides. "Passing through." He gives the name of his hotel. The cop waves Jacks forward. The flat of his hand indicates a strip of neutral territory between the two barricaded factions.

"At this point," the cop says, "turning back won't gain you anything."

Jacks tries to walk in a way that expresses a simple need to reach his lodging. The areaway between the opposing factions is less crowded than the street has been, but still fully occupied. People wielding large, professional-looking cameras rove this enclosure between enclosures, competing to capture Internet-ready scene bites. Students and teachers and for instance cafeteria workers hold their faces blank and down, scurrying through the contested corridor as if streaking for cover. No one who is not a cameraperson will look directly at the camera people. Everyone hurrying through the neutral strip pretends deafness to the greetings and exhortations of the camera people. Like Jacks, they appear to resist being pulled to one side or another of the passageway. Any deviations caused by camera people blocking direct forward motion are corrected immediately upon returning to the straight, narrow path.

Jacks sees the flow bunching up and stalling out ahead. Forward progress is culminating in a blocked scrum. He stops, trying to assess another way around. A reporter mistakes Jacks on pause for someone who wants to talk. Camera running, the reporter asks, "Which side have you come out to support?"

"If I were supporting a side," says Jacks, "shouldn't that be obvious?"

"Not really," says the cameraperson, happy for any engagement at all. "Look at the way you're dressed. You could go either way."

"Or I could go neither way," snaps Jacks. Then, as if in considered consolation, "It's not that I'm on the left or the right or even an independent. I'm absent from the process."

"Doesn't that seem irresponsible?" asks the cameraperson, moving with and focusing on Jacks, tripping a woman going the other direction.

"I can imagine having dinner with you," answers Jacks, "and six of your friends, and wishing I was somewhere else throughout the entire meal."

Jacks shoulders past the cameraperson, and doesn't get far. He sees what has happened to clog the passageway. Demonstrators and counter demonstrators have breached the thin barriers that separate them from lashing physically at the opposing side. Thought leaders from either wing have lined sneer-to-sneer out in the middle of the street. The spit of each viewpoint's invective splatters the faces of their opposites. Jacks pictures his photo from forty years ago, launching the double bird atop an upside-down trash can. Either side of the battle here might adopt that image, the right ones or the wrong ones, the good or bad ones, or both.

Jacks spots a thin, determined figure weaving among the clusters of protesters and counter-protesters. This person is striding toward Jacks. A dampened bandana clings to the bottom half of this person's face. Jacks tries to determine which side this person, a male person, has stepped out from, and cannot. The figure comes closer, definitely closing in on him, and lowers the bandana two inches. Jacks recognizes the eyes, the stride and shoulders. It's Mark. The boy steps tight enough to speak directly into Jacks's ear.

"It's time to be getting out of here," says the widow's kid, "according to your philosophy."

"Glad you see it that way. Let's go." Jacks turns and takes a few steps toward leaving. He has seen this madness, become entangled in it, and escaped it before. Jacks feels the spring of adrenaline. He's amped, not as amped as an underage L.A. kid out in the MacArthur Park bushes drinking beers on Saint Patrick's Day night. When the cops showed up and massed, he'd been animated by a surge of energy. The Worst had been billed to go on next. Thinking no big deal about the cops, Jacks had headed back toward the Elks Lodge to claim his set time. He'd seen two of the photographers who were always hanging around like awkward older siblings. Their prowling cameras had inspired him to stop for his trashcan photo op.

Jumping down from the trashcan, he had moved toward the fray. An older guy in a bigger band, Black Randy, heading the opposite direction had pulled him away from the forming battle lines. Randy had an album out and a clutch of singles, all eventually very collectible. He had cofounded a dangerous little record company. He steered Jacks by the arm. "I'm on next," protested Jacks. "Nobody's on next," answered Randy. Jacks made a move to shrug him off and join the kids at the receiving end of the charging phalanx of cops. Randy put on a tighter grip. "Look at those cops. I thought you were a smart person in a dumb crowd. Did I make a mistake?"

Now, forty-plus years later, the stakes should be less dire. Several calm people are leaving the area casually. That lack of hurry will not last. Malice and panic will swirl in soon. Jacks looks back to share this observation with Mark. He sees that Muriel's son has sheared off from his side. Half a dozen milling malcontents separate them. *If I shout,* thinks Jacks, *the kid will hear me. I don't want to shout.* People will look. People will notice. People will assign a side and a motive. Jacks keeps a bead on the back of Mark's head and shoulders. A curb rises from nowhere. Jacks half trips. He trains his eyes down to see where his feet can take a next safe step. He looks up and has lost sight of the kid in the crush.

A handsome young woman with a face set and grim aims her phone in Jacks's direction. She's up close. He can read the word PRESS on the bandanna around her forehead. A placard hangs from a lanyard around her neck. Jacks suspects the placard is little more than an all-access music festival pass. Obviously, she's someone with a blog, *like everybody*, thinks Jacks. She reads Jacks as potential content. "Who are you here to represent?" she demands of him.

Jacks has had enough. He's in a hurry. He'll give her what he thinks she wants. "Picking sides is like moving from the cancer ward to the tuberculosis wing."

"That's hyperbole and doesn't even make sense."

"You're right. Let me rephrase that. It is like preferring *Star Trek* over *Star Wars*."

The blogger wants to hit Jacks with a third question, but the population is fluid, like water in a washing machine's agitation cycle. Colliding clumps of dirty laundry have bobbed up between them. More to Jacks's concern, spry young men dressed all in black with their faces obscured by black ski masks have entered the contested grounds of the demonstrators and counter demonstrators. Jacks can't be certain. He believes he sees some demonstrators deftly switching their badges and signs, in effect crossing to the other side. In the distance, across two dozen surging shoulders, Jacks catches sight of a slight male figure yanking a black jersey over his plaid shirt and pulling a black ski mask to obscure the head. It could be Mark. It could be one of the other hundred kids like Mark.

Blacked-out new arrivals stream in from three directions and, as far as Jacks can sense, may in fact represent three totally divergent points of view. What he had taken for homeless characters huddled in darkened doorways drop that flimsy pretense and emerge clad in black, indistinguishable from the regimented streams of reinforcements, perhaps indivisible. The entire mass of anonymous combatants might also be one coordinated force split into three battalions. Jacks is chilled and stands still. Many of these black clad troopers carry batons, clutched in gloved hands.

Batons had changed Jacks's mind back in 1979. He had acquiesced to Black Randy's pressure, and followed the older fellow into a cheap chophouse with a view of the park where the police brutality would play out. Randy had sat Jacks down in a picture window booth and bought him a tough steak dinner. "Watch and learn," Randy had said, pointing out the window toward the rioting police and bleeding punks. "The first rule of keeping up a brave front, Jacks, is do not meet trouble halfway."

Too late now. Jacks has ventured more than halfway to trouble. He is unable to turn back. He is locked in pursuit of someone he believes to be Mark. Taking twenty steps deeper into the fray, Jacks loses his quarry. Ten strides later, he picks up the prey again. Jacks pushes people aside in his rush to catch up with Mark. He's not even sure it is Mark. Whoever it is looks back. To ascertain Jacks is still following? The chase leads Jacks away from the melee of the main crowd. There is a relief in not being elbowed continuously in the kidneys and liver and back and shouldered under the chin. Savoring that freedom from being clobbered on the run, Jacks loses track of where he's heading. He trots about two hundred yards up a side street and around an alleyway, following the lure of Mark jogging easily ahead of him. The prey stops suddenly and turns back at the pursuer.

Jacks pulls up short to orient himself. First, he looks behind. A rank of men, faces hidden, batons exposed, forms between him and escaping out the way he has come. Looking forward leads to an unpleasant discovery. He has been cut off at a dead end. In front of him, the person he had been chasing stands in front of a brick façade and peels back the ski mask. A young woman folds that mask in her waistband and confronts Jacks with condescending fury. "Infiltrator!" she yells.

Has he been chasing this girl? The woman's defining characteristic is that she is not alone. Several black clad figures, many of them male and armed, appear to either side of her and await the woman's command.

"Those clothes you're wearing," says the woman, as if she has caught Jacks in an obvious and irrefutable lie, "how convenient they are for aligning yourself with one side, and then the other."

"Are you picking on me because of the way I'm dressed?" asks Jacks. "Has my outfit confused you people about where to place me on your binary chart?"

"No one is picking on you," says one of the masked men. His outburst receives a stern side eye from the spokeswoman. The man's chagrin can be seen through his ski mask.

Clearly, Jacks has been singled out. A telephone is visible, of course, being wielded like a prop in the hands of a black dressed mime. This whole interaction is being preserved on video. Beyond being preserved, Jacks feels as if the entire confrontation has been orchestrated, engineered for optimal video presentation.

"This is only happening so someone can put it on the Internet," says Jacks. "I've been snared in a content farming scheme."

"We just want to know that you're on the right side," says the woman. "We can't tell by looking at you. Is there a reason for that?"

Jacks experiences a bout of physical dissociation. He's become the cliché out-of-body voyeur floating above the scene, looking down and recognizing his place in the tableau. That's him. There's Jacks, finally taking a stand. "Anyone holding a threat of violence in abeyance," he says, "doesn't care what I believe."

His inquisitor, Jacks suspects, is one of the demonstrators who became a counter demonstrator. Or does he have that backward? She's very good looking. Her face appears to have escaped so far any of the serious consequences life has to offer. Her surety of expression indicates she anticipates continuing to do so.

"Who in the fuck are you anyway?" asks Jacks. Maybe he really wants to know. Clearly he is tired and would be just as gratified not finding out and being allowed to walk on back to his hotel room.

"I'm the person who wants to know what side you're on, Jacks. Is Jacks with the anti-fascists or is Jacks against them?"

Jacks feels like he has been in the same argument his entire life. He is being asked one all-or-nothing trick question. His inquisitor is not revealing the preferred response. Lithe masked men in tight black hang on this reply. Jacks's wellbeing hinges upon what he answers next. All he knows with certainty, as he's known all along, is that his inquisitors won't believe a thing he says.

A LITTLE AFTERWARD: NOBODY
WANTS TO HEAR YOUR STORY

The divorced guy doesn't really want to go out and has a feeling he is not ready for socializing. His doubts started the very moment a handsome, optimistic younger couple, the girl much younger, welcomed him to the duplex and suggested he come with them to story night. The three neighbors stand on the steps to their communal front porch. A moving van has just left. The divorced guy's mind is still on it. "What happens at story night?" he asks.

"People tell stories." The girl says this as if she is humoring him now, as a joke. She is blonde and bobbed and alive with mobile possibilities in her aqua-patterned sundress and yellow-canvas sneakers. "It's in a bar. There are drinks and finger foods."

"So it's like comedians," says the new tenant. He imagines what he looks like to these new people. Holding onto his flat stomach. Holding onto his muscle tone. Holding his wry, blank, ragged good looks, and his unruly hair. He's all still there, no joking matter.

"Some of the people might be comedians," explains the girl's young man. He is neatly bearded. His build, posture and clothing are tidy and show no wear. He has the look of a moderately successful manager of brand partnerships who anticipates huge success. "The emphasis is less on doing bits," he explains further, "and more on telling stories."

"A lot of the stories have funny parts." The blonde laughs, like as a preview. "If you don't want to go, it's no big deal."

It's not as if the divorced neighbor doesn't want to go. The woman and her man seem predisposed to liking him. Neither is an outright fool. Beyond that, the new tenant will be seeing this couple every day, or be at risk of seeing them every day. Their ground-floor one-bedroom apartment is between the door to the leafy, craftsman-lined street and the stairwell to his second-floor two-bedroom apartment and its wide-pane views of that leafy street. Also, the laundry room is on the ground floor. "Great," the divorced guy decides. "Sounds fun. By the way, I'm Sandy."

"Hi, Sandy," says the young woman. "I'm Brie. This is my fiancé, Jake. Bring someone if you'd like."

"That would be great." Sandy scans the leafy street. There is no calling back the moving van. "I sort of just had a breakup."

Brie scrunches her pretty, round face into a sad emoji. "Oh that's too bad."

"It's going okay. I'm seeing a new person. Just we're at the stage where we're not ready to deal with anyone else beyond ourselves when we go out. I'm not sure that makes sense. I'm seeing that you could take that more than one way."

"Or no way at all," says Jake. His hand smoothes his sleek beard.

"Well," says Sandy, "I suppose you'll meet the new girl soon enough. Let's hope meeting her won't be more awkward than what I just put us through right here."

So all three neighbors have a laugh on Sandy, and everyone is on the same team when story hour rolls around. Of course, Sandy gets to the bar, wedged between his young neighbors at a tight table crammed against the low stage lip, cutting off ready escape, and it's all comedians expecting to be taken seriously. *Honestly*, Sandy thinks but does not say, *if they want to be known as storytellers, try writing a book.*

The first five storytellers spool out their tales of first skateboards and forgiven misguided parents in rote phrasing and telegraphed emotional misdirection that are portentous and void upon delivery.

Ninety minutes in, Sandy feels that he has been encased in a dried mulch chrysalis of beer and fried food. The sixth storyteller steps to the microphone. Sandy emerges from the enveloping stupor. *This is the one*, thinks Sandy with dread and annoyance. *I will physically hate this one. Everyone here will love him.* This one is dressed like a singer from a 1970s rock band, not any one particular singer. The storyteller has lifted and bound together signature looks from a half dozen icons. He flutters appropriated sartorial details onstage as if he is unfurling his icon certification documents. Looking at the guy, the audience eats it up. It's like he's arriving from a time before the Internet existed, as if his costume charade is not enabled precisely because the Internet does exist.

The story icon rolls out his personal recollection. Sandy sees the captivated audience strap itself in. The talker had played drums in a band. "It's something I have in common with Sam Shepard." He was traveling from town to town, telling himself he was a rock star touring. Basically driving all night in a van with six other guys. "Why did we do it? There wasn't even enough money for food. Were we all delusional?

"We made a demo. In the old days, that meant pooling your money to buy studio time. Now, it means your keyboard player is computer savant."

A waitress squats beside the lip-side table to watch, Sandy presumes, in disbelief. "This guy's name should be Sham Parsons," says Sandy to the waitress. "Am I right?"

The raconteur's demo did something unexpected, as Sandy might have expected. "We sent it to a record company," says the drummer. "They loved it. They wanted to sign us. 'When do we go into the studio?' 'No, no studio. Let's release the demo. We'll use the studio money for a new mix, and for mastering. You'll be amazed by your own work.' "

The waitress whispers to Sandy. "His name is Hunter Point."

"I'm not asking what his name is," says Sandy. "I'm saying that he should be called *Sham* Parsons."

"The record company got us a gig bottom-lining at a festival," continues Hunter Point. "Everyone else playing the festival was an established artist. It was a big deal. Our spot was an early spot, the first spot. Our spot was so early, it overlapped with the headliner's sound check.

"The headliner, Glenn Danzig, sees me," says Hunter Point. "He comes up to me and is so cool and encouraging. Halfway through our conversation, I realize Danzig has mistaken me for someone else. I'm not sure who. Just as my band is going on, he says, 'Tell your dad I said hi.' Glenn Danzig thought I was the kid of someone he knew."

Hunter Point pauses and gives the audience time to soak that in, which the audience audibly does.

"I don't understand you," says the waitress squatting at Sandy's ear. "Who is Sam Parsons?"

"No, I mean the shag hair," explains Sandy, "the western shirt, the boots, the laconic vocal delivery that stops short of dropping into a drawl? *Sham* Parsons."

Confident the audience is on pace with him, the storyteller resumes. "So we played the show. We killed it, of course. All sixteen ushers and the food vendor crews would back me up on that. For the encore, we loaded into the van and started on the fourteen-hour commute to the next gig. *I hate commuting*, I thought, looking around the van. *This is not a job for me. This is a job for some kid whose dad is friends with Glenn Danzig. Why am I following this dream?*

"We got home. I knew I had to follow my own dream. That's when I started doing standup and the pod casts and writing plays."

The waitress is on the job and needs to do more of that. She shoves off, leaving Sandy a smile that generally pulls in a twenty-five-percent tip.

"The point is," finishes Hunter Point, "Jerry Seinfeld doesn't come up to me at Comedy Store open mic and mistake me for Dave Chappelle's son."

Is that his ending flourish? thinks Sandy. *Is that finale grand enough to shake this crowd out of its suspended disbelief?* The answers to those questions, Sandy sees in glowing customer faces all around him, are yes and yes.

"Looks like you were making friends with the waitress," observes Brie.

"She reminded me of a story," says Sandy. Sandy's story is akin to this last storyteller's story. It's a story about interacting with a universally beloved musician under odd intimate circumstances. Sandy's narrative slant is perhaps more heartfelt, and contains greater detail and historical importance.

"She's probably heard it already," says Jake. "That waitress has worked here for a year. Every guy has a story for her."

"No, this is a real story," says Sandy. "My story pivots on a cameo by David Bowie, not Glenn Danzig."

"I knew it!" says Brie. "Sandy's story is crafted from superior raw material."

It's late. The bar's vacated tables are being wiped clean. No one is rushing to reclaim them. It's a work night. Everyone has somewhere to be in the morning. Sandy's account takes some time to tell. Better not to rush the finish.

Within the coming weeks and months, Sandy might have forgotten story night's Hunter Point, and his lackluster story, except the world won't let Hunter Point go. Paying customers are drawn to wherever Hunter Point appears in his raconteur drag and performs his raconteur routine. Hunter Point's social media accounts become known phenomena. While Sandy settles into his downsized two-bedroom apartment with tree-line views, Hunter Point enters a period of professional expansion, using his storyteller recollections as stepping-stones to rapid ascension. Based on his touring in a band van, Hunter Point becomes the knowing, familiar face of television and print campaigns for a disruptive computer product. Hunter's ad persona lands guest spots on three competing scripted TV series tracking the struggles of aspiring television comics. Sandy, by accident, catches portions of all three of Hunter Point's dramatic comedy episodes. Also by coincidence, Sandy opens a news alert on his phone. Hunter Point is developing a television program tracking an aging rocker's struggles as an aspiring television comic. The series has a six-episode order. Hunter Point will write, produce and star as himself. The actress attached as Point's love interest and the droll director signed on as co-producer were both previously admired by Sandy.

"These developments are all based on one sort-of-lame story," laments Sandy, softly, while at work, while on his commute, while waiting for his new girlfriend to finish in the bathroom. "It's all coming from that story he told that first night in the crowded bar. I have a story. I have a better story."

Sandy's story, its surface twist, its deeper meaning, its universality, its sex appeal and celebrity participation, its potential for wide dissemination and mass approval has became so big that it fills Sandy's entire two-bedroom apartment, night after night. Drilled mercilessly within his skull, Sandy's story is primed like a muscle memory to be sprung upon his current girlfriend the instant she unlatches the bathroom door.

"Let me tell you something," Sandy says. The current girlfriend joins him on the living-room sofa overlooking the tree line outside the wide-pane windows. Her name is Jenny. Jenny is brunette, striking with or without makeup and younger than Sandy, although old enough that nobody looks twice. Her skin is olive and oiled, encasing supple limbs and a flush, comfort-laden torso. All of her is damp and within reach bursting from a short, open terrycloth robe.

"Jenny," says Sandy, "did I ever tell you about the time I met David Bowie?"

"You know what's funny?" replies Jenny. "I always thought I liked David Bowie better than Prince. Like, whenever someone said, 'Who would you rather bring back to life, David Bowie? Or Prince?' I always answered, 'Bowie, no brainer.' But I was going out with this deejay guy. He left that Prince *Parade* album and *Sign o' the Times* at my place. The more I listen to those records, the more I start thinking, *Sorry, David, you're staying dead, for now at least.*"

Sandy waits for a spot to break in and tell Jenny his story. His narrative is in the same genre as Hunter Point's. Jenny takes a shallow breath. Sandy jumps in to set the time period of his David Bowie story and introduce the cast of characters. Jenny's attention drifts from the story to the bathroom. She's not sure she opened the bathtub drain fully and runs off to check. Sandy watches Jenny divert into the kitchen. Sandy realizes his David Bowie encounter is a story not everyone will appreciate.

Sandy joins Jenny at the open refrigerator. Together they inspect the contents, speculative, not expecting much. "Jenny," asks Sandy, "would you rather hear a true story from David Bowie, or a made-up story from Prince?"

"True or made up doesn't matter," says Jenny. "People judge a story by the storyteller. So, I'm thinking definitely Prince."

Sandy thanks Jenny for her candor and has sex with her one last time for sportsmanship and luck.

The couple in the apartment below comes into good fortune. A chunk of money has been released to them from a timed trust, and one of them, Sandy is unclear which, has had a breakthrough in the work life. Brie and Jake have put an offer on a house in the cool suburbs where Sandy lived before his divorce. The offer has been accepted. Brie and Jake's time in the duplex has been good time. They appreciate the neighborliness they've shared with the fellow upstairs. As a going-away gesture, the couple has secured tickets to the Hunter Point Farewell Raconteur Tour. These tickets have become hot properties.

Jake and Brie have seen Sandy spin through the breaking up and new date cycle three times in the past eighteen months. He appeared to be in the beginning stages with his latest date, not fully comfortable in public with other people, when she abruptly was no longer coming around. Jake and Brie talked it over.

"It'll be just the three of us," Brie tells Sandy. She and Jake have encountered Sandy at the base of the stairwell, as if by chance.

"Oh, like that first time," says Sandy. "That will be so nice." Brie and Jake truly have been fine neighbors. Sandy anticipates something approaching excruciation.

Hunter Point's acclaim has outgrown the funky venue of that first tight and intimate story night. A full-fledged club has been booked and sold out. Sandy follows Jake and Brie into the crowd, milling and young and charged with anticipation. The couple leads him up a steep set of stairs. They file into three seats up against the balcony guardrail, looking directly down upon the raised stage that is not empty for long. Hunter Point's disparate sartorial indicators have been woven into a fluid, integrated costuming. The drinks Sandy has ordered for everyone, doubles all around, arrive just as the raconteur introduces a story of being passed up by fame and fortune, of persevering right-sized outside the realm of acclaim, about living for the small personal satisfactions. Human relationships, insists Hunter Point, are what really matter. If people want to be smart, they should stop with all this chasing celebrity and riches and settle into moderate obscurity. If you're meant to land a series, you'll land a series.

"My friend Melanie is Hunter's stylist now," says Brie. "That's how we scored these killer seats."

"Melanie is the one who hooked up Brie with the costumers' union," says Jake, openly pleased to stroke his sleek beard, unabashed and proud of his girl's accomplishments and contacts.

Sandy from upstairs looks down on the nightclub crowd. He picks out the particular individuals who are held rapt by this storyteller. Sandy marvels at the power of smooth, plausible banality. The charmed faces are clean, alert, college educated, employed and unfathomable. Sandy knows a few of the people in the audience from the neighborhood or met through the young couple living below. These familiars have been sympathetic to him. Surely, one among them will listen to his David Bowie story and affirm that it is an important tale even though Sandy, the conclusion must be reached, lacks importance as a storyteller.

The raconteur finishes up. Sandy has been listening closely to himself. He misses the patented Hunter Point punch line. It is clear to see that the performance has been magical. Nobody moves to leave the club. They are all bound by a spell. Sandy re-reviews the familiar people in this particular, current place, one by one. He attempts to locate an individual who will feel his story. Sandy hits a drink hard, preparatory to launching his David Bowie story on his neighbors, the ones who will be moving away. He senses he is imposing upon them, like some guy insisting you watch him pirouette down the sidewalk after you've all been to the ballet. Sandy pulls back. Brie and Jake are impatient for the future. They have things to do before going places. Sandy thinks of all the places ahead of him and the people who will be in those places. There are so many people. Their indifference is unanimous, vast and disheartening. To avoid an awkward parting with Brie and Jake at their duplex door, Sandy takes leave of his neighbors at the club and calls a car to go off on his own.

You take your story with you, he thinks, knowing he's dramatizing, *wherever you go, everywhere you go.*

Humble Hunter Point does not fool Sandy. *This would be a good night to take up smoking,* Sandy thinks. He moves down the sidewalk fronting the club toward the Uber pickup spot. His car, the phone indicates, will arrive in three minutes. Two city buses roll past. Sandy expects to see promo posters along the sides of the buses advertising Humble Hunter Point and the small personal satisfactions of Hunter Point's upcoming television series. The Hunter Point bus-side promotions aren't there. Reality has withheld that nail-on-the-head literary license. It could still happen. In fact, it will. Within three maybe four weeks, Sandy would bet on it, he will see Hunter Point's humble fulfillment grinning out from the side of a bus.

A car pulls to the curb. Sandy sighs and sinks into the backseat. The Uber driver seems to want to talk. The driver came here from Texas. The new life in Hollywood is not what he had expected, although it does extend the themes of his life.

"What are those themes?" asks Sandy, playing along. He needs to protect his five-star passenger rating.

"Oh, you know," elaborates the driver, cheerful, optimistic, clueless. "The usual. The rise and fall and the rise again. The underdog that can't say quit. The redemption cycle. It's the eternal progression. You hear what I'm saying?"

"I hear you," says Sandy agreeably, not listening.

"Of course we're all just searching for love," says the driver. That catches Sandy's attention. "Love is all we're searching for," repeats the driver.

In the passing streetlights and headlights and the glow from the dashboard, Sandy sees the driver's face in profile as an average-looking, small-featured man of thirty-five with close eyes, a sharp, short nose and thin crimped lips, all components animated by hopeful expectation. The driver tells Sandy that driving a ride-share car is a brilliant, profitable way to meet people. From his seated position, the driver's height limitations and body-mass index are unavailable to Sandy's evaluations.

"Do you know how many people are out here?" asks the driver. "How many potential fares?"

"Don't tell me," says Sandy.

"Anyone you want to find, romance, love, quickies, they're all out there. Start driving. Sooner or later, you're bound to pick up whoever it is you're looking for."

Sandy, getting into the car, had held a fleeting notion that this driver might take to his David Bowie story. Obviously not. The driver is his own storyteller. The Texan drives to converse and to meet people who are interested in having interesting conversations. Again, Sandy is talking to himself, telling his best story, something he's hardly listening to, keeping his voice just far enough at bay that he can still believe it. *Think of all those potential fares. Think of you behind the wheel. Surely, if you stop to pick up enough passengers, you'll eventually capture someone who will hear out your story and ride with you to wherever it is you want that story to take them.*

ABOUT THE AUTHOR

Allan MacDonell is the author of *Prisoner of X: 20 Years in the Hole at Hustler Magazine* and *Punk Elegies*, which centers on characters and consequences met writing for 1970s L.A. punk zine *Slash*. 2018's *Now That I Am Gone* is MacDonell's memoir of his life as it carries on without him. *The Scary Parts* is his first book to not exploit himself as protagonist.

MORE BOOKS ON PUNK HOSTAGE PRESS

Danny Baker
Fractured – 2012

A Razor
Better Than a Gun in A Knife Fight – 2012, *Drawn Blood: Collected Works From D.B.P.LTD., 1985-1995* – 2012, *Beaten Up Beaten Down* – 2012, *Small Catastrophes in A Big World* – 2012, *Half-Century Status* – 2013, *Days of Xmas Poems* – 2014, *Puro Purismo* – 2021

Iris Berry
The Daughters of Bastards – 2012
!=All That Shines Under the Hollywood Sign – 2019
The Trouble with Palm Trees – 2021
Gas Station Etiquette – 2022

Yvonne De la Vega
Tomorrow, Yvonne - Poetry & Prose for Suicidal Egoists – 2012

Carolyn Srygley-Moore
Miracles Of the Blog: A Series – 2012

Rich Ferguson
8th & Agony – 2012

Jack Grisham
Untamed – 2013
Code Blue: A Love Story ~ Limited Edition – 2014 – *Paperback* – 2020
Pulse of the World. Arthur Chance, Punk Rock Detective – 2022

Dennis Cruz
Moth Wing Tea – 2013
The Beast Is We – 2018

Frank Reardon
Blood Music – 2013

Pleasant Gehman
Showgirl Confidential – 2013
Rock 'N' Roll Witch: A Memoir of Sex Magick, Drugs, And Rock 'N' Roll – 2022

Hollie Hardy
How To Take a Bullet and Other Survival Poems – 2014

SB Stokes
History Of Broken Love Things – 2014

Michele McDannold
Stealing The Midnight from A Handful of Days – 2014

Joel Landmine
Yeah, Well... – 2014
Things Change – 2022

MORE BOOKS ON PUNK HOSTAGE PRESS